INDISCREET

Alison Kent

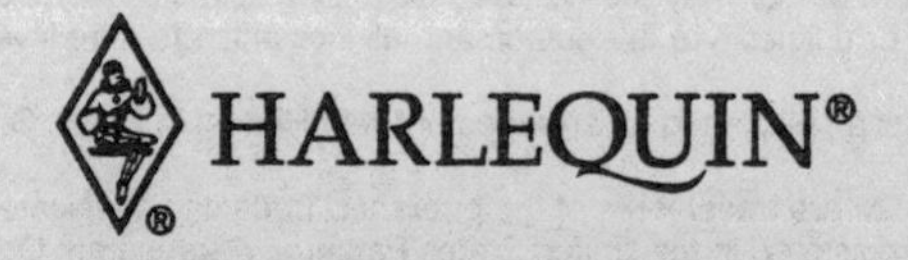

TORONTO • NEW YORK • LONDON
AMSTERDAM • PARIS • SYDNEY • HAMBURG
STOCKHOLM • ATHENS • TOKYO • MILAN • MADRID
PRAGUE • WARSAW • BUDAPEST • AUCKLAND

ISBN 0-373-79124-0

INDISCREET

This edition published by arrangement with Harlequin Books S.A.

Visit us at www.eHarlequin.com

Printed in U.S.A.

Behind every successful author stands a good critique group,
even better friends and a family that's the best.
As always, to Jan Freed.
A special thank-you to Bekke and Rey for respecting my voice,
for refusing to don kid gloves, for the nits and the giggles.
And to Walt, for loving me and all that entails.

gIRL-gEAR

urban fashions for gIRLS who gET it!

SYDNEY FORD
Chief Executive Officer

MACY WEBB
Content Editor
www.gIRL-gEAR.com

CHLOE ZUNIGA
Executive Coordinator
gUIDANCE gIRL

LAUREN NEVILLE
Design Editor
www.gIRL-gEAR.com

ANNABEL "POE" LEE
Vice President
gRAFFITI gIRL — the cosmetics line
gADGET gIRL — the accessories line

MELANIE CRAINE
Vice President
gIZMO gIRL — the technology line
gOODY gIRL — the gifts line

KINSEY STOREY
Vice President
gROWL gIRL — the party wear
gO gIRL — the active wear

The gIRLS of gIRL-gEAR
by Samantha Venus for *Urban Attitude Magazine*

Ahoy, my fine maties! Samantha Venus here again for *Urban Attitude Magazine,* asking how much did the pirate pay for corn? Why, a buck an ear, of course!

Here he is. The one you've been waiting for. The cocky frat boy turned savage beast who, by the way, dropped quite the treasure chest of cash to purchase Ms. Annabel "Poe" Lee at the gIRL-gEAR Halloween bachelorette auction. According to a message in a bottle, the two have been inseparable since!

A little bird named Polly told me that our studly young thing will be plying his cooking skills for the New Year's Eve showing at the Gallery at Three Mings. (And did I mention that incredibly sexy Devon Lee will be on hand? The man can invite me up to see his etchings anytime!)

Avast, ye scurvy landlubbers! Until we sail the high seas again, this is Samantha Venus, walking the plank.

1

THE HARDEST THING a woman had to do was tell a man to leave when she wasn't sure she wanted him to go.

Or so Annabel Lee decided as she stood in front of her office's wall of windows in the gIRL-gEAR complex, staring at the east-west headlights and taillights dueling down Houston's Southwest Freeway.

With one section of the miniblinds raised and the lights turned off, the darkness of her office blended with that of the night sky, creating an encompassing theater of black. The glow from the hallway outside her door provided the only illumination. She didn't need any more.

It was eight o'clock on Friday night.

It was the seventeenth of December.

Two weeks of vacation loomed ahead. Time she'd set aside to recover from the grueling study schedule she'd kept for the past month, a schedule that had helped her ace her finals, bringing her another step closer to completing her forensic anthropology degree.

Two weeks to explore her options—both career and personal. An exploration best done in solitude, no matter that her partners in the gIRL-gEAR fashion empire, where she held a vice-presidential position, insisted otherwise. They wanted to brainstorm, to role-play, to run aptitude tests, to make introductions, to initiate contacts.

Like Greta Garbo, Annabel simply wanted to be left alone.

She'd done all she could to limit disruptions to her self-imposed exile. She'd set an auto-response on her e-mail accounts, had vowed to check phone messages but once a day. Her voice mail gave emergency instructions on reaching her through gIRL-gEAR's CEO, Sydney Ford.

It wasn't as if Annabel wouldn't be seeing her partners at all during her time away from the office. She was hosting a casual Christmas Eve dinner for those staying home for the holidays, though the finalization of those details would be no more than a minor distraction. And, yes. She had an impending New Year's Eve catering disaster to divert, which would, unfortunately, take a bit of time and effort.

Neither of those, however, rivaled her most immediate crisis. Because tonight, during the four hours or so that remained between leaving the office and going to bed, she had to give up sex.

Celibacy had never before presented a problem. She wouldn't have gotten as far as she had in life without learning the value of discipline. She was thirty-three years old and hadn't been a virgin for a very long time. She'd experienced her fair share of devoted lovers as well as a few whose loyalties had belonged in another's bed. Never in her life, however, had she been swept away by a man's body.

Yet for seven weeks now she'd been drowning.

Taking stock of her life required total concentration, unwavering focus. The distraction of sex would be impossible to resist, the temptation to experience mindless oblivion insurmountable. At least this sex, this oblivion, and all of what she had with this man. She had to pour her energies into her self-assessment—not into bed nor a relationship that would never go anywhere beyond.

Arms crossed over her silk power blazer of cinnabar red, she lifted her chin, pleased at the strength she saw in her image reflected in the dark window. Pleased, in fact, with the total picture she made in her straight black skirt, which was short and tight—exactly the inaccessible fit he loathed—and her three-inch pumps in black leather.

Her dark panty hose were guaranteed to piss him off—as would her panties. He liked her to wear stockings and garters and nothing more, and the defiance of dressing exactly as he'd told her not to gave her an edge.

Tonight. She would tell him tonight. Before she left the office and went into hibernation she would call him, arrange to meet him for drinks, and tell him it was over. He wouldn't be happy. Hell, she wasn't happy. No sane woman would be, giving up sex that was spontaneous and heated, and cut so close to the heart of who she was.

She never climaxed without feeling she'd left too much of herself behind, and that he would use that weakness against her. That danger was a big part of the allure. She constantly wondered how far he would take her, but only half as much as she wondered how far he'd allow her to go.

Things had become more complicated than she'd ever thought possible after the first time he'd kissed her. The minute he'd backed her up against the alley wall behind the wine and tobacco bar hosting gIRL-gEAR's Halloween night bachelorette auction, she had known he would become her addiction. Much of her intuition came with the first touch of his tongue.

But she'd known even before she'd tasted him. He'd stood there, his hands flexing at his hips, his chest heaving. What the hell business was it of hers how he'd come by the money he'd used to buy her? That had been his demand in response to her query. The other words that had come out of his mouth had been raw and ragged and totally unfit for civilized ears.

That was when she'd admitted to the wild attraction and vowed to take him to bed. Nothing about him was the least bit refined. He was unpredictable, unruly, totally undisciplined and more than a little bit mad. He was the most intriguing man she'd ever met. He was also the most dangerous. To her, yes, but also to himself.

She was afraid part of her fascination was an urge to free him from the demons keeping him bound. What a stupid endeavor that would be. She knew nothing about the horrors he'd faced, even as she knew firsthand the impossibility of changing those blind to their own destructive behavior.

After all, she'd tried for years to change her mother.

Still, Annabel wanted him in ways that frightened her, despite knowing he could not possibly be a permanent part of her life. He was too capricious, too…damaged. And after surviving her childhood intact, she'd sworn to surround herself with sanity. If that wasn't possible, then she would live her life on her own.

So when, three minutes later, his long shadow fell across her from the office doorway, she damned herself for ever giving him the building's front door key. He came here often when she worked late into the night, tempting her by saying nothing, by being unpredictably spur-of-the-moment, by beckoning her away from the life of work and study that consumed her, to show her the world in which he lived.

A world of seedy bars with anonymous faces and the worst liquor imaginable. Of long drives down roads without end, of bowling and batting cages, of running at midnight through downtown streets in the rain. Of making out in the rain forest at the city zoo, with birds cawing and squawking and trilling all around.

A world no one she knew would ever believe she visited.

A world that wasn't real.

And here he was again, unexpected yet…not. She wasn't surprised, but neither was she ready. She hadn't been able to pull up the drawbridge to her protective walls. She needed more time to gird her loins before going into battle.

Yet all she could do was close her eyes and increase the pressure of her hands holding her arms to her body. She would turn and reach for him if she let go, and tonight she had too much to say.

With every step he took toward her the tension heightened, growing as thick as the flow of blood through her veins. Her pulse raced, an exhilarating rush prickling her skin.

His hands settled at the base of her neck, and it was all she could do not to step back into his body. He was hot; he was always hot, as if his temperature—much like his temperament—was not what most considered normal. But then, nothing much about him could be considered anything but out of the ordinary. And that was the crux of his appeal.

He squeezed the base of her neck; Annabel closed her eyes and called on her inner strength to pull away. And she would have. Oh, yes, she would have.

But before she could move, he slid his hands down her arms, massaging from her shoulders to her elbows. She let it go on too long and was lost because he touched her in ways no man had touched her at any time in her life.

When he skated his palms over her breasts to her collarbone and parted her jacket lapels, she allowed the intimacy even though she wore nothing beneath but a black silk camisole tucked into the short black skirt. Turning him down seemed great in theory, but the reality was he had her under his spell. She took a desperately needed deep breath.

"We have to talk."

"No. We don't."

Hearing the words come out of his mouth was as intoxicating as champagne bubbling on her tongue. So when he tugged her arms away from her body, she complied, letting him strip her blazer down and off. He tossed it into her chair as if it cost $2.98 rather than one hundred times that.

And then he pulled her camisole from her skirt, not even giving her the courtesy of a chance to tell him no.

No. A word the power and meaning of which he'd given her cause to forget.

The urge to slip her camisole up and over her head was an itch she resisted scratching. It was a small measure of control, but one she maintained and refused to give away. He had no need to know the strength of will it took to keep from lying back and inviting him between her legs anytime he came near.

His fingertips softly grazed her bare shoulders as he reached for the camisole's narrow straps. He rolled them down her arms using only his palms, binding her elbows with the silk and then with the grip of his hands.

He didn't understand his own body's power or the strength of his passion. He didn't understand so many things about civilized behavior. Either that or he didn't care.

Right now what she sensed was his struggle with the

savage side of his nature, the very side responsible for the tingling dampness between her legs. She knew him well enough to recognize his desire to get her out of her clothing without a care for preserving the fabric or the fastenings.

He managed to hold himself in check as he moved his hands to her skirt's rear zipper, though he still jerked it down forcefully. It would be a wonder if she didn't have to send it out for repair, anyway.

The price, she supposed, of taking a pirate for a lover.

When he pulled off her skirt to discover her wearing panties and panty hose, he cursed. He wasn't unkind toward her—never that—but toward the situation. He wanted her naked, wanted to bare the parts of her body to which he sought access. And like a child, he was often neither patient nor subtle when it came to getting his way.

She'd grown used to his demanding nature. It fit so well with her own, which made him work for what she wouldn't be above paying him to take. She kicked out of her skirt, but that was the extent of her participation in her own disrobing. The fact that she'd betrayed her vow to stay clothed was humiliation enough.

He shrugged out of his black leather bomber jacket, whipped his white T-shirt over his head. Then he moved in behind her, his hands holding her waist, and fitted his knees to the backs of her thighs, her bottom to the bulge of his sex. She shivered from the contact, the anticipation, as well as from his image reflected in the dark window—an image that relentlessly captured her thoughts with the same intensity his body devoted to taking hers apart.

His skin still glowed from three years spent under the Caribbean sun. His hair, bronzed and wildly untamed, hung to his shoulders. His ropey muscles spoke of hard labor; his physique hummed with a lean perfection. He'd left the States a know-it-all frat boy and returned with the hands and the mouth of a devil—hands that were making quick work of sweeping her camisole from her body to the floor.

In the mirrored window, she watched those same hands settle on her ribs before pressing upward to cover her breasts. At his practiced, near artistic touch, her neck arched. She rested her head on his shoulder, slid her back against the smooth skin of his chest. His heat was already too much to take, and her nudity offered a respite.

She longed to know the origin of his inner fire, but he refused to share the details of his captivity or his prior life. That got to her at times, the way he had of holding back even while so generously giving. She wasn't sure she understood the separation of his selves. She doubted even he was able to make the distinction.

Eventually he moved, his hips grinding in a way that brought to mind the sound of bongos and bass drums, his hands working their tortuous way down her torso to her panty hose. He slid one hand between her legs and fondled her sex until she swelled to the point of bursting. His other hand dug into his pocket.

The condom he came up with was followed by the production of a knife she was certain was illegal to carry. The click as the blade caught echoed like a shot. The reflection of the weapon in the window alarmed her only in that she feared he wouldn't wield it quickly enough.

The metal was cold on her stomach when he laid it flat against her skin. He slipped it under her waistband before flicking his wrist to slit the fabric of her panties and her hose. Another second, another flick of his wrist, and the switchblade point quivered, embedded in the windowsill.

After that, getting to what he wanted was easy. Yet he took his time, peeling down silk and nylon so that the tattered scraps loosely bound her upper thighs. He moved his hands back up her body, over the curve of her hips, until he reached her rib cage. The heels of his palms nudged her waist. He spread his fingers, turned her to the side and slid one hand down her belly, the other over her bottom.

Leaning forward and bracing herself on her desk, she spread her legs wider as he began to play. His fingers were nimble and exact in their aim, both hands meeting at her slick entrance and urging her apart. He pressed pulse points, stroked the intimate skin behind her opening before pushing one long finger inside.

The sound she made was a low sultry cry, one that told him of her pleasure and her need. Wanting more, she widened her stance, leaned farther over the edge of her desk, raised her backside toward the fly of his pants and rested her weight on her forearms.

His responding growl told her how much he enjoyed her uninhibited nature, her willingness to expose herself for his taking. She would give him anything, had given him everything. He had been equally honest in offering her his body to use at will. Yet his body was all he'd given her, and there were times that got to her, too.

At this moment, however, the way her body wanted his was the only matter of any importance. He entered her fully, one finger, then two, then a third when she pushed back against him and begged.

He continued to tease her clit while expertly stroking her with his other hand, a smooth in-and-out rhythm that in the past—before she'd learned the beauty and the skill with which he wielded his cock—would have sent her over the edge. She was spoiled and selfish and she wanted it all. And she told him so with a desperate backward press of her bottom.

She heard his laugh, one of satisfaction, not of humor, one that never made it to his mouth, but rumbled in his chest as if trapped there. As if he'd forgotten the relief of pure laughter and no longer knew how to let himself go.

He released her and stepped back; she heard the slide of his zipper and the tearing sound as he opened the condom packet. She glanced to the window, where she could see his jeans coming down and his cock springing free in the dark reflection. She sucked in a breath at the sight.

His body never ceased to amaze her, the aesthetics of his lean musculature, the lack of body fat to soften his hard lines. She rarely saw him eat, even the fabulous food he cooked, which everyone around him devoured. *Devoured.* That was all she could think of, watching as he rolled the condom to the base of his shaft, which appeared even more impressively long and thick jutting out from his solid rock of a body.

He moved forward; she pressed her forehead to her fists on the desk and, eyes closed, waited. He held her hip with one hand, guided his cock with the other, rubbing the tip of the plumlike head between the cheeks of her bottom, teasing her with a seeking pressure.

Later, she wanted to tell him. They'd take time for kinkier exploration when her hunger wasn't so fierce. But she didn't say any of that because there wouldn't be a later. After this, she still planned to send him away.

As the thought flickered through her mind, he drove home, filling her, nearly lifting her from the floor with the force of his first thrust. He paused, both hands on her hips, as if gathering his control, savoring the sensation of being buried alive.

He was hot, so hot. She squeezed him there where he pulsed in her body; his heat warmed her from the inside out. And then it began, the metered cadence she knew so well, the one he'd taught her to need. Leaning forward, he reached around to stimulate her clit, his fingers sliding down either side of the hard knot and tugging upward in time to the grinding rhythm of his hips.

The high heels she still wore provided the perfect angle and height for this raw mating of bodies. He pumped harder, faster, his fingers tightening on her clitoris, his grip on her hips sure to leave marks. She didn't care.

All she knew was the immense pleasure sweeping through her core, as if no other sensation existed but that deep between her legs. He filled her, stretched her, opened her in ways no other man had done, showing her a fullness, a completeness she desperately desired and wondered how she would learn to live without.

His strokes came close to taking her apart, and her fever rose. The buzzing along her skin followed, coiling tightly into one centered pulse of sensation further heightened with each of his thrusts. She blew out air in short sharp breaths, squeezing her eyes shut until she saw stars.

When her orgasm came, she shattered, hit with the force of the sizzling burst. Her skin burned; she tried to shake off his hold. He merely gripped her tighter, pushed into her farther, both of his hands now at her waist as he drove himself home.

His own climax came in silence, and she only knew because of the spike in his temperature. The heat of his cock had her shivering, even as he remained statue still but for the pulse of his throbbing release. For several long moments following, neither moved, their bodies fused, the thought of separation painful. Her breathing calmed, as did his orgasm's waves. She'd learned to wait for his finish, which was longer in coming than she'd known a man could last.

Finally he withdrew, tossing the condom and the wrapper into her trash, then reaching for his shirt. He pulled it on and leaned his bare backside against the windowsill while she dressed.

She wished she had a spare pair of panty hose in addition to the extra panties she kept in her desk. She buttoned her blazer, slipped her bare feet back into her pumps, smoothed down the edges of her newly cut hair. She turned around in time to see him fasten his pants and slip into his bomber jacket. Hooking her bag over her shoulder, she looked him straight in the eye.

"I can't see you anymore, Patrick."

"WHERE'S DEVON?" Annabel asked the hostess standing at her post inside the doorway of Three Mings, Devon Lee's restaurant in the heart of Houston's Rice Village.

"Good evening, Poe," the young hostess replied, having grown used to hearing people call Annabel by the nickname. "Your brother went upstairs twenty minutes ago. Should I ring the gallery?"

Annabel shook her head. "I'll find him, thank you."

She walked back out into the frosty night air and around to the side of the stand-alone building that sat on a quiet street off of University Drive.

The second story of Three Mings was an exclusive gallery where local artists' work was displayed, shown only on private tours and sold in silent auctions. A watercolorist himself, Devon also rented studio space to a few select clients.

After walking through the mazelike hallway of low ceilings and hardwood floors, off which narrow alcoves were lit strategically to enhance the work displayed, Annabel found her brother in a hushed discussion with an Indian artist whose specialty was exquisitely detailed henna body art.

Annabel stepped back to allow them the privacy to finish their conversation. Devon glanced up, his eyes crinkling at the corners as he smiled, and raised his hand to signal he'd only be a minute. Annabel turned to the wall behind her and took in the collection of photographs framed and grouped in a collage.

One photo in particular drew her attention, as always. The subject was costumed as a Japanese geisha, complete with *shimada-mage* hairstyle, white cream makeup and red lipstick she knew was infused with safflower extract.

The hair, she also knew, in this case was a wig, a *katsura,* but the makeup—from the application of the *bintsuke-abura,* the oil-wax combination allowing the white pigment to adhere, to the drawing of the thinly arched eyebrows in black and the added touch of red to brows and lids—had taken laborious hours to apply.

Annabel knew because it was her face, her eyes into which she was staring.

"That photo gets more attention than any other in the gallery, you know," Devon said, having silently walked up behind her.

"Considering the subject matter, I should think so."

"You really are wicked." He nodded toward the imprint of a woman's lips on the white canvas of Annabel's creamed-and-powdered cheek. "And your eyes always give you away."

She looked again at the photo, knowing it was the mischievous twinkle captured in her eyes as much as the kiss on her face that had garnered this particular photo so much attention. She had a session next week with Luc Beacon, the same photographer, and was anxious to discover who the client was and what they were looking for.

Right now she had more pressing matters on her mind, however, and turned her back on the display. "Devon, I'm in trouble."

Her brother shook his head knowingly. "Man trouble, no doubt."

"What makes you say that?" she asked, raising her chin ever so slightly. She knew her expression hadn't given anything away; she'd purposefully kept her face calm.

Devon lifted one sharp brow over eyes blessed with dark paintbrush lashes. "Your legs are bare."

She pointed the toe of one pump, glanced at her smooth ivory skin before rolling her eyes. "He hates my panty hose."

Arms crossed over his chest, Devon rocked back on the heels of his Italian leather loafers and stared down from his two-inch height advantage. "I'm surprised you wear them. I've always taken you for the garters-and-stockings type."

"Judging by your vast experience with women?" Annabel twisted her mouth.

Her brother shook his head. "Judging by the only thing I've ever seen hanging over your shower rod."

Annabel blew out a huff of breath. "I had the flu. I don't usually leave them out."

"Annie, lighten up. I don't give a damn if you leave

stockings out year-round.'' He narrowed his gaze, his jaw taut.

''Don't call me Annie.''

His sigh was sibling patience personified as he slipped his hand beneath her arm and guided her through the hallway maze and into his office. Once inside, he waited until she'd settled on his black leather love seat before closing the door to join her.

He faced her, one arm along the seat's padded back. ''Look at you. Arms crossed. Legs crossed. Whoever your mystery lover is, he's obviously chipping away at your walls of Jericho or you wouldn't be on the defensive.''

She kept all her body parts crossed, but did stop swinging her foot. ''I am not on the defensive. I'm simply irritated.''

''Because of a pair of panty hose?''

''No.'' She was irritated because when it came to Patrick Coffey, she'd lost the disciplined control she'd spent a lifetime honing. ''The caterer I hired for your New Year's Eve showing lost her best cook to a competitor and isn't sure she can manage her schedule without him.''

Devon continued to stare, lifting that one sharp brow the way he always did to signal he had a saint's fortitude when it came to waiting out her moods.

''I would think that might concern you,'' she finally said.

''I trust you implicitly.'' His expression shifted, settled in a concerned frown. ''But I am worried.''

She exhaled what she could of her tension. ''Don't be. I'll handle it.''

''I'm not worried about the caterer. I'm worried about you.''

She glanced away, studied the vase of yellow calla lilies centered on a red-lacquered accent table and flanked by scrolls of painted tigers rendered in *Sumi* ink and color on silk. The austerity of Devon's office usually fit her tack-sharp mood. Tonight, she simply bristled further.

"When you come to me and say you're in big trouble, I worry." Devon pushed up from the love seat and crossed the small room to lean on the corner of his matching black desk. The distance gave him the edge he needed; the position gave him the upper hand. "You haven't been yourself for several weeks now."

She waved off his concern with the flutter of one hand, wondering why she'd come here when she knew he wouldn't let her hide from his probing questions or continue to deceive herself that she was equipped to handle Patrick Coffey.

Then again, maybe that was exactly the reason she *had* come, she mused ruefully, getting to her feet. She needed the wake-up call to tell her she was doing the right thing in sending him away. "I was dealing with the stress of finals. Of course I haven't been myself."

Devon shook his head. "I've seen you stressed from finals. This is different. In your words, big trouble."

He was right, of course. How she'd even managed finals with Patrick disrupting her schedule, not to mention her concentration... Even now he was on her mind, and she just couldn't have that. He was getting too close; she was letting him in. She was *giving* in, when she'd determined that he had to go.

Turning her back on her brother, she made her way from the love seat to the window, opening the miniblinds and peering into the darkness for the second time tonight, as if she'd find her answers outside of herself rather than within.

Her sigh of admission was heavier than she'd intended. "Yes. It's a man."

"Glad to hear it."

She allowed herself a private smile. Her brother's reaction was no surprise. Over the years, he'd made his feelings on her dearth of personal relationships clear.

When she'd joined gIRL-gEAR as a partner, the champagne he'd sent had been more a celebration of her allowing the fashion empire's other women into her life than congratulations on the new position.

He didn't approve of her reasons for keeping her distance, and used every possible opportunity to tell her so. But those reasons were what had brought her as far as she'd come in her life. She hadn't survived their childhood as well-adjusted as Devon seemed to be. Or maybe he was simply pretending, as his own relationships never seemed to last, either.

He walked up beside her. "I was hoping that once you completed your degree, you'd be more amenable to settling down."

She couldn't hold back a full-fledged smile. "With a man, you mean?"

"Well, yes. I'm old-school. I admit it."

"Don't get your hopes up. At least not this time." She sighed. "I told him it was over."

"Hmm."

"What's with the 'hmm'?"

"I'm just wondering if you told him before or after you lost your panty hose."

"A lady never kisses and tells." Not that there was anything to tell, since she and Patrick hadn't taken time to kiss. "Besides, you should know better than to press me into a relationship. Last I heard, you were on the outs with that particular bliss. Are things okay now with you and Trina?''

Devon shrugged. ''What can I say?''

''You can say the two of you are working on it.''

''I'm not sure there's anything to work on.''

She shook her head in reprimand. ''Don't tell me that. I've never seen a couple more suited than the two of you.''

''Get real, Annie. What do you and I know about suitable couples? All we know is what happens when a couple doesn't work. And right now, Trina and I do not work.''

Annabel didn't have anything to say in response. Devon had made his point. And all she could wonder was if either of them would ever find a partner they could fall in love with as easily as they seemed to fall into bed.

2

STILL WEARING JEANS, a T-shirt and a bomber jacket, Patrick Coffey leaned a hip on the low railing that bordered Annabel's balcony, a bottled malt beverage sweating in one hand. He liked Houston in December. Nice and breezy. The perfect weather for stargazing and drinking himself flat on his ass.

Annabel wouldn't be expecting him, though arriving home to find him waiting wouldn't come as a surprise. She didn't approve of what she called his unorthodox behavior, trying to change him, fix him, turn him one way when he was headed another. At least she was finally coming to realize exactly what a pig's ear he was, and that she wouldn't be the proud owner of a silk purse anytime soon.

Leaning beyond the railing, which bit into his upper thighs, he glanced down, hovering over the edge, weaving from side to side until dizziness brought him back up. He lifted the bottle in a toast, celebrating his continued resistance to the temptation of taking a dive four stories to the ground below.

Another day, another...day.

And, oh yeah, another toast.

Earlier tonight in her office, after screwing the both of them mad, he'd walked out on her without saying a word, unable to respond to her statement about no longer being able to see him.

Hell, woman, he'd wanted to say. *For once, just open your goddamn eyes.*

But he hadn't said anything. He'd needed to get his thoughts together before putting them into words. He hadn't done a lot of talking the last few years, and what skills he'd once used to express himself had pretty much seized up.

Not a big loss, since he didn't have much to say these days. Neither did he have anyone wanting to listen. Really listen. Though, he supposed with another fine toast, he could probably find a willing audience if he were to make up a few horror stories about his captivity and exaggerate the reality of what had been a hell of a lot of boredom.

He couldn't help but wonder if the searchers would have made half the effort to find him had they known he hadn't been strung up by his balls at all. Instead, he'd spent a whole lot of hours flat on his back, napping in the sun, an ankle shackled to the base of a huge palm. And, hey. He'd lost a good forty pounds.

Yeah, he doubted that scenario would've garnered a lot of sympathy. Thank goodness he'd had his brother to count on. Ray had refused to give him up for gone. Three long years, and he'd put everything he'd had into the search, exhausting his finances, putting his own life on hold, working to right a very bad wrong.

He'd been just as conscientious since Patrick's return, making sure he had time and space to get his act together without the pressure of reporters and other inquiring minds butting in. Thing was, it was too much time and way too much space. Lately, they rarely spoke of anything more vital than football stats.

Oh, yeah. Rushing yardage and passing percentages were the things that made life worth living. Patrick considered his bottle, considered his brother. Hell. If nothing else, Ray's inability to shed the guilt eating him up deserved the biggest toast of the night.

He hadn't been responsible for the kidnapping, but nothing Patrick said made a dent in Ray's hardheaded insistence that he should have been more vigilant in plotting their course, in choosing a captain with a better sense of the region's criminal climate, in negotiating their freedom when the pirates boarded the schooner.

Patrick drained the bottle, reached for another, not feeling half the buzz he'd been aiming for when he'd grabbed the two six-packs on his way home from the gIRL-gEAR offices. *Home.* Now that was pretty damn funny, thinking of Annabel's place as home when she didn't even want him around.

As much as Ray sidestepped digging through the pit of Patrick's psyche, Annabel didn't even bother with a shovel, but plunged knee-deep through his crap. She expected him to be the man he was, the best he could be, no matter how many bamboo shoots he'd had shoved under his fingernails.

He smiled, a strange feeling he was still getting used to, remembering the night he'd bought her at the auction. Damned if that hadn't been some kind of night. She'd wanted answers: Why had he bought her? Where did he get the money? What was he expecting in return?

He'd had no answers to give. He'd simply herded her into the narrow alley behind the bar, wrapped her up in his jacket and backed her barely dressed body into the cold brick wall. He'd been healthy and horny. She'd been sex on stiletto heels. He'd kissed her until neither one of them could breathe, and his cock sat up and begged.

No surprise there.

What he hadn't seen coming at all, what had crept up

from behind and slipped a shiv between his ribs, was her appeal above the neck. After their bodies were spent, the brain sex took over. And it was every bit as addictive as conventional intercourse.

She was older than he was, independent, smart as hell. She was ballsy and brash and driven. In a horribly Freudian sort of way, she reminded him of Soledad—the woman who had been the one and only reason he'd held on to his sanity during those years away. And that was enough reason to let Annabel kick him to the curb.

Having one woman's blood on his hands was a sin for which he had a long time left to pay.

Thing was, it wasn't easy lately for him to separate past from present, because Soledad's death was the reason he couldn't let Annabel blow him off. Call it a hunch. Call it intuition. Call it thirty-six months kept captive in the hot seat.

Patrick's cushy homecoming was about to fall apart.

He didn't have anything solid to back up his suspicions, didn't have proof to take to his contact at the FBI, didn't have anything more than his instincts to rely on.

But he knew. *He knew.*

Russell Dega, the pirate leader who'd escaped during the confusion of Patrick's rescue, was here. The scum-sucking thief had come to close the one piece of business left unsettled between them: ending Patrick's life.

And if that didn't deserve another toast, he didn't know what did.

He finished off his fourth drink and had just reached for his fifth from the open six-pack sitting on the balcony's black-iron table when the whir of the loft's private elevator signaled Annabel's arrival. His gut clenched hard in response.

Using his knife, he pried off the bottle cap and tried

not to choke on the memory of what they'd done earlier in her office.

The disk clattered against the patio as the converted freight car stopped on the fourth floor. As he listened, Annabel lifted the elevator's rolling garagelike door, sliding it overhead on its tracks. He heard her unlock and slide back the accordion-style grate that opened into the dark room behind him. He lifted the beer, drank deeply, waited for the buzz that was way too long in coming.

Annabel was already stepping out onto the balcony and he'd yet to feel a thing.

"What are you doing here?"

He raised his drink. "Toasting my fine taste in women."

She waited a moment, then reached for the last bottle in the six-pack and tilted it his way. He removed the cap and, as she drank, their gazes met, stinging him with a keenly sharp buzz that he sure as hell wasn't getting from the alcohol.

He let the sizzle settle, watching her keep the table between them and move to sit in one of the balcony set's matching chairs. She shivered lightly, he noticed, when the cold metal bit into the backs of her bare legs.

Served her right for wearing the panty hose.

She drank again before glancing in his direction a second time and getting back to business. "You know me well enough by now to understand that I mean what I say."

"Yes, but here's to all the things you don't say." He tilted his bottle toward her in, what? His tenth toast of the night? Bringing the lip of the glass to his mouth, he swallowed a quarter of the contents, feeling…nothing.

Nothing.

Nothing but the same determination, the same wariness that had brought him here earlier. He wouldn't be leaving tonight until she was aware of... Hell. He wouldn't be leaving tonight period. Her awareness of anything wasn't a factor in the equation.

"What sort of things am I not saying?" she finally asked. "What do I need to say to make myself clear?"

"Give me a reason. Why can't you, or won't you, see me anymore?" He hated that his request came out sounding so candy-assed, but he was no good at conversation, and conversation was the only way to get from here to there.

"Having you here is inconvenient."

He sputtered at that. "Inconvenient? I'd say I've been about as convenient as you're ever going to get in a roommate."

"I don't want a roommate, and I'm not talking about the sex."

She wouldn't be. She never wanted to talk about the sex, simply engage.

Annabel was one of only two women he'd known who approached life—and sex—like a man. Then again, his experience with the opposite sex consisted of no more than a short list of adventurous coeds before graduation, and two older women intent on wearing him out since.

The thought brought him back to why he was here. Why he couldn't go. Until he put his dealings with Russell Dega to bed, Patrick would be as big a part of Annabel's scenery as downtown Houston's skyline.

Leaving her alone would seem to be her best protection, but if Dega were indeed here, the bastard would've picked up on Annabel being Patrick's Achilles' heel. He couldn't chance having her used as a pawn in a game that might end badly.

What little common sense he still listened to insisted

that his purpose would be best served if she were the one to suggest he stick around. Which meant she needed him here for a reason that had nothing to do with what he gave her in bed.

He thought a moment while drinking. Then, fingers laced around the bottle, he leaned back against the railing and braced the glass against the top button of his fly. Giving a little shrug, he said, "Guess I'm just surprised you'd give up such a good thing."

"And I'm surprised you didn't hear me say I wasn't going to talk about sex."

He gave another shrug. "I'm not talking about sex. I'm talking about food."

She crossed one leg, shifted her weight to her hip as he pulled out the second chair and sat. He kept the table between them because he was no stranger to body language and hers was screaming at him to stay the hell away.

He could respect that. Didn't mean he was going to abandon his plans to convince her she needed him around, though. Who'd've thunk Soledad's obsession with teaching him to cook would've come so in handy?

He stretched out his legs and leaned back, playing the part of a man on his way to a full-blown drunk. In reality, his senses were sharply honed. He wasn't only fighting for his survival—a badge of expertise he claimed proudly—he was fighting for hers. Knowledge he would dispense on a need-to-know basis.

"Who else would feed you grilled salmon with orange scallion salsa? Or puff pastry with shiitake mushrooms and Asiago cheese?" He sensed the smile she fought to hide. "Did I mention chocolate-raspberry pot pie?" He had her with the pie, but twisted the screw one more time. "How can you even think of giving up my cappuccino crème brûlée?"

Holding her bottle beneath her lips, she said, "You're the only man I know who can talk to me like that and not have me question your sexual orientation."

He tossed back his head and brayed. "And this from the same woman whose brother paints with watercolors."

"Happily affianced brother, I'll have you know."

"Happily? This the same brother you said was on the outs with his woman not a week ago?"

Tentatively, she returned the bottle to the table, as if distracting him with the slow motion, because in the next second she brought the glass down with a cracking thud. Then she snapped, "I hate how you do that."

"Do what?"

She growled and turned away, so that the light from the moon fell on her blue-black hair. The severely angled layers swung as she moved, the longest strands brushing her jaw.

The sharp razor cut was her first line of visible defense, a barbed-wire barrier keeping softness at bay. He wasn't fooled for a second. "How I can tell when you're not being honest? Or how I know when you're hiding something?"

"Either. Both." Her head whipped back, and he sensed her eyes narrow into stabbing pinpoints, felt them nail him to his chair.

He couldn't help it. Aiming to get a buzz or not, he felt the first stirrings of arousal as his balls shifted between his legs.

She used the neck of the bottle as a pointer and aimed it in his direction. "I am not going to fall for your tricks, Patrick."

"I'm not peddling any tricks over here."

"Of course you are. You think in seven weeks I haven't learned a thing or two about you?"

He forced himself not to stiffen; it didn't make for a convincing drunk. "Keep it to those two and we'll be doing okay."

Her exasperation was obvious as, with a deep sigh, she flopped back into her chair. When she said nothing more, he felt the first pricks of worry. Pissing her off was no way to get back into her good graces. And so he let her stew.

She stewed, but not for long. Her chin came up as she said, "I cut you off without warning. I admit that was hardly fair."

Her Annabel-ized apology only had him stiffening further. He waited for the "but" sure to follow—but nothing has changed, but you still have to go, but—

"But I have been thinking."

More dangerous yet. "Oh?"

"Perhaps we can come up with an arrangement of sorts." She held her bottle on the table, drumming her fingers along the label. "Temporary, of course."

"I'm all ears." Temporary would give him the time he needed to flush a certain nemesis from whatever shadows the bastard was using for cover. Yeah, temporary worked.

Although Patrick still couldn't help but wonder if that was all Annabel assumed he was good for.

"Cut your hair."

What the hell? "Cutting my hair is your deal?"

She shook her head. "Your comment. Being all ears. I just realized I only see them when you tie back your hair."

"Is this about your Delilah complex?"

"You're not exactly Sampson," she said softly. "Your hair isn't a source of strength. It might put off more people than you know."

Now he was getting irritated. "What people? The ones who are supposed to be considering me for work?"

Not that there were many of those—and there wouldn't be until he decided what he wanted to do with his life. He had money to live on for the moment, thanks to a combination of reward and bounty money, and it seemed a waste of time and energy to take a job for the sake of saying he had one. He'd learned a lot about priorities during the last few years, and doing for himself mattered a lot more than trying to please all of the people all of the time.

Annabel nodded. "Them. My neighbors. Little children on the street. Elderly ladies with heart conditions. Puppies—"

"Yeah, yeah." He shook back his hair, which suddenly seemed burdensome, if not a reminder of the savage life he'd known. "It's not my hair that's the problem."

It wasn't even the piercings or the tattoos. It was the expression in his eyes. And that he wasn't sure he could change.

"Not completely, no. But you do look like a thug. And if you want to cater the New Year's Eve showing at Devon's gallery, I can't have you looking like one."

He sobered completely. "Cater? Me? Are you out of your mind?"

Annabel's dark brows lifted. "Oh, that was another Patrick Coffey seducing me earlier with promises of grilled salmon and crème brûlée?"

"Seduction and catering are two completely different animals." Catering meant putting his work out for those other than family, appearing in public, behaving accordingly. People pointed out too often that his behavior mirrored the don't-give-a-damn look in his eyes.

"It's cooking, Patrick. Nothing more. Nothing less."

"The serving? The presentation?" She was handing him a silver platter loaded with a legitimate reason for her to keep him around. And all he could think about was the exhaustion of maintaining a civilized veneer despite the rude stares and speculation.

His survival skills told him he'd be borrowing trouble should he accept. His protective instincts quickly took charge.

This wasn't about him. This was about Annabel.

"I'll handle the arrangements," she was saying. "I have the menu already approved. All you'll have to do is prepare the food."

"And the back side of the deal?" The side he figured he would like even less than putting his passion out to be judged by strangers.

Annabel's closed expression confirmed his suspicion. "After the showing on New Year's Eve, we'll say our goodbyes."

Yeah, he'd had a pretty good idea that was going to be it, and it still sucked that she wasn't wanting to keep him around.

Annabel was the only one with the guts to tell him about his potential. She never treated him as a pariah. Whether or not she truly believed in him didn't matter. She'd given him reason to harbor a remnant of the same hope he'd held on to for three years.

He huffed. Maybe one savior per lifetime was all he deserved. And he sure didn't want Annabel suffering Soledad's fate.

Draining his bottle, he lazily pushed himself to his feet

and dug into his pocket for his knife. With Annabel looking on, he flipped open the blade. He stared at her for a long moment, looking for even a hint of apprehension, seeing nothing but a mild curiosity.

He wanted to damn her for being unflappable, but damned himself for letting her get to him instead.

As he raised the knife, the flame of a lighter on the street below caught his eye. His heart bolted; his blood raced. His muscles contracted, and he froze, watching the first bright glow of a cigarette catching fire. He couldn't make out any of the smoker's features—

"Patrick?"

—only dark clothing, dark hair. It could be Dega. It could be anyone, except the balcony seemed to be in the smoker's direct line of sight. Another long draw and the cigarette fell to the ground. The smoker turned and walked away, swallowed immediately by the shadows.

"Patrick?"

If he hit the fire escape, he could be on the street in seconds. He could make sure. He would know—

"Patrick!"

Annabel grabbed his wrist. Adrenaline shot him in the heart; he flinched. It was a long, tense moment later before he was able to force enough of a smile to put the both of them at ease.

With a roll of her eyes, Annabel released his wrist and shoved him away. "I hate it when you do that."

This time he knew what she was talking about: the way his feral instincts kicked in anytime he sensed danger. He glanced back down to the street, only to see that his hesitation had cost him what edge he might've had. Shit. A lot of protection he was going to be. Shaking his head, he turned away, slid his free fingers into his hair close to his scalp and pulled.

Only then did he use the blade.

He watched Annabel look on as the hunk of hair fell to the balcony floor. She watched as he sliced off another and another until he stood there with nothing but choppy tufts on his head. He returned the knife to his pocket. She returned her gaze to his face.

If asked, he would've denied the pleasure that rushed through him at seeing the encouragement in her eyes. When it reached her mouth, he couldn't help but tighten his grip on that one last remnant of hope. Maybe, just maybe, he deserved to have survived.

"I'll take that as a yes," she said, and when he inclined his head in answer, she turned on her heel and motioned for him to follow. "I'll get the clippers from my makeup case. You get the broom."

SHE COULDN'T TEAR her gaze away. She'd tried, truly she had. But he was entirely too compelling, making the task an impossibility when she'd thought herself impervious to his physical allure.

After she'd repaired the mess he'd made of his hair, they'd made love with the lights on. For the first time since he'd bought her at auction, she'd wanted to see his face while their bodies were joined. Until now, she'd imagined him as a fantasy, a mystery, a lover that came in the night when her defenses were down and her body an open book.

Their encounters were purely sexual, a disassociation from the rest of her life, an entertainment, recreation, an indulgence. Tonight that glass bubble had broken. He was real, a man, a beautiful male specimen of whom she couldn't get her visual fill.

Her sheets were fine white Egyptian cotton, the headboard an extravagant Victorian piece in dark wood. Patrick lay sleeping in the center of the bed, an arm beneath his head in lieu of a pillow, the barest edge of a sheet draped over his groin.

Dark hair tufted in the pit of his raised arm, ran in a line from his navel down beneath the sheet. His chest was bare, his legs lightly covered, while the thatch that cushioned his sex grew thick. Yet the lack of hair on his head was what drew her attention.

She'd clipped him close so that no more than a dark fuzz remained. That darkness served to highlight the deep bronze glow of his skin. The silver hoop in his ear matched the one piercing his nipple, and both looked as if they were simply an extension of his skin.

It was his tattoo that caused her to shudder. Not the intricate tribal art ringing his biceps. That one she'd discovered beneath more than a few white dress shirts on other men. Never in her life, however, had she seen anything like Patrick's snake.

The design was inked in multicolors: black, blue, red and green, with sharp highlights in yellow. The snake wound its way around his right thigh—she counted four coils—before arcing over his hipbone to end above the swell of his buttocks. With Patrick lying on his back, she had to visualize the fangs and the wicked, wicked eyes.

But even the remembered image was more than enough to cause her to shiver. She reached for the comforter, which had ended up on the floor earlier, and wrapped it around her shoulders. When she glanced again at Patrick, his eyes were open, even though he remained perfectly still.

"I hate the way you do that." His uncanny ability to come awake on full alert made her crazy. She hated the idea of him watching her while she slept, when she was vulnerable....

"Watch out or you'll give me a complex."

"*Give* you a complex? What about the dozens you already have?"

She'd lost count of the number of times over the past seven weeks she'd tackled one or another, hoping she could offer him more than memories of great sex to take away from their time together. She hated how he seemed to ignore his amazing potential. Especially his ability to adapt and survive.

A slow, sleepy grin spread over his sinful mouth, though it never reached his eyes. Using no more than his abs, he lifted his upper body off the mattress while stacking pillows behind him. It was only when he finally leaned back that she remembered to breathe. God, but he was beautiful.

"Dozens, huh? Guess I've never counted."

He was cocky and cute and too much of both. She'd determined that their time would be limited. She had even set the date for their end. None of that meant she couldn't continue to dig into his psyche while she had him here—though, knowing Patrick, she easily imagined him walking out stark naked.

She considered him critically. "Why do you never stay and eat what you've cooked?"

The expression in his eyes gave nothing away, even as his smile seemed to freeze. "I always eat what I've cooked."

"But you don't eat with the people you've cooked for. This past year I've had dinner at Sydney and Ray's at least once a month. As soon as the meal is served, you walk out of the room."

"I've forgotten my table manners."

He didn't even flinch when he said it. He didn't break eye contact, and he kept a totally straight face. Either he was a hell of a liar or he truly believed that he was the savage beast he claimed to be. A part of her heart broke for him.

Another part wanted to slap him and tell him to get over himself already, that she was immune to his act. Except that would make her an even bigger liar than he.

Another few silent moments passed, moments she spent wondering what his three years of captivity had been like, if he'd had friends, if he'd had lovers, how many he'd had. If they'd appreciated his intensity in bed the way she did. If one of them had taught him the skills he so expertly plied.

Funny, the jealousy sparked by that thought. Not so funny that she recognized the full grip of the unhealthy emotion.

"And it seems you've forgotten that it's impolite to stare," he finally said, interrupting her fruitless musings.

When she realized she was doing exactly that, she forced herself to pull away. "Your facial bone structure fascinates me."

"If that's a come-on, it's the lousiest one I've ever heard."

"It's not a come-on," she said, even as her pulse quickened. "I was simply visualizing your skull's inter-ocular and bizygomatic breadth."

He knew as well as she did that craniofacial anthro-pometry was the last thing on her mind. Yet she couldn't find the strength to turn away when he whispered, "Show me."

Letting the comforter fall, she moved toward him, en-joying the flare of his nostrils as he took in her nudity and her complete comfort in baring her body. She crawled up to straddle him, dislodging the sheet so that she sat atop his thighs, settling over the softness of his scrotum, his penis tucked close to her sex.

She placed her hands on the smooth skin of his torso, sliding her palms upward until making contact with his jaw. Her fingers explored the structure of his face, moving from one point to another.

"This is the bizygomatic breadth," she said, measuring from the most lateral point on one cheekbone's zygomatic arch to the matching point on the other. "And this is the biocular width," she added, moving her left hand to span the space between the far corners of his eyelids. "A forensic sculptor would use these measurements as well as others in reconstructing your face."

She pressed her fingertips to each spot until Patrick closed his eyes and moaned from the pleasure of her touch. She wanted to moan, as well, because his cock had stirred against her belly, his shaft thickening and rubbing over her sex.

"I can see why you liked studying this stuff. Who knew the human skull could be such an erogenous zone?"

"Our study subjects didn't feel a thing," she countered. "They were dead, and quite unconcerned with eros."

Patrick lay still for several moments more, allowing her to explore the fit of the skin on his face, the structure of his skull, until the room seemed to echo with their dueling heartbeats and their husky breathing.

She stopped the exploration of his jawline, her thumbs pressed to his cheekbones, as his erection began to firmly make its presence known there where her belly tingled. When he opened his eyes to catch her staring, she moved her hands to her thighs.

Strange, this nervousness making her uneasy. Yes, he

constantly surprised her, but she wasn't used to being caught off guard. "It's like you're someone I don't know. You look so different without all that hair."

"A good different?"

"An effective different."

"So consider me the variety spicing up your life." He said it with a wiggle of both brows, which stood out against his perpetually bronzed skin.

That, he certainly had done, she admitted, moving her palms from her thighs to his abdomen, pressing lightly the taut muscles there. When he groaned, she felt the hum from her fingertips to her elbows.

Yet oddly enough, she wasn't wanting sex as much as she wanted to explore his body. Considering that he was quite the randy young man, she wouldn't be having her way completely, she mused without complaint. She had never known such intense satisfaction, and in reality would hate seeing him go.

But she had long since learned the importance of cutting free dead weight.

And behind those uncanny beautiful eyes and wickedly sparkling wit, she feared that was exactly what she would find instead of the artist's soul her foolish heart insisted he hid. Better to die not knowing, than to know...and die a little more inside.

The older, wiser Annabel approached relationships anticipating their inevitable end. An end that was all too near for her and Patrick, giving her the freedom to enjoy his body without the guilt of self-betrayal.

Or so she worked to convince herself as she leaned forward to grab a condom from the bedside table. Patrick opened his mouth over her breast, but she pulled back before he could do more than wet her skin with his tongue.

Tearing open the condom packet, she moved from straddling Patrick's thighs to kneeling between them, caught by the fire that stirred in her belly simply by looking at him. Yet it was nothing compared to the fire of taking him into her mouth.

Leaning forward, she parted her lips over the head of his cock and sucked him between her lips, holding him there while running her tongue along the sensitive underside seam. Her mouth burned from his heat; her pulse raced in response to the visceral sounds he made.

He thrust upward. She took him to the back of her throat before drawing her lips firmly from the base of his shaft back to the head. Once there, she teased him again, her tongue circling and swirling around his glans until, in a sharp panting breath, he begged her to stop.

She did stop, but she didn't remove her mouth. She left her lips pressed beneath the ridge of the head and slipped a hand between his legs to fondle his balls. Then the soft skin of his sac, the weight of his testicles, the swollen extension of his erection that formed a ridge all the way back to his anal opening.

She loved all of it, loved the feel, loved learning where to press, where to stroke, where to tickle, where to squeeze. He was an incredible canvas of tactile sensation, and he aroused her beyond belief simply by being.

When he drew up his knees and opened his legs wider, she knew he was ready, just as she knew she could no longer wait. Their accord as lovers couldn't possibly be more perfect, and she wondered over it yet again while rolling the condom down the length of his shaft.

Catching her lower lip between her teeth, she crawled up his body, lifting onto her knees, then lowering herself over his erection. For as long as she was able to manage, she remained unmoving, staring into Patrick's eyes, which glittered with all that he felt, and with a promise to give her exactly what she wanted.

It was that unspoken vow that choked her up, that way he had of telling her he would always be there, would never let her down. That he was the real deal, as real as it got. Not the polished perfect product of wistful fantasy.

And that was when she closed her eyes and began to move. The sex she could count on. Counting on anything else, anything more, would be simple stupidity. No matter what his eyes said. She knew better.

She knew…knew…knew nothing any longer but the surge of desire, the purely physical lust that consumed her, that seemed to take away her mind and leave nothing but her body.

Sensation surrounded her as she lifted and lowered her hips, selfishly setting the rhythm that would bring her relief. Patrick held her, his fingers digging into the muscles of her buttocks and urging her to increase her speed.

The tendons and veins on his neck stood out in sharp relief as he strained to match the pace she set. He thrust upward to each of her downward strokes, and she braced her hands on his shoulders, loving the way his muscles bunched as he grasped her hips to direct her movements.

It was too much—the combination of looking into his eyes, seeing the way he wanted her, watching his struggle to hold his own completion in check.

She tossed back her head, riding his body as the swell of orgasm became the center of her world. Shuddering, she cried out, digging her fingers into his shoulders as the heat of his release filled her.

Still shivering, she glanced down, caught defenseless by the emotion brimming in his eyes and the arm he brought up and hooked behind her neck.

He pulled her down for his kiss, grinding his mouth

to hers even as he ground their bodies together. His tongue swept into her mouth, branding her, claiming her, marking her as his possession.

For once in her life, she didn't pull free from such a demanding kiss.

Or back away from the idea of belonging to only one man.

3

"CHLOE WILL BE HERE in ten minutes to go over the details of our Christmas Eve dinner. Are you thinking of dressing today?"

Patrick glanced from the omelette pan to Annabel's face, then down to his gray jersey athletic shorts, which were threadbare and lacking support. The absence of a jockstrap or briefs didn't improve matters any. Especially since his thoughts had been wandering to the bedroom, and his cock was of a mind to head back that way.

"A T-shirt ought to do me. Maybe a bucket of ice water. But you'll have to watch the omelette." He lifted a brow, indicating the eggs, cheese, tomatoes, cilantro and chorizo simmering on the stovetop.

Annabel tightened the belt of her silky robe, the creamy white-and-blue-green swirly patterns reminding him suddenly of Caribbean waters beneath endless skies. A reminder that took his thoughts back to the cigarette butt he'd picked up from the sidewalk outside the loft at dawn.

He tensed but refused to glance at the evidence of his suspicions lying on the countertop. He'd been planning to deliver breakfast in bed to Annabel. If he'd known she'd be up and dressed before he finished cooking, he'd never have left the butt in plain sight.

Stupid, stupid, stupid.

Annabel walked closer and pinched a square of diced

tomato from the cutting board next to the stove. Her mouth gave a little twist as she considered his suggestion. "Why don't I get you the clothes, and you finish fixing my food?"

"Hungry woman," he growled, hooking an arm around her neck and pulling her away from the counter into a kiss.

It was a fiery kiss, full of tongues and warmth and a satisfaction that their mouths fit so well together. Yet the kiss was a distracting ruse as much as anything, and he kept his eyes open.

With his arm still around her neck and his face nuzzling the skin beneath her ear, he used his free hand to slide the omelette from pan to plate. He then set the pan on the counter, covering the cigarette butt, before turning his full attention to the woman in his arms.

Dodging his affections, she grabbed another bite of tomato, this one out of the omelette, complete with a dangling string of cheese. She reeled in the cheese with her tongue, chewed and swallowed, afflicting him with that smart-ass smirk that never failed to tie his gut in knots.

Thought she was going to get the better of him, did she? She'd better be thinking again. This time when he grabbed her, he didn't let her squirm free, but delivered another hard, teasing, drive-by sweep of his tongue through her mouth.

"You taste like tomatoes," he murmured, wrapping his arms around her waist. He pulled her close for a kiss that was leisurely and lingering, that swept him away with possibilities and promises—until fear came crashing in, the fear that she would drown his ability to scent danger.

Still he kissed her, pushing his hips against her so that

his erection found and settled into the softness of her belly. He pulsed there, throbbing, aching, and he backed her into the edge of the counter for a more secure hold.

She wound her arms around his neck, one hand at his nape, the other pulling his head down with forceful insistence. Her hunger matched his own. Her tongue tangled with his, and her taste set him on fire.

For all her sass, she tendered a sweetness that stole his breath, reminding him that he was a man and that he had survived. She was a huge reason he was finally grateful for the latter; he'd gone so long not giving a damn.

While the idea of remaining a part of her life kicked his self-preservation instincts awake, the idea of leaving triggered something more compelling—the need to protect what was his and no other's. In a matter of weeks, Annabel had become an addiction his sworn enemy wouldn't fail to exploit.

The thought gave him pause. Maybe he *should* run as far away from this woman as time allowed before the inevitable happened, before he lost the edge that had kept him alive, and Annabel paid the price.

He started to break the kiss. With a sound of distress, she cupped his jaw so tenderly he couldn't pretend that all she felt was lust.

That all *he* felt was lust.

He growled into her mouth, seeking more of what she was always so ready to give...then perversely grinding away every trace of gentleness until only raw passion remained. He didn't even release her when the bell rang and the loft's private elevator whirred in the shaft, signaling Chloe's arrival.

Annabel moved her hands from his neck to push against his chest, and tore her mouth free with a gasp. Then she glared at him. "I hate it when you do that."

He feigned an indifferent shrug, reached for the omelette plate and cast a pointed glance at the front of her robe, where her nipples had risen to the occasion. "Yeah. I can tell."

"Arrgh!" She balled her hands into fists, turned and stomped toward the door, but not before glancing down and adjusting the folds of her robe.

Patrick peeked around the floor-to-ceiling lava lamp sculptures that divided the kitchen from the main room of the loft and watched her very fine ass swish away. Sending her off with a long, low wolf whistle, he tossed the pan into the sink and snagged up the omelette and the cigarette butt.

Making his way through the back of the kitchen to the hallway, he headed for Annabel's bedroom. Shimmying out of his jersey shorts, he kicked them into the corner of the walk-in closet where she let him keep a few things. Standing there bare-ass naked, he scarfed down all of their breakfast while deciding on an action plan.

Clothes first, then down to the street to seek out more clues. There was a massive chance that the Jamaican-made cigarette was a coincidence, even though in the eighteen months since his return he'd never found a store that carried the brand.

And he'd looked, because he'd gotten used to taking an occasional drag to relax.

After setting his empty plate on Annabel's chest of drawers, he dug into his duffel for a T-shirt, jeans and the knife few people knew he had—a knife he'd taken from one of Dega's men and kept hidden behind a loose chunk of cinder blocks supporting the barracks.

If Russell Dega was actually here on the hunt, Patrick had damn well better be ready for a showdown.

"SORRY TO HAVE DRAGGED you out of bed," Chloe Zuniga said as Annabel closed the elevator's sliding grate behind her. The two women headed for the kitchen, Chloe giving Annabel a thorough once-over. "I thought you'd be expecting me, not still be in bed getting all kinds of lucky."

"I was expecting you, and I wasn't in bed. I was in the kitchen. I didn't get much sleep last night, and Patrick is making me breakfast." Annabel rounded the corner into the open kitchen area and stopped.

"Or he *was* making you breakfast," Chloe said.

Annabel took in the omelette pan in the sink and the total lack of anything left to eat. Not even a scrap of the diced tomatoes or shredded cheese. "Hmm. I'm going to send that boy a grocery bill if he's not careful."

"Boy?" Chloe pursed her pink lips. "I doubt there's another woman alive who would call Patrick Coffey a boy. Then again, I imagine you know him better than anyone else."

There were times Annabel thought so, times she wondered too much about the other women he'd known, when she had no business wondering any such thing. "Honestly? I'm not sure I know him at all, and I plan to maintain that status quo. You want coffee?"

"Sure."

After casual chitchat while filling their cups, and Annabel's quick check of the bedroom, where she discovered Patrick's vanishing act down the fire escape, she led Chloe back into the loft's main room and settled on the opposite end of the sofa.

"So," Chloe began. "Would you like to explain that status quo comment?"

Annabel lowered her cup. "About getting to know Patrick? What's there to explain?"

"A lot."

Annabel shook her head. "I don't think so. I simply see no need to know him better than I do when this isn't a long-term relationship. We've had our fun." And she really had done her best to make him see the truth of his destructive behavior. "But I have a lot of decisions to make that are best made without having Patrick around."

Chloe's blond bob swung as she tilted her chin. "If you were a man, I'd accuse you of not being able to think with your big head."

Smiling privately, Annabel blew over the surface of her hot coffee before she sipped. "I'll admit to seeing things through sex-colored glasses these days."

"I'll bet." Chloe stared into her own cup. "I'm the same way with Eric."

"Yes, but you and Eric are involved, committed—" a strange twist of envy caught at Annabel's midsection "—and in love."

Chloe nodded as she lifted her coffee, but her tremulous expression—one totally out of character—was more telling than the motion of her head.

Annabel frowned. "Chloe? Are you and Eric having trouble?"

"Oh, no," Chloe hurriedly insisted. "We're fine. We're great."

"If I didn't know you better, I'd believe every word. But your face is telling an entirely different story." Annabel paused to let that sink in. "You forget how long I've known you."

"Oh, no, I haven't." Chloe's brow lifted sharply. "I was there every step of the way while you were busy stealing my job."

Annabel huffed. "You weren't exactly laying down your life to save what you had. Your interest wasn't there, and I took full advantage. I remember having this discussion with you then.''

Pulling in a nervous breath, Chloe said in a rush, ''I'm afraid that's what's happening with Eric. That his interest isn't there. And that I'm going to lose him.''

''What are you talking about?'' Annabel's chest grew tight with worry. ''You adore him. He adores you—''

''I'm not so sure anymore.''

''How can you say that? I was at your place Tuesday night. I saw the two of you together. He can't stand for you to be out of his sight.''

''That's the thing. I've been so busy with the gUIDANCE gIRL program that I've neglected him, neglected us. And I readily admit that....'' Chloe's sadness was virtually palpable. ''Did you know Macy's pregnant?''

''No. I didn't.'' But the revelation certainly put Chloe's funk into perspective. ''Do you want to have a baby?''

''Yes. No. Later, maybe.''

''And Eric?''

''I've always thought so. It's just that recently he's stopped talking about the Little League team of his loins, when he used to tease me about babies all the time.'' She tucked her feet beneath her protectively. ''I'm not sure what to do.''

Even knowing her girlfriend was hurting and wasn't trying to be funny, Annabel couldn't help but chuckle. ''One thing you can do is get ready to kiss those perky boobs goodbye.''

Chloe frowned. ''That's not funny.''

So much for trying to lighten the mood. ''I know it's not. But what sort of friend would I be if I didn't point out the obvious?''

"Well, think of a different obvious, would you? Like the one I keep missing when I try to figure out what's going on with him." Chloe's hands gripped her cup so tightly Annabel feared the china would break.

She'd never seen her girlfriend so emotionally distraught. Chloe usually tossed off problems in a flurry of foulmouthed curses and gutter talk. She was not the type to fret or to stew. Especially not when it came to her relationship with Eric Haydon.

Annabel, unfortunately, was the last person to dispense advice on dealing with men. She was certainly no shining example of sticking with anything long term.

Even so, she was hardly unfeeling enough to change the subject now that Chloe had confided her fears—no matter that those fears struck at the heart of Annabel's own decision to cut Patrick out of her life.

"Look, Chloe. I'm the least qualified person I know when it comes to relationship issues. All I can say is that from an outsider's perspective, you don't have a thing to worry about with Eric." She went on, nipping Chloe's objection in the bud. "But maybe you need to discuss this with him instead of me. Does he know how you've been feeling?"

Chloe went back to nursing her coffee, refusing to meet Annabel's gaze. "Every time I get up the nerve to talk about it, he changes the subject. It's as if he's totally indifferent. And I can't help but worry that it's not just the babies he's losing interest in."

"You think it's you."

Chloe nodded, looking so miserable and lost, Annabel couldn't doubt her friend's sincerity. Which was why it came out of left field when, cup empty, Chloe slid the china across the coffee table and bounced around like a depressive on a manic rebound. "Never mind about me.

I started my period, and I'm moody because I thought an accidental pregnancy might be just the solution.''

She couldn't be serious. ''When is an accidental pregnancy ever a solution to anything?''

''I'm kidding. I'm hormonal, I told you,'' Chloe insisted. Though Annabel wasn't convinced about the kidding part, she watched Chloe dig through her bag for her Day-Timer. ''Anyway, let's go over the rest of your Christmas Eve dinner details. I think we're set, but with my luck, I've totally forgotten something major.''

''Actually,'' Annabel began, wondering the best way to make this last-minute request, ''I was hoping we could skip discussing Christmas and go straight to New Year's.''

''Sure,'' Chloe said with a shrug. ''I'm game, and I'm easy.'' She tapped her pen on her calendar page. Then she looked up questioningly. ''What I'm not is clairvoyant.''

Annabel released a wry smile. ''Newvale's canceled on me.''

''For Devon's showing? You're kidding. What's the deal?''

''One of their cooks took a walk. Or was asked to take a walk. Whatever.'' She set her empty cup on the coffee table, leaned back and cinched her robe tighter. ''I'm stuck with sixty RSVPs, a truckload of booze and no servers.''

''Servers, hell.'' Chloe's expression grew wide-eyed. ''What about the food? I can't believe Newvale's didn't sell the contract to another caterer.''

''I have the option, but have to let them know by Monday.''

''And something tells me you have an alternative up your sleeve.''

"Patrick's agreed to cook."

Chloe's smirking expression of moments before went carefully blank. "I see."

Annabel bristled. "You don't think he's capable?"

"Of cooking? Sure he is. Of handling possible crises until the last guest leaves?" Chloe shook her head. "Not on your life. A year and a half and he hasn't stuck around to eat a single meal he's cooked. The man is an island."

Chest constricting, Annabel forced a smile and pushed away the unaccustomed protective instincts urging her to defend her lover's good name. He didn't have one, after all, leaving her with nothing to safeguard but her feelings, which were in conflict with her goal of their imminent parting.

"He doesn't have to leave the kitchen or mingle with the guests. All I need is for him to cook and for you and the other girls to help me serve."

STANDING IN THE boarded-up doorway of the small video-rental store across the street, Patrick stared up at the fourth-story balcony of Annabel's loft. He'd been here once already, earlier this morning, but couldn't help it. He'd had to come back.

If anyone had been wanting a clear look at him last night, this would've been the place to get it. Not a single telephone pole or electrical line or billboard blocked the view from the sidewalk to the loft. It was a straight shot from here to there, and he didn't like the idea that he'd been as exposed as he had, that Annabel had been exposed at all.

Mostly he didn't like the idea that he'd been so stupidly reckless, that he'd been drinking and feeling sorry for himself when he knew better. The first didn't do him a bit of good, and he'd had three years of doing the second to prove it wasn't worth the hassle.

Thing was, until he'd picked up the cigarette butt this morning, he'd been halfway convinced that looking over his shoulder was more a waste of time than a precaution. He'd been home for nearly a year and a half now and hadn't seen so much as a shadow other than his own. And looking for shadows was something he'd gotten used to doing pretty damn fast.

For the first couple of months after being hijacked off the schooner and watching his brother and Ray's two fraternity buddies sail away, Patrick had flinched at the slightest shift from light to dark. Or, he thought with a sharp laugh, from dark to light.

He'd jumped at everything, truth be told, until he'd met Soledad. When the pirates had returned to the island three days into his captivity, she'd boarded Russell Dega's powerboat and dragged Patrick up out of the cargo hold, demanding the bandit bastard cut him free from his bonds. Dega had, but not out of the kindness of his heart.

He'd laughed at her saucy, rapid-fire orders and used the same knife Patrick now carried to slice through the ropes he'd had three days onboard to get used to wearing. Patrick had listened then to the two of them arguing in a mixture of English and Spanish, Soledad snapping at Dega that he was about profit, about money, not about sport or revenge.

For some reason, once Soledad came into the picture, Dega seemed to forget the enmity he had for Patrick, treating him as a curiosity, a joke and then as a new toy he'd tired of winding up and watching squirm. It was as if Soledad was the baby-sitter Dega hadn't trusted any of his men to be. That was Patrick's first clue that she wasn't just another of the women who waited for their men to return from a hard day's looting at sea.

During the three days Patrick had been kept on the boat, however, Dega had been quite clear that he had zero patience with self-important college boys determined to muck up his operation by trying to play the hero. As if Patrick was going to sit back while the pirate crew boarded and trashed the schooner, threatening his brother and Ray's buddies?

Even Dega's threat to teach Patrick a lesson didn't stop him from locking the main cabin hatches behind him as he bolted down the companionway. He'd been after a flare gun, a bullhorn, a handheld VHF radio—anything to signal their distress. He'd run into one of Dega's men instead, and had been blasted with the rented schooner's own canister of pepper spray.

Hero. Right.

He'd ended up being the only one dragged away.

The pirate gang numbered in the low twenties, as best Patrick had been able to tell once shuttled from the hold of the powerboat to the remote—though civilized—camp that served as their land-based operation. And that was where he'd stayed for most of his three years away.

He'd been free to wander through the compound, to swim in the cove surrounding the private dock, to fish the reef along the island from one of the flat-bottom boats. At least until the night he'd rowed out into open waters and fired up the outboard.

He really thought he'd calculated his timing, having clocked Dega's comings and goings for several weeks. But he'd thought wrong. He hadn't been out of the cove ten minutes when he'd looked up to see Dega's boat bearing down on him. The searchlights had blinded him, had guaranteed that Dega saw him, but the boat continued forward at full throttle.

Patrick had taken a dive he'd been certain at the time would be his last. He'd sunk like a rock as the propeller churned the water over his head, the boat coming to a stop and circling directly above the spot where he was trying not to drown.

He'd been wrong about the dive being his last, and had ended up with a lot of time to figure out how things had gone from bad to worse while the shackles binding his ankles kept him landlocked. Now, however, the task at hand was to figure out how to keep the situation from traveling any farther south, and how to bring Dega down for the very last time.

Wishing for a cigarette, but only half as much as he wished for a drink, Patrick stepped out of the doorway alcove onto the sidewalk. Lost in thoughts he'd like to lose permanently, he'd forgotten that it was barely ten o'clock. Hardly the time to be chugging down a cold one no matter that his drinking was more about the situation than the hour of the day.

He supposed he could toe a sober line for the next couple of weeks to make Annabel happy and keep her quiet. She didn't like his drinking much, or at least she didn't like not knowing the reasons he drank. But the day he answered her questions was the day she owned more than his willing body.

And sobriety was a small price to pay for a soul. Even a sorry-ass one like his.

Heading back across the street, he pulled open the door to the hallway leading to the warehouse's bank of elevators. Even in daylight, the high, narrow windows provided scant illumination, barely more than the wall lamps that were supposed to finish the job. Patrick couldn't figure out why such a classy woman as Annabel would want to live in such a dump of a neighborhood.

No one was asking him, but *revitalization* appeared to be nothing but a fancy word for *rip-off* if she'd paid even half of what he imagined. Still, he had to admit he would miss the place. He felt safe here, as weird as that was. Felt as if he fit in, instead of sticking out like a big fat sore thumb the way he did in Ray's neighborhood.

Yeah, they'd both grown up in the house Ray and Sydney now lived in, but Patrick had lost his suburban blinders a long time back. He no longer saw the same world as his brother, and that hurt, losing that connection over a freak disaster that was no one's fault.

It hurt even more knowing Ray blamed himself for the entire vacation gone bad. That was one delusion Patrick needed to make sure got cleared up, and soon. Annabel had been right to chew him out.

Approaching the elevators, he fought a smile at the thought of her brutal honesty. Surprisingly refreshing, since everyone else seemed to tiptoe on eggshells around him. But not her. Oh, no. She crunched her way straight to her in-your-face point.

Namely that Ray's self-inflicted punishment had gone on four years too long already. And if Patrick didn't "snap out of his moody self-absorption and help his older brother forgive himself," she wasn't sure they'd ever be able to make up for lost time, much less get back the bond they'd once shared.

Hands braced on the hip-high elevator railing, Patrick hung his head and studied his boots. How she'd known about that brotherly bond was no mystery. Anything Ray knew, Sydney knew. And anything one gIRL-gEAR partner knew, they all learned eventually.

Stupidest damn thing Patrick had ever seen, and sure to get one or more of them burned.

It wasn't that he didn't like Annabel's friends, because he did. He just couldn't imagine trusting that many people so implicitly. And with Ray growing more and more distant, the one person Patrick might've felt free to confide his fears to couldn't be counted on not to spill the gory details.

He spat out a mouthful of curses as his mood turned foul. Yeah, it was more than past time to make things right with his brother, but he wasn't going to solve a thing standing inside a box going nowhere.

The elevator jerked upward once he finally hit the button for *four.* When it lurched to a stop, he yanked up the door until it caught and slid open on its tracks. Then, pulling back the folding grate, he stepped into the loft.

Chloe and Annabel still sat on the sofa; both women stared in his direction as if expecting his return to bring world peace, when he'd come back with nothing but his instinct for survival running high.

Still the two women stared, and his hackles rose. He hated feeling as if they'd been discussing him, analyzing him and finding him distinctly lacking.

"It's just me. Your friendly neighborhood thug."

"What happened to your hair?" Chloe asked.

"Annabel scalped me," he said, running a hand over the top of his head. "She's on a mission to improve my acceptability rating."

Annabel gave him that look that made him feel as if he were a lost cause. Or maybe his perception was simply an extension of his mood. Either way, he needed to get out of here before he tossed out the smart-ass remarks on the tip of his tongue and pissed her off.

He took two steps down the long hallway that ran past

the kitchen toward the bedroom before she stopped him. "Walking out on a conversation, or on a guest, doesn't exactly win you any points. Just in case you're interested."

Mouth twisted with sarcasm, he met her gaze. "Nope. Not interested in the least."

"I see," she said, all snotty and managing to look down her nose at him from her place on the couch.

If he hadn't been watching closely, he might've missed the flicker of hurt in her beautiful eyes. He damned himself for that, for causing her pain, knowing he should pack up his duffel and go—no matter that he'd just spent an hour detailing the reasons he couldn't walk out of her life.

But he sure as hell could walk out of the room.

And he did.

4

"OKAY, SPILL. What was all that stuff going on back there with Patrick?" Chloe asked, having followed Poe in her own car as they'd driven from Midtown through Rice Village to Three Mings.

Earlier, Poe hadn't wanted to talk about Patrick's weirdness. She'd simply gotten dressed in the guest room, grabbed her bag and herded Chloe to the parking garage, using some excuse about needing to go over the setup for the New Year's Eve showing at Devon's gallery.

Now that they'd arrived, and Poe had had the twenty-minute trip across town to cool her jets, Chloe vowed that she wasn't going anywhere without first getting the scoop.

Poe slammed the driver's-side door of her low-slung black Jaguar. Her expression might've fooled others, but Chloe saw beneath the cold mask to the seething fire.

"It's exactly as I related earlier. I told him he has to go, and he's pissed off," Poe said, walking around the front of the car.

"Patrick being pissed off makes sense." Chloe fell into step beside her girlfriend as they headed for the staircase leading to the building's second story. "But I still say that you blowing him off doesn't."

Poe cast a glance over her shoulder as she began the

climb. "Actually, it makes a lot of sense. He's been a nice distraction, but it's time for me to move on."

"Move on to what?" Chloe asked, following Poe. "A nunnery? Because I can't imagine that Patrick Coffey doesn't know his way around a bedroom."

"It's about moving on with my life. *My life.* It has nothing to do with Patrick or the bedroom." Poe reached the second-story covered landing and glanced back. "How many times have we talked about this recently? You know what I'm facing."

"Yeah. A midlife crisis at age thirty-three." Though thirty-three wasn't as bad as the crisis Chloe was having as she neared twenty-eight.

"It's hardly a crisis. I'm simply preparing for life after graduation."

"So you're determined to leave gIRL-gEAR?"

"You and I talked about this long before I was made partner. It can hardly be a surprise to anyone. But especially not to you."

Chloe shrugged. "You're right. It shouldn't be. But it is."

Poe crossed her arms over her chest and faced her friend directly. "This degree has taken me twice as long as it should have. I've worked full-time. I've modeled on the side, all to pay for this education. Why would you think I'd change my mind after the effort I've put in?"

"No reason. Just wishful thinking. We'll miss you," Chloe admitted, hating the thought of losing a friend. It was hard enough to face the idea of losing Eric. *Oh, God.* "*I'll* miss you," she said, her voice a strangled mess.

"Good Lord, Chloe. I'm not leaving the country. I'm not even leaving the city. At least not yet. I'll certainly still be around."

"You won't be at the office." She pursed her lips,

deciding to put an end to this depressing conversation before she sank any further into a morass of self-pity. "But nothing you've said explains why you're dumping Patrick."

Poe rolled her eyes before giving Chloe a look that throttled her as effectively as a pair of hands. "Our being together is not...healthy. You've seen how Patrick is."

"Yeah. Sexy as hell. Moody and intense. Wickedly intriguing."

"Not to mention quite unstable and more than a little bit wild. He's unpredictable, to say the least, and I'm running short on patience dealing with his disposition." Poe put an end to the conversation by turning away and opening the gallery's front door.

But Chloe wasn't that easily fooled. She'd seen the harsh pain in her girlfriend's eyes and knew there was a lot more going on here than Poe, being Poe, would ever admit. With the subject of Patrick Coffey summarily closed, Chloe walked into the gallery.

The first thing that struck her was the coolness, then the silence and then the sense of calm. Closing the door behind her, she shut her eyes and breathed in the scents of hardwood floors and fresh flowers and oils on canvas.

Or she imagined the latter, because she couldn't quite identify the source of a more earthy and elemental smell. No, even that was a lame description and not accurate at all. The scent was rich and sharp and...*arrgh!*

She gave up trying to isolate what it was relaxing her so, and simply...relaxed.

"Chloe? Are you coming? Devon's probably in his office."

Chloe shook her head; her eyes drifted open slowly. "I'll catch up. I want to look around. I haven't been here before, remember?"

Poe smiled. "Sure. I'll find Devon and be back."

Chloe couldn't even find the energy to wave the other woman away. She knew she was being overdramatic, or flaky à la Kinsey Storey—the most recently married gIRL-gEAR partner—but it was as if Chloe could literally feel the tension of the last few weeks seeping away. Ridiculous, really.

She was much too practical to believe the ambience of a room could soothe her stress. Then again, *soothed* was exactly how she felt as she held her clutch purse at her waist and made her way slowly into the gallery proper.

It had to be the simplicity, the contrast to the recent chaos of her life, lending an air of tranquility to her surroundings in ways the supposed aromatherapy candles she burned failed to do.

Candles. Ha! Yes, she'd been that desperate, that hopeless, that lost of late that she'd turned to candles and bath oils and massages, looking to ease the nerves burning an ulcer into her stomach.

The massages had helped; sex would've been better.

But Eric never came to bed anymore until long after she was asleep.

"That watercolor is called *Missedtakes,*" said a voice at Chloe's shoulder.

She glanced from the painting she hadn't even noticed to the man who had spoken, the man without a trace of an accent, but whose beautiful almond-shaped eyes told her he was Devon Lee.

"I've thought of moving it farther into the gallery because visitors find it hard to walk away." As he spoke, he studied the depiction of a woman staring into a pond, gazing at what wasn't her reflection but a man's retreating back. Devon didn't look at Chloe at all.

She turned to the framed canvas again and listened to Poe's brother; his voice lulled her further into a strangely hypnotic state.

"I suppose there's a sadness about it, but I prefer to see the hope that comes with moving on."

Moving on. The very words Poe had used earlier. Chloe felt conspired against, though such a feeling was absurd. Neither Devon nor his sister knew all the details of the uncertainty plaguing her relationship with Eric, how she feared he'd fallen in love with who he thought she was and not the truth of who he'd since discovered her to be....

"It doesn't appear to me as if she's doing anything but wondering what went wrong." Ugh. She'd barely managed to raise her voice above a whisper and still it had cracked.

Devon stepped closer, hovered behind her yet made no contact. "Or maybe she sees it exactly, and he's the one who is blind."

Emotion gripped Chloe's throat and made it hard for her to swallow or to speak. She wondered what Eric would see in this painting, or if he would be as blind to any possible interpretation as he was to her.

No. That wasn't fair. He knew she was restless, searching, unsatisfied. That was why he never came to bed. A funny way to go after all those babies he'd once claimed to want so badly. A claim she was coming to believe had been a lie.

Chloe turned and stared into Devon's dark eyes, seeing a sensitivity that complemented rather than compromised his incredible masculinity. "You painted it, didn't you?"

His lips quirked in a wry smile. "And here I worked so hard on disguising my signature."

She shook her head. "I didn't see your signature. It's in your eyes."

Slowly, he moved his gaze from the canvas to her face. His black brows drew into a slashed V above a very straight, very aquiline nose. His lips were lush and eminently tempting, and his teeth fairly gleamed.

"I wasn't aware I was that transparent," he said softly, his voice low and seductive, even if he hadn't meant it to be.

Or perhaps she was simply longing to be seduced. She tried to shrug it off. "You caught me in a receptive mood."

"Are you sure that's all it is?"

She tilted her head ever so slightly. "Why do you ask?"

He drew closer without seeming to move at all. "I hear it in your voice."

Oh, boy. This was not good, this feeling of anticipation sweeping the length of her body. The unexpected excitement, the sudden giddy rush of blood to her head.

She reached deep inside to find the punchy sarcasm, the acerbic sense of humor that always served her well...and came up with nothing. "Then I suppose I ought to keep my mouth shut."

What she really needed to do was turn and walk out the door, to wait for Poe at the car, to refuse to have anything to do with the New Year's Eve showing that would mean time spent in this man's company. She was hurt and raw and too susceptible to his flirtation, to the feeling of having what a man might want when she'd so obviously disappointed Eric.

"Devon Lee," he said, and held out his hand.

She took it and replied, "Chloe Zuniga."

"Ah. Annabel's friend," he murmured, taking far too long to release her.

Chloe nodded. "She thought she'd find you in your office. I told her I wanted to look through the gallery."

He held out his arm, gesturing for her to precede him into the low-ceilinged maze. "Then it would be my pleasure to give you a tour."

Doing her best to ignore the warmth of his attention, Chloe turned, only to come face-to-face with Poe. "Poe, hey. I found your brother."

"So I see," she said, with a remarkable lack of pleasure in her tone at finding the two of them so chummy.

Devon cleared his throat. "I was just about to walk Chloe through the gallery."

Poe looked from Devon to Chloe and back again before facing them with crossed arms, a posture that nearly caused Chloe to cower.

"The only stop on this tour is your office," Poe said to Devon, turning to Chloe and tapping into her guilt with what might as well have been an accusation. "We have work to do."

UPON RETURNING to the loft, Annabel shoved the elevator grate closed just as Patrick came out of the kitchen. He was wiping his hands on a towel, and smells of onions and garlic followed him. The guarded look he wore told her she wasn't in for a fun-filled evening at home.

It really was too much for a Saturday. No breakfast, refereeing Devon and Chloe and now back to face her pirate and his mercurial moods. Wondering what had happened to her nice, relaxing two-week vacation, Annabel tucked her car keys and sunglasses into her bag and tossed it to the sofa.

She arched one brow. "Are you finished sulking?"

Patrick waited for a moment, staring at her, unmoving, the glint off the silver hoop in his ear as bright as that in his eyes. With his hair cropped close and his face exposed completely, she had no trouble seeing the tic in his jaw as he bit down on his answer. Finally, he turned and walked back to the kitchen, leaving her unsatisfied and frustrated and on the verge of turning right around and walking back out.

Of abandoning him to his own devices. And abandonment was one thing of which she was incapable.

Circling the near end of the sofa, she picked up the wooden memento box she kept on her coffee table. Twelve inches long, four inches deep and covered with a Chinese almanac print, the box had belonged to her mother, a gift from man number seven and a keepsake that meant no more to Annabel now than it had to her mother then.

She'd kept it...she didn't know why. It was as false in its representation of her Asian heritage as were her mother's never-ending promises to stay.

Inside, however, was a rectangular jade pendant inscribed in gold with the Chinese character for love. The pendant had belonged to Annabel's grandmother, who had willed it to her and it meant more to her than any single memory of her mother that remained.

Her grandmother had done all that she could for both of her grandchildren, finally moving them to Houston to be near more of her own family when it was clear their mother had left, never to return. Annabel couldn't have asked for a better example of serenity in patience and purpose.

Inheriting more of that attitude would have served her well, but at least she knew that when she parted ways with Patrick, she would do so having given his redemption her very best shot. If she failed in her efforts, it would be because he wasn't ready to be redeemed. She stroked her thumb over the smooth jade before returning it to the box and going to salvage what she could of her Saturday night.

"Listen, Patrick," she began, rounding the wall of lava lamp sculptures and entering the kitchen. Once again, the empty kitchen. She sighed heavily and turned off the fire beneath the skillet of braising garlic.

On the countertop next to the stovetop, she found the New Year's Eve menu notes she'd left on the coffee table earlier in the day. This time her sigh was even heavier, as was the weight of her heart. She recognized his effort to apologize for being an ass this morning.

He'd taken the initiative and jumped right to what had to be a trial run of the recipes, taking care of what she wanted him to do. Holding up his end of the bargain they'd made. The only reason she'd agreed to keep him around.

That thought shouldn't have caused her such grief, such a sense of foul play. She certainly shouldn't be thinking of taking it all back—and she wasn't, really. She was simply surprised to find Patrick so deeply under her skin.

Steeling herself for what she'd find in the bedroom, she walked out the kitchen's back entrance and down the short hallway. He stood at the bedroom window. Even though it wasn't yet dusk, the interior remained dim due to the cloudy evening skies.

With the miniblinds open but left down, stripes of what light there was outside fell across the hardwood floor and across Patrick's body. From the rear, he appeared more as a silhouette than a three-dimensional man.

His head hung down, his focus on the floor rather than the street below. Having his hands in his pockets seemed to add more width to his already impressive shoulders. He stood with his feet apart as if he were on point, ready to pounce.

The bronze of his skin, the black of his T-shirt and jeans, his crop of dark brown hair combined in a sort of camouflage. She could so easily see him in the tropics, in the jungle, fighting to stay alive. He had the look of a freedom fighter, a guerilla, and he stirred her emotions as well as her blood.

She drew in a full breath to steady her shaky nerves, and approached slowly. She wanted him to hear her steps; she'd learned from their first night together not to surprise him. It was best for both their sakes.

He stiffened. She saw the slight shift in the set of his shoulders, saw him tighten further the closer she drew. It wasn't until she slipped her arms around his waist and pressed her face to the center of his back that he relaxed at all. The breath he exhaled seemed to deflate his entire body until she thought he might fall should she let go.

Breathing deeply, she inhaled his scent, looking to calm herself with his familiarity, but remembering too many other times when she'd held him this close without the burden of clothing between them. Separating the sensual from the sexual had become an impossible task.

She embraced the aesthetic feel of his body, the muscles that bulged, that rippled, that stretched into elongated contours beneath his skin. Yet another part of her knew this body simply as the one that brought her such pleasure.

Her own now reacted, her breasts tightening, her thighs clenching hard in response to the rush of inner heat and dampness waiting to spill. Patrick finally moved his hands from his pockets to cover hers, which were resting over his midsection. The simple gesture brought enormous relief.

"Guess the haircut didn't do much for my civility."

A little bird told her that this was not the time for that conversation. Instead, she tightened her hold. "No, but it's done plenty for your sex appeal."

"Yeah?" he asked, and she felt his cocky grin.

She couldn't see his face, but she didn't have to. His entire body relaxed, as if accepting her forgiveness of his transgression.

"So," he began in that rich voice that rumbled through her, holding him as she was. "If I'm so sexy, why aren't you busy jumping my bones?"

This time she was the one who grinned. "You really do have a one-track mind."

"Yeah, but at least that's one thing about me you don't hate."

If only things were that simple. "There are more than a few things about you that I don't...hate." Didn't he know? The breath he obviously held said he needed to hear the words. "I do not hate your kitchen skills."

He huffed.

"Or your passion. I certainly do not hate your wit, your intelligence or your ability to take yourself lightly, though you need to work on doing that more often. And I do appreciate that you don't hold a grudge against those who aren't sure what to make of you."

He huffed again and growled. "I'm more interested in what you make of me."

She sighed, doing no more than enjoying this moment of holding him close. An enjoyment that took on a heightened sense of pleasure when he grasped her hands and moved them from his midsection to the fly of his jeans. Very impressive.

"Okay," she admitted. "You're very hard to resist."

"*Too* hard to resist, I hope."

"Hmm. I don't know." She pressed her palm to the length of his growing erection and squeezed. "Ah, now it's getting harder."

"You like flirting with danger, don't you? I can feel your smile on my back."

"You could feel it much better if you'd pull off your shirt."

He wasn't two seconds in taking her up on the suggestion. He unbuttoned his jeans while he was at it, then braced both hands on the window frame and leaned his weight into his arms, silently inviting her to have her way.

Ah, the responsibility of his surrender. She thrilled to the fact that he trusted her as far as he did, and wished that he trusted her fully. Or perhaps it was himself he still wasn't ready to trust.

She supposed that should have frightened her a bit. Had she not lived the life she had, that might well have been her reaction. But she was beyond being intimidated by a man who denied his own suffering.

She pulled her hands away from their tactile enjoyment of the bulge behind denim and soft cotton and pressed her palms to his sides, to his rib cage, just above the slack waistband of his jeans.

The smoothness of his skin never failed to amaze her. With all that he'd lived through, she always expected to find him as hard and coarse as his outlook. But he was a beautiful male specimen, and she slid her hands from his ribs to his armpits, enjoying the shudder that rattled through him.

When she moved her fingertips to his chest, circling his flat nipples embedded in the hard muscles of his pecs, and tugging on the one silver ring, his shudder grew stronger. This time she shuddered, too, and released him just long enough to skim off her silk sweater and bra.

Oh, yes. So much better, feeling his skin with her own, on her own. He stiffened and then slowly relaxed, as if easing into the contact and knowing she was in no hurry to complete what they'd begun.

That was one thing she enjoyed most about this man. She was seven years older, and she saw the age difference in his cocky playfulness, yet never in bed. He was mature as a lover, patient, taking care of her pleasure, savoring their time and allowing nothing to intrude.

With her breasts pressed to the center of his back, she turned her head and placed her lips on his spine, kissing him softly, tasting his skin while making circles with the tip of her tongue. She moved her hands ever so slowly down his abdomen, teasing him by never reaching beneath his clothing, though he lifted his hips and urged her to do so.

She couldn't wait to take his penis into her hands, to stroke the thick shaft, to marvel over the softness of the mushroomed head, to absorb the warmth that always seemed on the verge of burning her hands. But there was so much more of his body to be cherished first.

"Take off your boots," she ordered, and he bent to unlace and remove them. She kicked off her own pumps, losing two inches to him.

"Now your pants," she added, once he'd straightened. She swore she heard a dangerous chuckle as he stripped. The sound served to tighten her tautly strung nerves even further, to heighten the room's tension until the air became hard to breathe.

He stood, braced his hands on the window frame again as if needing the solid hold to keep from falling. Or to keep from letting go all the truths and emotions he kept bound tightly inside.

Determined to break through before letting him go, she shimmied out of her pants and kicked the black linen across the floor along with her black lace panties, tickled at her ability to mistreat her expensive clothes.

Patrick Coffey was a very bad influence, and she wouldn't have him any other way.

Starting at his shoulders, she drew her fingertips down his back to his buttocks, and then down farther, skimming her palms over the backs of his thighs as far as her reach allowed. Her own skin prickled with gooseflesh; the room was cool, but the reaction was strictly due to Patrick's heat. The temperature contrast added an extreme dimension to the sensory stimulation that consumed her.

Slipping her hands around to the front of his thighs, she tickled and teased her way back up his body, brushing her fingers only briefly through the thicket of hair at his crotch. He growled, thrusting his hips forward and keeping his hands where they were on the windowsill, accepting her challenge to wait.

This was what she enjoyed most about sex with Patrick. His patience outlasted even hers, as did his endurance, making for a wicked combination in bed. She played across the ripples of his abdomen, tugging at the hair that grew beneath his navel, drawing ever-expanding circles out toward his hipbones.

And then she dropped to her knees. While her hands ran down his thighs, she bit at the firm flesh of his backside, healing the light nips with tender kisses and wet swirls of her tongue. He clenched his buttocks, relaxed again once he realized she'd stopped.

"I hate it when you do that," he whispered gruffly, even as he spread his legs wider to give her better access.

She slipped a hand between his legs and cupped his tight balls from behind. "You're lying to both of us, Patrick."

"Yeah," he admitted with a shudder. "I know. It's just a guy thing. You're getting too close to the goods."

"And you love it." She pulled her hand from his balls and ran it along the ridge of hard flesh behind, skimming over the "goods," as he put it, until his shiver reached his knees.

Nothing gave her greater satisfaction than knowing she affected him so. A heady thing, this power, and she was wet with it, wet with wanting him, wet with the thrill of the wait.

Nipping again at the curve of his ass, she wrapped one arm around his thigh, slipped the other back between his spread legs and closed both hands around his engorged shaft. She held him tight and he stood still, his muscles rigid, his skin so hot it grew damp.

She held him until she thought his body might snap, until a bead of sweat dropped from his forehead to her wrist. Only then did she begin to stroke, using the release of moisture from the slit in the tip of his cock to ease the slide of her hands. He thrust into her grip, and she pushed her forearm up between his legs, spreading him open the way he so often spread her.

The motion of his body, the low panting growl that rumbled up from his throat, the slickness he continued to release all served to heighten her desire. When she couldn't take it anymore and the scent of her own arousal grew strong, she released him, crawling around him on hands and knees to open her mouth over his cock.

He groaned as she took him to the back of her throat, groaned again as she pulled away, leaving her lips wrapped around his swollen head and casting her gaze up to his. His eyes appeared to burn with a blue flame. His skin glistened with sweat. She took his erection in her hand and swirled her tongue around the tip, never breaking eye contact as she sucked him back into her mouth.

This time she watched as his eyes rolled and his jaw clenched so firmly she imagined the pop of the bone. Her enjoyment of his taste and his texture was interrupted when he pulled free from her mouth, grabbed her upper arms and lifted her to her feet.

He shoved his erection between her legs, his tongue into her mouth. The bruising crush of his fingers held her still, and she simply placed her palms over his heart. The beat of his blood thudded through her. His kiss consumed her until dizziness swept her into a place between cognizance and unconscious thought. His mouth was hard and demanding, his tongue a rough source of amazing pleasure.

But it was the driving thrust of his cock between her thighs making her crazy with want.

"I hate tasting myself in your mouth," he growled, having torn his lips free and moved to nuzzle her neck.

"Well, I can't get enough," she admitted with a whisper, knowing she was speaking of much more than he was. She couldn't get enough of his ability to take her to a place where thought ceased to exist and pleasure became the center of her world.

He took her there now, making his way to her breasts, sucking on one nipple, then the other, while his hands kneaded and squeezed. She braced her hands on the window ledge; her head fell back and her legs opened. Patrick took the hint and continued down her body, his tongue circling and dipping into her navel before he licked a straight line down her belly to her clit.

When he sucked her into his mouth, she gasped, biting down on the begging cry that he take her now, take her roughly, take her until her legs lacked the strength to hold her upright. She bit down because she refused to reveal to him any of her weaknesses, knowing that made her a hypocrite for deriding him when he did the same.

Right now, she hardly cared what her actions said about her character. All she cared about was Patrick's exceptional mouth. She curled her fingers around the sill, boosted her butt onto the edge and moved the soles of her feet to his thighs.

He took hold of her ankles, imprisoning her with his hands while his tongue swept down her slit and entered her. He thrust in, pulled out, using his skillful tongue as he would his cock, before returning his attention to the hard knot of nerves ready to burst.

A whimper escaped her mouth before she could stop it, and Patrick hummed his appreciation of her reaction into the center of her sex. She loved what he did to her, even while she hated him knowing the power he wielded. She didn't want him to think she would ever give up so much of herself outside of the bedroom.

When his hands began a slow slide from her ankles to her calves to the tender skin of her inner thighs, she trembled with a needy anticipation. And then his thumbs were there—*yes, oh, yes, there, right there*—opening the lips of her sex to expose her slick inner flesh.

He slid two fingers through her folds and into her core as deeply as she could take him, pushing in, pulling out, just as he'd done with his tongue. He knew exactly what to do every time, all the time, to bring her to the edge without letting her plunge over. He always made her wait. Just as he waited. Sex between them was a battle of wills as much as physical bliss.

He fingered her so deftly, finding her G-spot and caressing the swollen pillow even as he sucked on her clitoris, lightly tonguing his way around the hard bud. He stroked and licked and suckled, and she dug her heels into his thighs, pressed her palms to the window ledge until she thought her arms would break.

But she knew he wouldn't stop. Not when he had her so close, when she was the one shuddering and he was the one in charge.

She clenched her inner muscles and pulled her hips farther back on the window ledge. Patrick glanced up, frowning, giving her a long moment to catch her breath and to slip the toes of one foot down beneath his balls.

His frown deepened, just before his eyes closed and his hands moved down between his own legs to take hold of his cock. He stroked himself, as if he was the only one who understood what he needed, the relief he sought and where he'd find it.

She slid from the window ledge into his lap, straddling his thighs with her own. The tip of his cock settled into the cleft of her sex, and she desperately wanted to take him inside. But not yet. Her hesitation wasn't about the lack of a condom. Birth control wasn't an issue, and the sex they engaged in was safe. No, she waited for him to return to the moment. She wanted him with her all the way.

He opened his eyes, and she swore they glistened with unshed tears. Either that or a redness born of unbearable frustration and a sadness he rarely released. Wrapping her arms around his neck and pulling him close was suddenly more important than joining their bodies.

She soothed him with tiny kisses, with strokes of her palm over the back of his head. He buried his face in the crook of her neck and inhaled, waiting, resting, finding whatever strength of will he needed to fight the demons that raged within him.

When he looked up again, when this time he met her gaze, his eyes seemed to burn with an inner fire, a dangerous fire that sent her heart racing. And then he drew the tip of his cock through her sex, finding her entrance and plunging deep.

She cried out, but he caught and swallowed the sound with his kiss. He surrounded her, consumed her; he burned her inside and out, and she thought she might die.

His cock remained still but for the throbbing pulse she could feel all the way to her womb. His tongue, however, swept madly through her mouth. He held her head so she couldn't move, trapping her between both of his large hands, and kissing her feverishly, as if his life depended on what she offered.

She moved her hands to his cheeks and kissed him back, giving him all that she was capable of giving without opening up her own stores of hidden needs. Right now, at this moment, nothing mattered more than saving Patrick's soul.

It was when his urgency lessened, his kiss softened and his hold relaxed that her body began to ache. The muscles in her widespread thighs burned from straddling him so awkwardly.

Yet every time she adjusted her position, she was reminded how completely he possessed her. Her sex had never felt so full, and even the tiny shifts of her hips increased the friction of his thick shaft against her swollen clit.

She couldn't take any more of the pressure urging her toward orgasm, the sensation of coming undone. And so she pulled her mouth free and stared into his beautifully sad eyes.

"Let's go to bed."

5

PATRICK WONDERED if he'd ever again be able to enjoy a woman the way he did Annabel.

He lay above her, his upper body braced on his elbows, his lower body tucked soundly between her spread legs. Legs, in fact, wrapped tightly around the backs of his thighs as if keeping him from pulling away.

That wasn't going to happen. He was buried exactly where he wanted to be, and could see himself growing old like this. Well, not exactly like this. Eventually, he'd shrivel up and then he'd have to move. But, yeah. The concept of staying around indefinitely was worth thinking about.

Annabel didn't agree. She wanted him to go. She had this bug up her butt about him getting in her way, being a distraction, keeping her from taking her life forward. As if he were some sort of detour or something.

He thrust forward, thrust deeper. She gasped, her head arched back, her eyelids fluttered. His gut clenched hard. He got off majorly on making her crazy. Making her want him.

Want *him*.

She reminded him that he was alive, and that counted for more than the way her body turned his inside out. She knew exactly who she was, and she didn't need him for anything. But, God help him, he needed her. To make him remember that it was time to do more than simply survive. To make him feel safe and sane and whole.

When she raised up on her elbows, he shifted his weight to his hands, suspended above her, his breathing as unsteady as the tremors in his legs, which came from holding completion at bay. He pushed into her even harder, not caring that he was as deep as physically possible.

He needed to own her, to make her aware of what she'd be missing once he was gone. To imprint on the both of them the reality that what they had together was rare.

The corner of her mouth quirked, and he gritted his teeth, feeling her inner muscles tense around his cock. His balls drew close to his body, yet still he held on, playing her game of endurance, easing back until only the head of his erection teased her.

Her expression grew desperate. Score one point for him. A point she matched when she slid her feet down his thighs to his calves and locked her legs over his. She held him there, using her feet to spread him apart when he much preferred the leverage of holding his legs together.

He reared back, pulled out and made his way south, settling his mouth over her beautiful sex and breathing in her unique scent of salty warmth. She tasted way too much of him, but he could deal, what with the way she writhed and enjoyed.

He swirled his tongue through her folds, pushed into her opening, pulled out and went at her again. He loved how wet she grew when he concentrated his efforts. Though this sort of effort required no concentration at all. It was a purely erotic pleasure.

When her hips arched urgently and her breathing was

no more than frantic panting, he crawled back up her body, driving his cock back into her willing warmth, his tongue into her mouth in a mirror of their mating.

They came within seconds and together, Patrick moving his mouth from hers to bury his face in her pillow. He shuddered, feeling the center of his body surge with a release that was powerful and primal, and took him apart. The base of his spine tingled. The base of his cock pulsed. And beneath him Annabel's skin dampened with sweat.

He waited until she'd stopped quivering before he rolled off and collapsed. He was going to die. No, he was already dead. Moving any part of his body ever again was not going to happen, though getting his hands on a cigarette sounded damn fine. Of course, with Annabel bouncing around the way she was, a busy little bee stacking pillows behind her, his postcoital-man disease was curing rapidly.

She settled back and sighed. "You are amazing."

Lying on his back, Patrick tossed one arm across her lap and squeezed her thigh. "Is that a compliment or an invitation for a second helping?"

"Both, I suppose," she answered, twining her fingers through his. "But, actually, it's a question."

Groan. "Let me guess. Who taught me what I know, right?" Eyes closed, he shook his head. "Why is that what women always ask?"

She seemed hesitant before replying. "Maybe because we like to think your talents are individually inspired."

"You do inspire me." There had never been a more certain truth.

But she kept on. *Pick, pick, pick.* "As did obviously so many others."

Patrick groaned audibly this time, rolled out of bed and to his feet. "I'm not going to talk about this."

She didn't even argue, but came right back with a quick and almost apologetic reply. "You're right. It's none of my business. I shouldn't pry."

Then she followed him out of bed, pulling the bedclothes with her and balling them up to wash, changing the subject with a rapidity that had his head spinning. "We should make a run out to Central Market. We're almost out of coffee."

Cocking her head and holding the sheets to her midsection, she stood there naked and gorgeous and rumpled, and more than his dick began to stir. Especially since she hadn't even seemed to think twice when including him in their shared coffee dilemma. He liked that, liked feeling as if she considered him a part of her life, even if only a temporary one.

Yes, she deserved more details about his captivity than he'd been comfortable sharing so far. He'd tell her—he would, and soon. Just not right now. "Good idea. I want to make a practice run at a few of your menu's recipes, so I'll put together a quick shopping list."

"Do you think you can pull this off with only two weeks to prepare?"

Standing there as naked as the day he was born, he grinned. "With you nagging me every step of the way?"

She narrowed her eyes, obviously trying to keep him from seeing the glint of amusement, the same one tugging up the side of her mouth. "A woman must do what a woman must do. Just answer the question."

"Sweetheart, as long as I'm on that list of things you must do, I can pull off anything." He lunged for the crumpled sheets and pulled them away from her clutching hands, tumbling her back into bed, where she squealed. She actually squealed.

Oh, yeah. It was going to be a hell of a fine day.

PATRICK READILY EXPECTED the stares of other shoppers while he and Annabel cruised the aisles of Central Market on this busy Sunday morning. Being judged on his appearance was something he'd used to his advantage for years, from the first time he'd been made aware that his looks were worth a bundle.

As a cocky college frat boy, he'd found his blue eyes and dimples got him laid on a regular basis. The same way his shaved head and unfortunate expression of having lived a stark horror now sent women running.

He had to laugh. Good thing they couldn't see his tattoo or the ring piercing his nipple. They'd be offended right out of their lily-white Keds. Hell, they should've seen him eighteen months ago, wearing no more than threadbare khaki shorts held on with a rope, his hair a knotted mess, his right thigh a palette of caked-on blood and colored ink.

It had taken Soledad months to complete the tattoo, but it had been a way to pass the time, talking, laughing, loving—

He cut off the thought because love hadn't been a part of his relationship with Soledad. She'd been his sanity, yes, his bedmate and, in the end, his savior. But thinking about her now was akin to selective memory. She had been but a part of the overall horror. The one good part. The only good part.

And he needed to remember the bad if he expected to flush out Russell Dega and see to Annabel's safety. Keeping that in the forefront of his mind was all that mattered.

"If we work this right," Annabel said, interrupting his musings and bringing him back to the present, "we can have this entire store to ourselves."

"How do you figure that?" he asked, dragging the two-tiered grocery cart behind him through the market's bakery. He frowned at the display of baguettes and *bâtards,* thinking about the menu's tenderloin cocktail sandwiches.

"I'll send you on ahead to clear the aisles. We won't have a single basket blocking our way." Annabel read the label on a package of imported focaccia and tossed it into the cart, shaking her head as yet another shopper reversed direction to avoid them. "This is ridiculous. I can't believe you have to put up with this."

He followed as she continued browsing, shelving the focaccia while her back was turned, wondering about the impatience in her tone. He'd learned to shrug off the less than subtle glances he received from a large segment of the phobic public.

As bright as she was, she should've known a haircut wasn't going to change things any more than losing the earring he wore. "I've gotten used to it."

"So was I wrong?" she asked, frowning when she realized he'd replaced her focaccia with a loaf of brown bread and a fresh-baked *bâtard.* "Is the shaved look more off-putting than the wild Tarzan hair?"

"Hard to tell."

"How so?"

"Having you here legitimizes me."

"Really?" Displaying her fickle moods, her face brightened at that. She seemed to like the idea. A lot. "So, it's as though I'm keeping you on a leash, then? And you can't attack unless I let you go?"

She stopped and gave him a grin that staggered him

like a left hook to the jaw. ''Would that make you my bitch?'' she joked.

''Funny,'' he said with a growl, and she cocked her head in a bowing acceptance of the compliment. Even though he hadn't meant it as one. ''I like to think of it as having made a pact with the devil.''

They moved into the produce section, and Annabel huffed, handing him a plastic box of fresh dill. ''If I were the devil, I would have long since corrupted you.''

''And you haven't?'' He brought the dill to his nose before placing the herbs in the cart. Then he bowed his nearly shaved head, running a hand from his forehead to his nape.

She huffed a second time. ''A simple haircut is hardly corruption.''

''Simple? Simple?'' With the tic in his jaw loud enough to hear, he rounded the cart that sat between them and backed her into the plantain and mango display. ''What exactly about this haircut do you find simple, Ms. Lee?''

She sighed, a full-body capitulation that made his knees weak even while notching up his protective instincts. The reaction would've had him laughing if it didn't feel so damn real. He was not going to let Russell Dega lay a hand on this woman.

''I know the haircut was my idea, but I didn't want anyone judging you by your rather savage appearance,'' she said, pressing her palms against his chest.

He loved the feel of her fingers, so strong yet so tiny. ''And you don't think that's what they're doing now?'' He cast his gaze to the side, where more than a few of the shoppers who skulked near the bins of Rio Grande Valley grapefruits and oranges stole quick glances his way.

Annabel ignored all of them, boldly sliding her hands from his chest up to his shoulders, one palm moving to cup his nape. "You're a beautiful man. It's their loss if they can't see that."

"Yeah, that's it," he scoffed, even while her compliment had his heart beating faster.

She tilted her head and studied his face. "I'm serious, Patrick. You're observant about so many things. I'm surprised you don't see your own appeal, even if others don't have the sense to notice."

He waited for one heartbeat, two, then a third before he stepped out of her clutches. "And what appeal would that be? The fact that I can fill your stomach and your body and kill both those hungers without thinking twice?"

"Must you always be so crass?" she asked from the other side of the cart.

"I'm simply acknowledging my appeal. I thought that was what you were urging me to do," he said, knowing full well she wanted him to peel away the protective coat he'd worn the last four and a half years and expose the raw nerve endings beneath.

She turned and headed to the refrigerated cases of fresh and packaged seafood. "You know I was talking about your physical appeal. And, yes. Your looks are simply one part of the total picture. But you have this bad habit of using your appearance to intimidate." She finished considering the smoked salmon and moved to the shrimp. "You could use it instead to get what you want."

She was baiting him, and he would gnaw his leg off to keep from being caught in her trap. "Isn't that rather shallow?" he asked, though he'd admitted to himself moments ago that he'd done that very thing for years.

"Expecting my wishes to be served on a silver platter because of my nose, my eyes and my all-American jaw?"

"Of course it is," she readily agreed. "But it's the way of the world. It's refreshing, at least, to see that you recognize the value of your deeper qualities."

He wasn't doing so well with the gnawing. "What? You think I actually have redeeming values?"

"I've always known that you do." She gestured to one of the fish market's employees. "I just wanted you to acknowledge them," she added, quickly flipping her attention back to Patrick before he could say a word. "And I'm not talking about your kitchen or bedroom skills."

"I'm pretty sure I was there last night when we signed our catering contract." A fool's contract. "And I'm fairly damn confident those two reasons are the only ones you gave for keeping me around."

"Do you want to call this off then? I need to give the caterer my decision by Monday." She stepped back to let him select the shrimp and the salmon, as if choosing the seafood would be the formal binding seal on their agreement. He would cook, she would serve and then good night, Saigon.

With his forearm braced on the chrome butcher case, his other hand at his hip, he stared at her, standing there with her arms crossed over her chest and her lips bowed up in the snotty pout he adored and hated, her weight leaning into one cocked hip.

The fingertips of one hand tapped the opposite forearm while she waited for his order to be weighed, wrapped and priced. While she waited for him to give her an answer that was about a whole lot more than catering. That was about cleaning up his attitude and getting the hell on with living his life.

He was damned if he did, damned if he didn't, and was faced with the swift death of breaking things off with her now, or the sweet torture of two more weeks in her company. Not quite the live-or-die situation he'd faced with Dega—

Dega.

The one word put an end to Patrick's hesitation.

The salmon and shrimp joined the breads and herbs in the cart, which he twirled around and dragged behind him with one hand, his other wrapped around Annabel's upper arm. He propelled her toward the coffee bean alcove and sent another three shoppers scurrying away as he rounded the corner with his cargo in tow.

Her chest was heaving when he faced her, and he knew it wasn't exertion because neither one of them had exerted much of anything on the quick trip through the store. Yet his own chest rose and fell just as rapidly. This woman made it damn hard for a man to breathe.

"I'll cook for your damn party, but you're mine until then. Anytime, anywhere, any way I want you. Agreed?"

He saw her swallow as, wide-eyed, she nodded. "Agreed."

"Good." Because sticking to her side was his best guarantee of keeping her alive. And he would keep her alive. He'd failed with Soledad. He wouldn't fail again.

PUTTING HER JAGUAR into gear and pulling out of the market's parking lot, Annabel wondered what the hell she'd just agreed to.

Patrick Coffey was a train wreck, the sort of unfolding disaster that piqued curiosity while inspiring charitable instincts. Yet she'd agreed to his mad scheme because, more than any man ever had, he made her feel alive.

A totally emotional response that had no place in

their...*agreement,* she supposed was an apt description, because she refused to think of what they shared as a relationship.

When he'd first come into her life, she'd dug out and shaken off the savior complex she'd stored years before, after realizing the futility of helping those unwilling to help themselves.

Her mother had taught her that lesson so well, Annabel had graduated with honors. No refresher course was needed, no matter how many times and with how many arguments her body insisted otherwise. Just like her mother, Patrick would continue to live in his insular world as long as he was coddled.

Kicking him out of her life represented her defiant refusal to coddle.

So why was she less than confident about her plan's chances for success?

The ride back to the loft from Central Market continued to pass in total silence. No. That wasn't quite right because, as she drove, she heard everything Patrick wasn't saying. She maneuvered her Jaguar back down Westheimer, seeing the expression on his face that said he was plotting the many ways he could use her.

She hated him for that, for making her shiver and sweat with the heady anticipation. For making her weak with wanting him. Because she was. And she did.

She pulled into the garage and parked, popping the trunk and wordlessly reaching for the grocery bags. Patrick, cursing under his breath, slammed the car door and followed. Having apparently given up his vow of silence, he grabbed all but the one bag she already held.

She closed the trunk, lifted a brow, prepared to demand that he leave his attitude here in the garage or she would send him packing now and agree to Newvale's replacement caterer, last-minute hassles be damned. She had no idea what was going on in Patrick's shaved head, but she was tired of his mood swings, the ups, the downs, the in-betweens that raised her hopes when she knew better.

She knew better.

But just as she opened her mouth to speak, Patrick's head came up. His eyes grew wide. His body froze. And then his head, nothing more, slowly turned. His eyes blinked once, then narrowed. His nostrils flared as if he were a fox sniffing the air.

''Patr—'' was all she got out before he cut her off with one sharp shake of his head.

He slowly lowered the grocery bags to the concrete floor, soundlessly crept along the length of her car. He stopped beside the support post in front of the Jag's bumper. She heard the click of his knife blade latching in its grip, and her heart shot into her throat.

Knees locked, she stood unmoving at the rear of her car. He peered around the post's corner to the street below. He was so still it was as if his heart had stopped beating. As if his lungs had ceased to inflate. As if his eyes no longer needed the blinking wash from his eyelids. He was a jungle cat, the picture of a predator, stealth standing on two feet.

And she could barely breathe.

Her hands grew damp as she instinctively waited for his word that she was safe. Safe from what, she had no idea. But Patrick's demeanor left little doubt that he sensed a real threat. She'd never seen him like this. Frightened barely defined what she felt. She couldn't even work her throat to swallow.

His body flat to the concrete pillar, he switched his lookout from right to left. Annabel hadn't moved a muscle, wasn't sure moving a muscle was even a possibility. Her arms burned from holding herself and the groceries unnaturally tight and still.

He looked down then, dropped to one palm and one knee and reached beneath her car. She heard the sharp scratchy clinck of metal on concrete as he stabbed the knifepoint into the garage floor. Seconds ticked by before he pushed himself back to his feet and pocketed the blade.

Dusting chalky dirt from his knees, he walked back to where he'd left her standing. He took the bag she still held and she shook her arms until tingles of feeling returned.

Rolling her head from side to side on her shoulders, she nodded toward his free hand. ''What did you find?''

He opened his palm to reveal a cigarette butt.

She stopped moving; her rapid heartbeat resumed its pounding against the wall of her chest. ''All of that for a cigarette butt?''

He shrugged. ''I thought I smelled something burning.''

She was going to kill him. Kill him where he was standing. ''For God's sake, Patrick. It's just a cigarette butt.''

He brought the brown-papered butt to his nose and inhaled. ''Yeah. I guess it is.''

But Annabel heard his voice, saw his eyes. And she knew that wasn't even half the truth.

WHAT HE HADN'T TOLD HER was that the cigarette butt wasn't cold. It wasn't hot, but it hadn't been out long. And if the aroma of that tobacco blend hadn't been a part of his life for three years, he'd never have noticed it at all.

He carried the bags of groceries from the elevator across the loft's main room to the kitchen and dining alcove, setting the whole lot on the dividing bar. Annabel helped him unload the menu ingredients straight to the red-and-aqua-tiled countertop. No need to shelve what he was about to use.

She picked up the first paper bag and began to fold it along its original lines. "Patrick?"

"Annabel?" He tried to match her tone of inquisitive accusation as he reached for the breadboard and bread knife.

"Tell me what just happened."

"Well, we bought smoked salmon, fresh dill and brown bread, for one thing." He counted out the items, using the knife as a pointer. "I'm not sure I want to use a branded crème fraîche or make my own—"

She grabbed the loaf from beneath his extended hand. "I'm not talking about our shopping trip."

He thought about hedging, but gave up after a quick self-reminder of who he was dealing with here. "The garage."

"Yes. The garage." She set the bread off to the side and picked up a second bag to fold.

"The garage." He reached over and turned on the oven to heat up the precooked beef tenderloin he'd chosen from the market's kitchen. He'd cook his own for the party, of course, but for this test-drive—

"The garage, Patrick. The garage," Annabel repeated, threatening him with the wedge of Gorgonzola he needed for the mayonnaise.

First divesting her of the cheese and moving the green-olive flatbread out of her reach, he pulled the food processor from the bar's storage well. When he straightened and faced her, he knew he owed her at least a partial truth.

"I'm not sure what happened. I only know that for at least a week now I've felt as if I were being watched." Honest enough. Vague enough. It worked. The last thing he wanted to do was scare her.

"Watched," she repeated. "Watched by whom?"

He shrugged, measuring out the gourmet mayo he'd purchased and enough Gorgonzola to keep the flavor combination on the mild end of the spectrum. He hit the puree button; the motor whirred...then stopped as Annabel pulled the plug from the socket.

"Who would be watching you, Patrick?"

"No one you would know."

"I see."

She didn't see, of course. She no doubt thought he was out of his mind, headed for the loony bin, a fruitcake of the first order. Interesting, however, how he saw nothing in her expression that smacked of fear, or even a tentative reticence to challenge his claim.

It wasn't exactly that she didn't believe him, more a case of been there, done that, yet... "You don't believe me."

"What's to believe? If you say you feel as if you're being watched, then you feel as if you're being watched." And at that, she shoved the food processor's plug back into the socket.

Patrick jerked on the cord and nearly pulled the entire faceplate from the wall. Whatever the hell was going on with her, he wasn't up for her games. "The cigarette butt is a Jamaican brand. I found another one across the street from the balcony."

Annabel lifted one shoulder, hardly impressed. "It's a

culturally diverse neighborhood. I'm sure you would find several others if you walked the block."

She was right, of course. Then again, so was he. What they had was a classic standoff, a no-win situation, a silent and tacit agreement not to voice the frustration each felt at the other's refusal to remove head from ass and wake up.

He returned the plug to the socket and let the Gorgonzola and mayo mix while he toasted a slice of brown bread before removing the single serving of tenderloin from the oven.

With Annabel looking on silently, he spread a diamond of toast with the Gorgonzola mayonnaise and layered the shaved beef on top. He handed her the open-face cocktail sandwich, but refused to let go until she looked up, and he knew he had her attention.

One timely pause and he stated the one single truth she needed to hear. "If it's who I think it is, then he's here to kill me."

CHLOE ZUNIGA PULLED her lime-green VW Beetle into the parking lot of Three Mings. For a very long moment she seriously considered blowing off her appointment with Devon Lee and simply stuffing her face with General Tso's chicken.

Fighting with Eric always made her want to eat. And not eat normally, but enough to drown her sorrows in pools and puddles of sugar and salt and vats of liquid chocolate. Alcohol, thank goodness, she only used when she partied. Alcohol was all about fun, and fun was not at all what she was having today.

Hell, who was she kidding? she mused, slamming the car door and adjusting her sunglasses in the glare of the winter sun. She hadn't experienced fun in weeks. It was getting so bad that she hated going to the office. All the newlywed, affianced and bloated pregnancy bliss was getting on her nerves.

Especially since Eric refused to talk about their own relationship, where it was headed, where they might want to take it, where he saw them a year, five, ten from now.

He accused her of being desperate and swept up in the lives of her girlfriends. He said her obsession with marriage and babies wasn't about their life together at all, but a case of self-inflicted peer pressure.

He didn't know shit about what he was saying, and she wasn't going to apologize for slipping into her recently broken potty-mouth habit. Her desires were not a part of the gIRL-gEAR partners' trend-setting reputation. She loved Eric and wanted to make a life with him.

And until recently, until he'd started working so many hours and coming home long after she was asleep, she'd thought he felt the same.

But since she knew food wasn't going to do anything but kindle her heartburn, she headed for the stairs to the gallery and her appointment with Poe's brother, unable to deny the thrill of anticipation where indigestion had once burned.

Devon Lee was a hell of a sexy man. He was a bit taller than Poe, with more of a sense of humor twinkling in his eyes. His Asian-American features were sharply defined, and Chloe couldn't help but wonder about the root of the Caucasian half of his genes.

She climbed the stairs slowly, doing her best to rein in the runaway emotion she had no business entertaining. She was here for Poe, to give her friend a hand salvaging the party, and that was it. Whether or not Poe's brother revved Chloe's motor was not for consideration.

Even so, when she stepped through the front door of

the gallery, she could think of nothing but the unexpected sizzle of her last encounter with Devon and the trouble she'd had getting him out of her mind since.

Yet the simplicity of the gallery's rooms was calming. She found herself unwinding, felt the upheaval that had unbalanced her since she'd left home this morning leveling out. She breathed deeply, inhaled a potpourri of aromas. Her stress ebbed to the point where she hardly remembered the source.

All she knew was serenity and, eyes closed, she smiled.

"It's nice to see my patrons benefiting from the gallery's ambience."

She couldn't help it; she shivered from the soothing sound of Devon's voice. "Benefiting? How so?"

"Your shoulders are nowhere as tight as they were when you first came in."

At the interesting revelation that she hadn't been alone in her musings, she turned to him and asked, "Are you in the habit of stalking your visitors?"

He shook his head. "Not stalking. Observing."

"A student of human nature?"

He inclined his head. His dark eyes twinkled. "I managed to get you up here to see my etchings, didn't I?"

No. She was not going to fall for his charm, or the flirtatious banter she missed now that Eric rarely smiled anymore.

"Actually, I think I'm here to photograph your main room." She held up her digital camera. "My fiancé—" wouldn't Eric the commitment-phobe just cringe if he heard that "—owns a bar and will be supplying the tables and linens for your New Year's Eve showing. I want to give him a visual of the layout."

This time Devon gave a slight bow. "Then I owe him, and you, my thanks."

Chloe took a minute to study Poe's brother, willing her pulse to calm. There was no reason his simple expression of gratitude should cause such a frisson of awareness to tickle her skin.

But it did.

"Just don't fool yourself into thinking this is about the goodness of my heart or anything." What it was about was not having to spend New Year's Eve at Haydon's Half-Time while Eric played hotshot host to the sports groupies who couldn't get enough of ESPN. Or of him.

Devon laughed at that, the sound deep and almost musical. "Of course not. It's simply you helping Annabel and my reaping the benefits, for which I am eternally grateful."

Chloe nodded, still feeling Devon's laugh where she hadn't felt anything now in weeks. "Just so we're clear."

He gestured for her to precede him down the hallway toward the main room. She did, listening to his quiet steps behind her. Observing, indeed. This was stalking, plain and simple. No other explanation existed for the tremor traveling the length of her spine.

But there was, her former bad girl self insisted. A very logical, very obvious and very sexual reason. Being emotionally committed to Eric did not mean the death of her body.

When she turned the fourth corner in the gallery's maze of hallways, she found herself facing an alcove where a woman of Middle Eastern descent sat flipping through what appeared to be a binder of tattoo designs.

Curiosity had Chloe hesitating just long enough for Devon to take the cue. "Mina Sayid? Chloe Zuniga."

Mina glanced up, then stood and smiled, meeting

Chloe halfway as she entered the alcove. "Welcome to my tiny corner of Devon's world."

Chloe returned the other woman's handshake and smile, taking in Mina's Birkenstocks, jeans and long-sleeved slate-blue thermal top. The outfit seemed incongruous with the ruby embedded between her arched brows, black as her waist-length hair, yet somehow worked.

And then Chloe saw the artist's henna-stained palms, taking one hand in her own and studying the intricate design. "One of my co-workers wears Mehndi art like this. It's absolutely gorgeous."

"Mina is one of the city's best," Devon said, moving to stand at Chloe's shoulder. "She has quite the clientele for both her henna art and her tattoo designs."

Chloe met the other woman's soft gaze and smiled. "Pencil me into your appointment book. I've been lusting for weeks over the work Macy had done."

"I can pencil you in right now if you'd like." Mina swept her arm toward her empty studio. "I had an unexpected cancellation, and the rest of my afternoon is free."

Chloe quickly considered what remained on her own calendar for the day. Oh, right. Nothing. Eric was hosting a Houston Texans night at the bar and had been quite clear that it would be the wee hours before he made it home.

She didn't mind that so much as she minded that he hadn't asked her to come with him. In the past, he'd always had.

She wondered if Devon would be spending the rest of the afternoon at the gallery. She wondered why she even cared, just knew that she did. Decision made, Chloe nodded at Mina. ''Let me do what I need to do here with Devon, then we'll talk.''

Devon crossed his arms and leaned back against the alcove's wall. ''Her work doesn't come cheap.''

''Devon!'' Mina cried.

Chloe glanced from Devon to Mina and back, more certain than ever of her choice. ''Believe me, sugar. I'm worth it.''

And after a long hot moment, Devon replied, ''So we shall see.''

6

ON MONDAY AT NOON, Annabel walked out of the Joseph A. Jachimczyk Forensic Center into the bright December sunlight, wishing more than anything for a hot shower and copious suds.

The tour, both fascinating and informative, left behind a definite ick factor along with a sense of exhilaration. Even now, reaching into her bag for her sunglasses, she knew that her heart had never beat with this sort of excitement in response to her work at gIRL-gEAR.

Listening to the coroner and forensic sculptor discuss reconstructing and identifying recently discovered skeletal remains was akin to coming home. A strange thought, since neither Annabel nor her brother had ever experienced the true meaning of the term.

Most of their childhood had been spent living with their maternal grandmother in her Tacoma, Washington, duplex until she'd finally moved them to Houston. She was the caretaker of choice when their mother went running after whichever man had most recently walked out, certain she knew what had gone wrong and how to win this one back.

Annabel had figured out by the time she was ten years old that her mother would always return alone. Whether or not she would return at all had become a running bet between Annabel and Devon by the time they reached their teens.

Neither had any idea if they'd ever met their father, though doubted they shared their paternity. Devon had an easygoing nature in contrast to Annabel's prickly personality. Since they had grown up in the same environment, he teasingly attributed their differences to the quality of the donated sperm.

After losing count of the number of men who had come into their lives and stayed through Easter or Thanksgiving, but never both, Annabel had very dramatically decided not to risk making their mother's bad relationship choices. On her twenty-first birthday, she'd quit dating.

Instead, she began taking lovers who would please her physically, but not require that she involve her emotions. Emotions meant putting her heart on the line, to be swept away and then summarily squashed when she burned the toast, or was late to pick up the dry cleaning, or gained too many pounds.

She was much too smart for that.

On her thirtieth birthday, alone with Jose Cuervo and chocolate chip cookies, she'd had an enlightening epiphany before nausea struck. All those years during which she'd thought sophisticated wisdom had kept her detached and uninvolved, she'd simply been incapable of falling in love.

She could lust her brains out with the best of 'em, but losing her heart was not—and never would be—an issue. She was immune. Superior, yet somehow…deficient.

Or so she'd thought until the night Patrick Coffey dragged her out of Paddington's Ford and branded her with the heat of his body and the fire of his mouth. She'd responded instantly, shockingly, every cell, nerve and emotion fully engaged.

Crossing the parking lot now, she settled her sunglasses in place and fished her keys from her bag. She hated these juvenile emotions. Expectations were a ridiculous drain; one was better off managing independently rather than looking to another for fulfillment.

Jerry Maguire had it all wrong. No one person could complete another.

She didn't buy for a minute the happily-ever-after of her six gIRL-gEAR partners. Chloe made for a perfect example. Their wake-up calls would come soon enough, a call she would never have reason to anticipate as long as she stopped flirting with an attachment sure to cause her immeasurable grief. And doing so with a man who defined instability.

Though, even as she made the accusation, she doubted the accuracy. There were moments when she saw Patrick with the clarity of a diamond. Unfortunately, she mused wryly, most of the time she saw a thug.

Squealing tires brought her head up in time to see, hear and feel a souped-up muscle car roar into the parking lot. She frowned as the classic El Camino pulled in next to her Jaguar, with none other than the thug himself behind the wheel. She stood with her keys in her hand and remained unsmiling—not an easy task when Patrick looked like hell on wheels and she knew him so very intimately.

Her stomach fluttered as if defying her efforts at staying unattached, uninvolved. Even her hands trembled, holding her keys as she was, and she clenched her fists tighter. It was her knees, however, that gave her the most trouble. She took a step in reverse, backing smoothly into her car door, telling herself she was simply moving out of harm's way.

Patrick cut the engine, turned to her and grinned the biggest, baddest grin she'd ever seen spread over his face. The silver hoop in his ear twinkled, as did his eyes when he pulled his sunglasses from his gorgeous face. But it was his expression of boyish delight that was her undoing. This was what he'd looked like before something—or someone—had robbed him of his innocence, Annabel thought dazedly.

She drew in a breath that took far too much effort, and gestured toward his vehicle. "What is this?"

"My car." He climbed out and slammed the heavy door against the equally heavy frame. "Don't make 'em like this anymore."

"Thank God for that," she said, recognizing, as she did, that no other car would fit him. They shared a definite *bring-it-on* attitude. "You've had this in storage all this time?"

He shook his head, ran his palm lovingly across the bright red roof. "Bought it this morning. Got tired of hitching in your cat there."

She ground her teeth until her molars ached. "You just went out on the spur of the moment and bought a classic El Camino."

"Totally restored. A beaut, isn't she?"

A smile pulled at her pursed lips. "And I'm sure you've given *her* a name?"

That devil's grin again. "I was thinking of calling her Annie. She's sleek, sexy—" he waggled his brows "—and hot under the hood."

Oh, but he was cute. She folded her arms and strove to look stern. "Where did you get the money?"

"Same place I got the money to buy you, sister."

Hel-lo. "I would like to know." Patrick made no effort at finding work, yet never lacked for obscene amounts of cash.

His grin vanished, replaced by a slow-growing wariness. "Why?"

"Fine." She turned back to the task of unlocking her car door. His suspicion shouldn't have hurt. She hated that it did. "Don't answer me. God forbid I know anything personal about the man who's sleeping with me."

Two more weeks—no, less than that. Ten more days and he would be out of her life. She could easily replace him in her bed; she needed him for nothing. *Nothing,* she insisted, infuriated at the sudden sting of tears.

"I'm sorry, Annabel." His fingers kneaded her neck, rattling her further when she needed to remain cool and detached. When she didn't answer, he lifted his hand. "Every penny I have is on the up and up. Trust me."

Her chest constricted. She whipped her gaze to his. "How can I possibly trust you, Patrick, when you still don't trust me?"

He remained unmoving, unsmiling, poised as if on a precipice between saving himself and sharing what might be enough for her to take him down. When he glanced away, over and beyond the roof of her car, she knew he'd made his decision. Still, his expression remained grim.

"The money is mine, free and clear. There was a bounty on Russell Dega's band of pirates." Patrick narrowed his mouth, looked toward her, then away. "I would've split it with the gang's informant. But she didn't make it out alive."

Oh God. *God.* Intuition told Annabel this was the reason for his lost innocence, the crux of his anger and pent-up pain. He was hurt, dammit, but she did not know how to offer comfort. Sex wouldn't repair any of Patrick's damage. Or any of her own.

Her heart began to race; her breathing quickened. Her world turned upside down with the force of what she felt. And so she did the only thing that seemed right. She turned to him and slipped her arms around his rib cage, pressing her palms to the center of his back between his T-shirt and jacket. Her cheek she pressed over his heart, which lurched and began to beat as rapidly as hers.

She heard a strangled noise echo in his throat as his arms went around her. They stood like that for two minutes at least, unmoving, focused and close. She was aware of him in ways she'd never before taken time to examine, ways that were physical yet went beyond.

Today she wore flats. Patrick, as always, wore biker boots, putting the top of her head just under his chin. He rested there, so that she felt the grinding force of his jaw. She felt, as well, the bob of his Adam's apple as he swallowed the rest of the sound she was sure she hadn't been meant to hear.

A part of her wanted to ask what had happened, who had been the informant and how she had died. But a less munificent part didn't want to know anything about any other woman who'd shared his affections. Annabel knew this one had in extraordinary circumstances, and her own jealous thoughts made her feel very small.

She tightened her hold, nearly able to number Patrick's ribs. He was that lean, that spare and hungry, given to no excesses other than the occasional drink and his performance in bed. She knew with clear certainty that he hadn't been this way...before. That he'd been a party boy, rowdy and as benign then as he was dangerous now.

And so, as clear as she'd just been with herself about not prying, she went ahead and did. "Tell me about her."

A laugh that was sarcastic rather than joyous rumbled in his chest. "Seven weeks and you're finally asking for details."

She'd always been curious; she knew no one who wasn't. But until now, until this moment, she hadn't been sure she wanted the responsibility of safekeeping his secrets or sharing his pain. Now she had no choice.

Rejecting his tentative trust would kill the last trace of the boy inside him, and that she couldn't do.

She breathed deeply, drawing in his warmth and the heady scent of wildness he exuded. "Tell me about her," she said with more conviction. "I want to know everything."

THEY ENDED UP SITTING across from one another at Mission Burrito on Alabama, sharing a black-bean-and-chicken burrito dripping with salsa.

Talking softly over a front porch corner table made more sense than having this conversation in the middle of a busy medical center parking lot, even though Patrick could've stood with Annabel tucked close to his body the rest of the day.

Thing was, he hadn't wanted to risk giving anyone watching the bright idea of getting to him through someone he held close. And he couldn't imagine feeling closer to anyone than he had to Annabel then, holding her in his arms and hearing her ask him about Soledad.

He'd been home eighteen months, and Annabel was the first person bold enough or brave enough to want the specifics of his captivity. Ray had insisted Patrick take his time, talk when he was ready. Sydney had followed Ray's lead, though hadn't quite managed to hide her expressions of curiosity or pity.

The pity was what drove Patrick crazy, inciting the temper he'd spent three years in the islands controlling by walking away. His obvious hostility, even in absentia, completed the huge cause-and-effect circle that kept everyone at a big fat arm's length.

And now Annabel wanted to know about Soledad.

Annabel, being Annabel, had opened her half of the burrito and was eating the chicken, rice, beans and vegetables with fork and spoon. His longneck dangling from his fingers, Patrick sat and watched her dainty destruction of her food in the basket. She looked up and caught him staring with what felt like a ridiculously goofy grin on his face.

"You find me amusing?"

"Not so much amusing as a contradiction. You eat with much more gusto in private."

"In private you've usually worn me out and left me starving."

"Good to know you enjoy my work."

She balanced her fork on the edge of the burrito basket and blotted her mouth with a napkin before she answered. "I know this is going to come as a shock, but I enjoy *you*, Patrick. Your work, as you put it, is simply a part of who you are."

He brought his bottle to his mouth because he wasn't sure he could say anything, what with the way his throat felt so tight. Getting down the beer he'd just swallowed was going to be hard enough.

He was glad when he saw Annabel prepare to go on without waiting for him to reply. Even if he'd been able to speak, he'd yet to come up with anything to say. She enjoyed him, and that was more than anyone had offered in the way of accepting him for who he was now—not for who he'd once been.

"That said," she began, all uppity and prim, "we're at different places in our lives. Or maybe we're even at cross-purposes. I'm not sure. All I know is that I've reached the point where I have to move forward to get what I want, and that means leaving the past behind."

"gIRL-gEAR?"

"If necessary."

"Me?"

"Ditto."

He swirled the liquid remaining in the dark amber bottle. "And your closets? Are you cleaning out the skeletons?"

"I don't have skeletons." She threaded her fingers through the handle of the frosted mug holding her frozen margarita.

"We all have skeletons, Annabel." He narrowed his gaze and focused, determined to see every nuance of her expression as he told her his truth. "Mine died because I wasn't fast enough on my feet to save her. Her name was Soledad. She'd once been Russell Dega's mistress. And the night before she lost her life she told me that she loved me."

Annabel swallowed hard; he watched her work the knot from her throat, watched her pulse beat there in the hollow. "The informant?"

He nodded.

"What happened?"

He shook his head. "Tit for tat, sweetheart. Skeleton for skeleton."

She reached for her fork and went back to picking through her rice and beans. After several seconds of doing nothing but moving food left to right, she calmly replaced her fork on the basket's edge. "My mother."

Now, this was interesting. "A living skeleton?"

"I don't know. Neither Devon nor I have heard from her in years." Annabel brought her straw to her mouth and sipped, then grimaced. "God, this is vile."

"The drink or the conversation?"

"Both, actually."

"Then bottoms up." He lifted his beer. "You're not yet numb enough to face the bones or the bad booze."

"Is that why you drink as much as you do? To face the bones?"

What should he tell her? The truth? That he rarely felt the effects of alcohol, but keeping a bottle in his hand gave him a reason to explain away his behavior? "I'll quit drinking if you'll quit looking down your nose when you talk to me."

She started to do it again—to stick her nose in the air and cut him off at the knees. But she stopped, stared into the drink she hated and shook her head. "I practiced that move for years to get it right. It seemed such an adult way to distance myself from unpleasantries."

What was wrong with this picture? "What was so unpleasant that you couldn't even be a kid?"

She sipped more of her margarita, frowned and swallowed. "Dealing with my mother. She knew absolutely nothing about nurturing relationships. Not with her children, nor with the men who came and went. She couldn't even take care of herself. I don't know how she ever thought she could care for me and Devon."

"You and Devon. You took care of each other?"

Annabel shook her head, but it wasn't an answer. She was simply cutting off his question. "Skeleton for skeleton, Patrick. Your turn."

Back to Soledad. Blurting the truth out quickly seemed the road best traveled. "Once Dega got tired of keeping me on his boat and threatening to toss me overboard, he dumped me off at the island where his operations were based. A commune of sorts. Or a survivalist camp, though with all the modern amenities. He gave me to Soledad."

"As a gift?"

He shrugged, having no idea what instructions Dega had given. ''More or less to do with as she saw fit.''

''And what did she find fit to do with you?''

Patrick continued to slosh the beer in his bottle from side to side. ''She used me as a canvas, for one thing.''

''The tattoo?''

Nodding, he upended and drained the longneck.

''That had to have taken—''

''Forever,'' he answered, finishing her sentence. ''Didn't much matter. I wasn't going anywhere. In fact, if not for Soledad, I'm pretty damn sure I'd be rotting on the island in a shallow grave.''

Annabel gasped. ''What?''

Patrick snorted. ''Dega didn't have any use for me, which he made perfectly clear more than a few times. Soledad was the one who wanted to keep me around. I was her entertainment, I suppose.''

''Wait a minute. Slow down or I'll never catch up.'' Annabel held up one hand. ''Dega giving you to this woman implies she had his trust. Yet she was the FBI informant?''

''She contacted them on a trip to Key West to pick up ink and needles her father sent her from Miami. A post office box, illegal as hell to ship that stuff, I'm sure.'' He upended the bottle and pulled at the last of his beer. ''At least that's the best I can figure. She'd made the run a couple of weeks before the raid.''

''So Dega did trust her. Enough to let her off the island, right?''

Patrick nodded. ''After I was rescued, I found out during debriefing that she'd refused to tell them where I was until they agreed to pay me the bounty if anything happened to her.''

''But the feds let her go—''

Patrick cut her off when he realized the scales weren't tipping his way. "Nope. No more. Time to offer up some tit for that tat, sister."

Annabel rolled her eyes, picked up her mug, then frowned when she reached the end of her margarita with an unladylike slurp from her straw. "I don't really have anything else to tell. My mother was classic bipolar, but refused medication or counseling. It was always about the next man. He would be the one who would see beyond her illness to her true self, who would understand her, who would fall for her madly and never leave her side."

"And when he did?"

"Then she left Devon and me with our grandmother and went after him." Annabel grew melancholy, her face darkening, her brows lowered. "Devon ended up dating every woman who crossed his path, looking for whatever it is motherless boys are missing, I suppose."

"And you?" Patrick asked, because he was much more interested in how—and why—Annabel had become the woman she was.

"I swore never to be used by a man. Any relationship I was in, I would be the one doing the using."

"Whew. That's good to know. I was beginning to take it personally."

"It's not about you at all. It's about me. About the child I once was who thought all men would eventually leave, and the decision I made not to ever let that happen." She sighed. "That's why I'm having such a hard time with this."

"This?" His heart blipped. "You mean this *this?* You and me?"

She nodded, her eyes filled with sadness and regret. Unlike any woman he'd ever known, Annabel was always in charge of her emotions. So now, sensing her struggle with her usual control sent him climbing another few knots up that dangling remnant of hope.

"If it helps, I'm not having it much better." He toyed with his empty bottle. "I never thought we'd be together beyond that first night."

One of Annabel's brows arched. "You put up a lot of money for no guarantees."

He shrugged. "A donation to a good cause."

"But why me?"

What should he tell her? That she had reminded him of Soledad, and he'd been looking for a connection to the one good part of the last three years? Three years that seemed to have wiped out every single one that had passed before?

He barely remembered who he used to be. "It was the way you always looked at me. Like you saw right through my bullshit."

"I did. I still do."

He ignored her halfhearted smirk. "And you never back off or turn away. I don't frighten you."

"Are you trying to frighten people, Patrick?"

He shook his head. "There's a big part of my old life I'd like to have back, you know? The part where I was treated like everyone around me."

"You don't make that easy to do."

"And that's the new me that I don't want to change. I have less patience with the seven sins than I once did. Living shackled to a palm tree or a truck fender for three years gives one a new outlook on gluttony and sloth."

"You were kept bound for three years?" Her voice was barely more than a whisper, no louder than the breeze rustling tree leaves overhead.

He shrugged. "Off and on. Depended whether the extra manpower was needed. Unloading the day's haul. Digging an irrigation trench. And then there were the days Soledad was in the mood to cook and needed a hand. Or was feeling more artistic and needed a leg."

At that, Annabel smiled. "How long did the tattoo take?"

"A good couple of years. But it wasn't like she worked on it daily." He paused to think back on the moods that had driven Soledad to ink. "She'd add to it usually after Dega had gathered up a load to take to the States to be fenced."

"Did you sleep with her?"

"Sure." Here was where he felt the need to tread lightly, not wanting Annabel to come away from the conversation thinking he'd simply used her to replace Soledad. Maybe in the beginning. The very beginning. But not now. Not any longer.

Not since that first night.... "It was a long three years," he said gruffly.

"What happened to her?"

"We were fishing off the end of the pier, soaking up rum and the sun. The drinking had started the night before. Dega and most of the men had long since passed out. But I've got this tolerance problem. I just don't get drunk."

"I've noticed."

"Yeah, well, I try. It's not like I don't try." And it wasn't like he didn't wish he could obliterate so many of his thoughts with a bottle of Jack. "Soledad and I were just goofing around, beyond tired but both sober. She was giving me a hard time about being such a piss poor fisherman. She wouldn't let me go to bed until I caught our breakfast."

He remembered laughing. God, but he remembered

laughing. It was the one thing that stuck with him most about that morning, he realized, rubbing a hand over his face. Drunk on the realization that he was alive and, for the moment, free.

In a warped sort of fantasy, he'd pretended he and Soledad were vacationing, teasing and flirting, surrounded by beautiful blue water and early morning skies. It was at that moment that he'd known he'd be okay. That he had what it took to survive.

"Patrick?"

He glanced back up at Annabel, blinked burning eyes and turned his head as a sporty sedan pulled out of the parking lot. Watching the car was a legitimate distraction, giving him the time he needed to pull himself together.

"Sorry," he said finally, clearing his throat. "I haven't thought about it in a while." A lie, because he thought about it daily. "And I sure as hell haven't talked about it to anyone." That was the absolute truth, and a conscious decision. At least until Annabel's interest had him upending the well.

"I was bitching about our lack of luck when this speedboat blasted into the cove and straight to the dock, waking up every one of Dega's men. You can't imagine what it's like to be in the center of an AK-47 firestorm. I've yet to see a movie get it right."

The remembered sounds assaulted him as if he were back on that dock, flat on his belly, his hands over his head. He'd inched toward Soledad; she'd given him a wry grin and a ridiculous thumbs-up while lying in a mirror position.

He'd heard his name shouted over a bullhorn, seen flak jackets emblazoned with the letters *FBI,* others with the words *United States Coast Guard,* and he'd known. Soledad had given him up to the authorities and, in the process, spat in the face of Russell Dega.

Patrick couldn't say another word. He could hardly breathe. When Annabel reached across the table to wipe the tears spilling from the corners of his eyes, he flinched and grabbed her wrist, wanting her to see, needing her to know. The truth. All of it.

"Don't try to make this easier on me. It will never be easy. It will never go away. Every day I hear Dega yelling out and see Soledad getting to her feet, using herself as a shield so I could make a running dive for the boat. And then he shot her. He just…shot her.

"She went off the side of the pier and floated there." Facedown. Skirt billowing. He remembered too many details. "And then the boat was too far away for me to see anything more. The feds came in after that. Cleaned out the operation. Rounded up the bad guys. All but Dega. I found that out during my debriefing, too."

"And now you think he's here."

Patrick nodded, reaching down and finding the same inner strength that had served him so well. "He's here."

"Why would he come after you now? It would seem to serve him better to disappear off the radar."

"I don't know. I couldn't find my way back to that island if I tried. I have no idea where I was. What I *know* is that I'm not taking a chance with you. The cigarette butts weren't a coincidence, and nothing you say will change my mind about that."

"I believe you," she said softly, and Patrick's world ceased to spin on its axis, coming to a stop so that nothing existed but her words. She believed in him.

And that belief, that faith, was going to see him through.

PATRICK WAS NOT GOING TO let Russell Dega steal away another minute of his life. Nor would the bastard ruin the lives of those Patrick held close. It wasn't going to happen, not as long as he had the strength to breathe.

He and Annabel had left Mission Burrito's patio sober in mind and in body, and silently headed for their cars. He'd walked her past his El Camino to her Jag, where they'd stood for several minutes, unspeaking and in each other's arms. He'd longed to kiss her, wanted more than anything to kiss her, to press his body to hers and never let her go.

Instead, he'd watched her get into the Jag and pull out of the narrow parking lot, wishing he could follow her home and take her to bed. Their lunch had brought a turning point of sorts, one he longed to hold on to, driven to keep that connection alive.

In the end, he'd let her go home alone. He'd had to. Just as he'd had to wait for her to drive away before he was able to bend down and retrieve the cigarette butt from the pavement beneath his car door. He couldn't believe it. He'd been sitting there telling Annabel the story of Dega with the bastard a hundred feet away.

Third time being the charm and all, Patrick wasn't taking chances that he could handle Dega on his own. With all three butts now in a Baggie in his pocket, he shoved his sunshades into place, dropped down behind the wheel and put the car into gear.

It was time he made a visit to the FBI.

During his time spent with her, he'd learned that she'd once been Dega's mistress. Even after their falling out over Dega's treatment of the sailors he victimized, Soledad remained in an almost matriarchal position over the camp. Which was why Patrick had never understood her interest in him.

It certainly hadn't been about taking him protectively under her wing, though she had been the one to teach him to cook. Neither had it been about her acting as a shield between the two men. From day one, Soledad's interest had been purely about enjoying Patrick's company. As if he'd brought into her life an excitement that had been missing.

He still choked up when he thought of all she'd done for him, from making his captivity bearable, to teaching him more than he'd ever thought to learn about women, and then to giving up her life. He wasn't sure he would've done the same for her.

He'd do it for Annabel in a heartbeat.

And he'd do it for Ray.

Downshifting for a red light, Patrick couldn't tell if the rumbling in his chest was adrenaline or the roar from the glass pack modification to the El Camino's muffler. The thought of anything happening to his brother after the way Ray, with Sydney's father's help, had brought Patrick home caused no small measure of terror to flush away his more mellow thoughts of Annabel.

He couldn't let this estrangement with his brother go on. Things needed to be set to rights—the way they'd been when the two of them, along with Ray's two frat brothers, had boarded the schooner to celebrate Ray finishing up his Master's thesis all those months—correction, all those *years* back.

Damn, but that had been a long time ago. A lifetime ago. Patrick grabbed his cell phone and dialed Ray's.

"Ray Coffey," his brother answered on the third ring.

"It's Patrick."

"Hey. What's up?" His tone was wary, distant.

"You busy?" Patrick held his breath.

"Not too. Why?"

"Meet me somewhere?"

"Where?"

"FBI office?"

"When?"

"Now."

"Ten minutes." He was all business. "I'll be out front." Ray clicked off.

Patrick did the same. It was a start.

7

EXITING THE FBI OFFICES with Ray at his side, Patrick shoved his sunglasses into place. An hour spent going over his suspicions had brought him no closer to any sort of usable truth.

The feds had received a tip that Dega had been seen in New Orleans four months ago, but a tip was all they had. That lack of detail didn't do a lot to make Patrick feel better. Especially since they hadn't been forthcoming with the info until he'd shown up in person to ask.

Discovering the extent of their silence hadn't sat well with Ray at all. He'd paced Agent McCandliss's office, furious with a system he blamed for making Patrick a target by failing to get Dega off the street.

Seeing his brother's distress, Patrick had been the one to decide it was time to go. And now they were heading to their respective vehicles out in the parking lot.

Until today, Patrick hadn't shared the investigation's details with anyone. Now he wondered if handling things totally on his own wouldn't have been for the best. He'd known Ray blamed himself for the disastrous vacation.

What Patrick hadn't known, however, was how deeply his brother's guilt ran. Feeling waves of unhealthy emotion pulse even now from Ray's body, Patrick reached over and slapped him on the back.

"C'mon. I want to show you something." He led the way to where his El Camino sat parked one row away from Ray's crew-cab dual-axle pickup. He unlocked and opened the driver's-side door, gestured for his brother to slide behind the wheel and give the girl a go.

Ray simply stood and stared. "What the hell is this?"

Patrick shrugged. "My feet were hurting."

"Your feet were hurting."

"Yep."

"So you bought a classic muscle car."

"Yep."

"Dude, you are some kind of out of control." Shaking his head, Ray gave a low chuckle, one just loud enough to cause the closest heads to turn before he ducked inside to check out the tucked-and-rolled leather interior.

Patrick had watched the same reaction happen whenever they spent time in public together. He saw it now, just as he'd seen it thirty minutes before when they'd entered the FBI offices. People looked, as if knowing that Ray was a true American hero. Funny thing, the choking sort of pride Patrick felt at sharing that same blood.

With a long appreciative whistle, Ray got out, slammed the door and circled the car, running his hand over the smooth hood, where blue flames licked over the bright red paint. "I guess this means you don't hold it against me for getting rid of your Bronco."

"Are you kidding? You would've spent a small fortune keeping the gas from gelling and the tires from going to rot on that thing." Patrick shook his head. "You were right to get rid of it. It was turning into a real piece anyway."

"Too many trips between here and College Station, maybe? Waiting till the last minute to head back to campus all those Sunday nights?" Ray smiled wryly.

"Business administration. What a waste of four years."

"You got your degree. That's not a waste."

"Lot of good it's doing me." Patrick snorted. "Since I'd tagged after you to A&M anyway, I should've gone on to firefighting school. Done something more productive."

He wanted to laugh at the irony. On that fateful day three years ago they'd been drawn to the pirates' powerboat by the crew's frantic signals and what looked like a hell of a fire. The smoke billowing out of the hold ended up being a controlled burn in an oil drum.

Patrick cringed, realizing what Ray must've been dealing with all this time. A trained emergency responder, and he'd still been had. Patrick tried to think of a change of subject that wouldn't be too obvious, but Ray's thoughts were elsewhere.

"You went to A&M because I did?" he asked, his voice raspy and gruff.

"You kidding? I could've slacked off anywhere. Knowing you were there to kick my ass if I flunked out was the only reason I stuck it out." A truth as real as it got. "I was a screwup, but you didn't quit on me. Ever."

Ray bit off a sharp curse and looked away. "Right. That's why the minute I moved back into the house I got rid of your stuff. Even after Mom and Dad had left everything in place all that time."

Patrick pressed his lips together, stared at the bright chrome of the El Camino's grill. "Ray, this beating-yourself-up business is really getting on my nerves."

He huffed. "So you've said more than a few times."

"Think about it, man. Can you see me fitting in with the crap I used to have? High school team pictures? Championship trophies? All those baseball caps?"

A corner of Ray's mouth lifted as he glanced back

in Patrick's direction. "Uh, no. But I did keep most of the caps."

"Good. Use them. I never expected my room to end up being a shrine." Thinking about it now, he decided it was past time for another trip to Arizona to see their folks. "I understand it. It's just...weird."

Ray shook his head, leaned his butt on the car and crossed his arms over his chest. "Mom and Dad couldn't deal, imagining what you were going through. If you were even alive to go through anything. The room gave them...hope, I guess." He shrugged with uncertainty. "A sense of things being normal. As if you'd bust through the door any minute with half your moron buddies in tow."

Normal. Patrick wasn't even sure he knew what that meant. "You know, I haven't looked up a single one of those jerks since I've been back."

"And you say I can't let it go."

Patrick's shrug was less about uncertainty and more about facing what he'd spent too long avoiding. "I guess we both have our demons. I'm just not liking the way they've gotten wedged between us."

Ray dragged both hands down his face in an expression of weary exhaustion and shoved away from the car. "Yeah. I know. I'm glad you called."

"Me, too," Patrick said, and meant it. "I just want you to be aware of anything should it go down."

Ray's head came up. "You think that's going to happen? I mean, I know Agent McCandliss says he's doing what he can. But it bugs the crap outta me that he doesn't have a better handle on Dega's whereabouts."

Patrick wasn't going to argue with that. He simply nodded. "It'll happen. I don't know when or where, or what he wants from me. But there's obviously something."

"Hmm. Soledad, maybe? She was Dega's girlfriend, right? Could he think she spilled her guts while winding that snake around your leg or something?"

Thinking about Soledad... Patrick took a deep breath and shoved it out, turning to lean across the roof of his car. He drummed his thumbs on the warm metal, admitting that he'd used her, plain and simple, while she'd claimed to have fallen in love. He'd felt alive when with her, had needed to hold on to that fleeting sensation to make it from day to day. He'd feared that, otherwise, he'd rot like the tires on his Bronco.

What he'd never considered was that she'd been using him, as well. That he'd been her tool of revenge against Dega. And that she'd been willing to give up her life to bring the bastard down. "If she shared details, they slid into one ear and out the other."

"Nothing about offshore accounts, contacts in the States? An address? A phone number? Anything, a hint even, that might give us a clue as to where he's holed up?"

"Believe me," Patrick said, shaking his head. "I've thought back over everything." Thought back too much, remembered details better left buried. "Mostly she talked about her own life, how she'd come to end up with Dega."

Ray adjusted his sunglasses, rubbed at his eyes beneath. "There's gotta be something—"

"I've tried, Ray. I swear I've tried." Patrick shrugged. "Nothing's making sense."

Ray was quiet after that for several long seconds, finally blowing out a long breath as if admitting defeat.

The Harlequin Reader Service® — Here's how it works:

Accepting your 2 free books and mystery gift places you under no obligation to buy anything. You may keep the books and gift and return the shipping statement marked "cancel." If you do not cancel, about a month later we'll send you 4 additional books and bill you just $3.80 each in the U.S., or $4.21 each in Canada, plus 25¢ shipping & handling per bo and applicable taxes if any.* That's the complete price and — compared to cover prices of $4.50 each in the U.S. and $5.25 each in Canada — it's quite a bargain! You may cancel at any time, but if you choose to continue, every month w send you 4 more books, which you may either purchase at the discount price or return to us and cancel your subscripti

*Terms and prices subject to change without notice. Sales tax applicable in N.Y. Canadian residents will be charged applicable provincial taxes and GST. Credit or Debit balances in a customer's account(s) may be offset by any other outstanding balance owed by or to the customer.

If offer card is missing write to: Harlequin Reader Service, 3010 Walden Ave., P.O. Box 1867, Buffalo NY 14240-1867

BUSINESS REPLY MAIL

FIRST-CLASS MAIL PERMIT NO. 717-003 BUFFALO, NY

POSTAGE WILL BE PAID BY ADDRESSEE

HARLEQUIN READER SERVICE
3010 WALDEN AVE
PO BOX 1867
BUFFALO NY 14240-9952

NO POSTAGE NECESSARY IF MAILED IN THE UNITED STATES

Then he cleared his throat, his tone softer as he asked, "What about you and Poe?"

Poe. Every time Patrick heard Annabel's nickname, he had to stop and wonder what Edgar Allan Poe fan had come up with it. Didn't they know Poe had written the poem "Annabel Lee" for his dead wife? Creepy. The name, not the woman. "What about us?"

"Are the two of you making sense?"

"Today? Yeah. It's interesting. Tomorrow?" He shrugged again, saying nothing about their New Year's Eve bargain to part ways. "Who the hell knows?"

"Hmm."

This time he turned his back to the car in order to face his brother. "You got something to say?"

Ray dug into his pocket for his truck keys. "Just that Sydney's worried about you both. Says it's like putting a lamb in a lion's cage. Only the lamb thinks it's a lion, too, which will only prolong the inevitable slaughter."

Patrick raised his brows. "That's quite a theory."

"Yeah, well, Sydney's quite a woman." Ray pulled out his keys, his expression a bit awed. "Smarter than me, that's for sure. I tend to agree with her most of the time."

"And this time?"

"This time I agree that it's a good analogy, but disagree with who she thinks the lamb is." Ray's dark eyes clouded with concern. "Be careful, little brother."

Well, hell. Guess that answered that. "I do a fairly decent job of taking care of myself. One good thing I brought home from the island experience."

Ray let out a long string of pretty nasty curses, but Patrick interrupted him before he could go off on one of his guilt trips. "Look, forget it. Annabel's fine. And I'm obviously doing a lot better than you are."

It took Ray a lot longer to come back. When he did, his voice was low and raw. "I have a hard time thinking of what you went through as a vacation."

Patrick scuffed a boot across the pavement, looking down because it was easier than facing his brother's heartache. "If I blow it off, it's not to make it easier on you. It's to make it bearable for me. It's the way I deal." He forced up his gaze, his throat tight. "You gotta let me deal, Ray."

"I know, it's just..." He rubbed again at his eyes. "You shouldn't have to deal. The whole thing never should've happened."

"Yeah? So? People shouldn't die in fires, either, but it happens. You don't save them all...am I right?"

Ray's sudden pallor and grim mouth was answer enough.

"The point is," Patrick continued, "if you focused on the victims you've lost in the past instead of the people who need rescuing today, you wouldn't save anyone, bro. Much less have a wall full of commendation awards."

"Yeah, I'm a regular hero," Ray said bitterly. "Everyone thinks so."

"Everyone knows so," Patrick corrected. "Especially me. And in case you haven't noticed, I've got some pretty huge fires to put out now. So, are you gonna help me here, hero, or milk the martyr thing till we're all ready to burn you at the stake?"

Ray snorted, his eyes suspiciously bright. "Asshole."

"Dickhead," Patrick retorted, the response as affectionate as it was automatic.

Bouncing his keys in one hand, Ray glanced beyond Patrick's shoulder. "When we got to the place Dega told us to pick you up? I wasn't surprised you weren't there. I knew I wasn't going to see you again, no matter what twenty-four hour bullshit he fed us about letting you go. Watching that powerboat speed away was about the hardest thing I've ever done.''

''Yeah. I didn't even want to think about what must've been going on in your head then.'' Patrick swallowed hard. ''That was the toughest part, you know. Being pretty much okay all that time, but dealing with you and the parents not knowing.''

The silence grew thick and awkward, a nostalgic fog of emotion that had them stepping back and clearing their throats and sharing a profound sense of kinship and relief.

Ray was the first to recover. ''Look,'' he said gruffly. ''You even see a shadow you think might be Dega, you call me. Day or night, I don't care. You call the feds first, but then you call me.''

Patrick nodded. ''Will do,'' he answered, watching his brother nod curtly before turning to walk off.

And then there was nothing more to do but dry his own eyes and head back to Annabel's loft, a cage that seemed more welcoming than the house in which he'd grown up.

Whether that made him the lion or the lamb was anyone's guess. Patrick sure as hell didn't know.

PATRICK DIDN'T RETURN to the loft for hours. Annabel half expected him not to show at all after exposing himself as he had. He'd revealed more today than he had during their past seven weeks together, and no doubt regretted every word.

Especially the admission of holding tight to his past.

It was obscenely tragic, yes, and a past she would never expect him to forget. But he'd told her not to try to make things easier on him. She couldn't help but take that to mean that he wasn't willing to move on. And she had always been about moving on, doubly so these days.

In fact, she'd spent the quiet evening online exploring career opportunities on job-search Web sites. She'd managed, as well, to get a peek at the workings of the crime labs in several cities via newsgroups and message boards where professionals shared stories and discussed the methodology of forensics.

Unfortunately, a peek was all she'd gotten, as her concentration skills were shot. No matter that she'd convinced herself Patrick would distract her from deciding what direction best suited her future, she was rapidly becoming her own worst enemy in that regard. Too often she caught herself wondering what he would think about leaving Houston should work in her new field take her out of state.

The third or fourth time she'd entertained such aberrant thoughts, she'd admitted it was time for sleep. Her loss of focus, she'd decided, had to be directly related to this afternoon's lunch and the revelations he'd finally made about his rescue and Soledad's death.

How he'd lived with that for so long, carried it for all these months…

The longer she'd spent dwelling on his memories, the colder her skin had become. Rather than heading straight to bed, she had ended up soaking in a hot tub of bubbles, seeking warmth and a release of the tension keeping her wound tight. Finally she'd slept, waking hours later to the grinding slide of the elevator grate as he'd opened it.

She'd lain still, her heart in her throat, listening for his movements. A ridiculous endeavor, as he made no sound at all. Obviously she had dozed off again, because when he finally entered the bedroom and slid into bed, she woke suddenly, her breath caught as she settled into the heat of his body.

Telling Chloe that a relationship with Patrick was unhealthy had been the clearest truth Annabel could speak. She could support him, encourage him. What she couldn't do was fix him. He had to not only admit to his demons but be willing to fix himself. So why did that proven truth now seem murky, when nothing about their situation had changed?

Nothing but Patrick's willingness to open up in the bright light of day.

In the time they'd been together, he'd grown from a bitterly recalcitrant ass to a man with a depth of character she couldn't help but admire. A depth that few men ten years older yet knew. A character that showed more promise than that of any man whose path she had crossed.

She loathed tears, her own more than anyone's, but was unable to stop them from spilling between her tightly closed lids. She shed enough tears to wet her pillow and to cause her to sniff. And not a soft unobtrusive sniff, but a ridiculously loud and unladylike snort.

"Are you crying?" Patrick asked, his voice low yet not a whisper.

Feeling morosely unable to cope with emotions she didn't understand, she simply shook her head. She hated the sense of having no self-control, after priding herself for so many years on that very thing. And then she sniffed again.

"You are crying." His hand, which had been resting on the curve of her hip, moved to her middle. He splayed his fingers beneath her breasts and waited. "I can feel it. You're crying."

"I'm fine."

"You're not fine. What's wrong?"

She shook her head, inched away. He pulled her right back.

"Annabel?"

"Yes, Patrick?" Her voice hardly quavered.

He growled beneath his breath. "Don't be an uppity snot with me. What the hell is going on?"

"If you don't mind, I'd like to go back to sleep."

This time his growl was loud and seemed to rumble through his limbs as well as his torso. He moved so fast she had no time to consider a defense, finding herself pinned on her back to the mattress, his weight and his very strong arms holding her in place.

"I do mind. Tell me what's going on."

The room was dark, the only illumination that of the moon shining between slats of the miniblinds. She hadn't closed them fully once she'd given up her vigil of watching for him to return.

The light wasn't much, just enough to see the gleam in his eyes. "Why?"

He frowned. "Why what?"

"Why do you want to know what's going on with me?"

"What kind of question is that?"

"A simple and straightforward one."

"Fine," he snapped, his jaw grinding. "Because."

She blinked, staring up. "Because what?"

"That's my simple straightforward answer to your simple straightforward question. Why? Because." He shifted above her, his thighs moving to the outside of hers, his hipbones settling against her own. "I can be as coy and reticent as you."

"You? Coy?"

A grin tipped the corner of his mouth. ''Sure. There's still a frat boy lurking beneath this thug.''

''I can see you as a cocky frat boy, but I will never think of you as coy,'' she said, wishing unconscionably that she'd known him then, before his exterior persona had hardened into a shell.

He considered her a moment, released one of the wrists he held pinned to the bed, and brushed a chunk of hair from her forehead. ''Do you think of yourself as coy?''

''When it suits my needs, I can be.''

''So I see.''

She smoldered when he didn't say anything more. ''Why do you do that?''

''Do what?''

''Play games to get what you want.''

He paused a moment. ''Games? You mean like Answering Twenty Questions with Twenty Questions? Or Let's Make a Deal the Annabel Way?''

''That's not funny.''

''Never said I was funny, sister. Simply horny and hung.'' He ground his hips against hers as if to prove a point.

Thing was, his penis remained soft, obvious in its bulk, but not aroused. Her traitorous body warmed and grew liquid, yet she kept her response to herself.

''I want to know, Patrick. Why do you care what goes on with me?''

He gave an evasively careless shrug. ''We thugs are like that.''

''You're not a thug.''

''Since when?'' he asked, frowning.

This time she was the one to employ evasive tactics by refusing to respond.

Patrick sighed. "We're not going to get very far here if you won't talk to me, sweetheart."

The term of endearment, so commonly used, slid over her like a sweetly delivered Italian caress. She'd thought herself able to fend off such a ridiculous reaction; how sincere could a frat boy be?

She knew Patrick was much more than she'd ever expected. Yet still his wild streak, his seeming instability, ran too wide and too deep. She wasn't ready to risk the high stakes of her future on a gamble with no guarantees.

She tried to roll away—and succeeded. He let her go and this time remained flat on his back on his side of the bed. He didn't try to scoop her back into his body. In fact, after several long minutes of uncomfortable silence, he left the bed. Then the room. Then the loft.

Again he did it all with nary a sound except for what could have been a fist slamming into the elevator wall as the door closed.

ANNABEL TOOK A MINUTE to breathe deeply, absorbing the serenity of Devon's gallery, a serenity her tempestuous soul welcomed more than ever this particular Tuesday morning.

She'd had her life course set for years, yet suddenly seemed rudderless, as if she'd been boarded by a pirate of her very own. Which, in a manner of speaking, she had.

She'd meant what she'd said to him last night about him not being a thug. She wasn't certain when she'd changed her mind and, yes, that left her rather disconcerted. For the most part she was able to catalog her feelings. Or she had until Patrick left her so thoroughly blindsided.

She'd been staring at Devon's *Missedtakes* for several

minutes, amusing herself with a litany of "what if's"...*What if Patrick was only acting out and not the least bit wild or untamed?*...when she realized she could hear quiet laughter in the background.

Female laughter. And male. The latter being her brother, but the former... Was that Chloe?

Annabel knew Chloe's attention to detail with any project in which she was involved meant she would do a great job on the catering for Devon's showing. But with Chloe and Eric, not to mention Devon and Trina, on the outs, Annabel sensed the gallery a fertile breeding ground for rebound romance.

And breeding of any sort was the last thing Chloe needed to flirt with. Pulling her attention away from the watercolors, Annabel headed toward the voices.

The tête-à-tête she'd been afraid she'd find was, instead, a ménage à trois. Devon stood in the alcove of Mina Sayid's studio while she applied henna to the tops of Chloe's feet. The attention of both women was fully engaged in the process.

Devon, however, had glanced up as Annabel rounded the corner of the mazelike hallway. She raised a finger to her lips; he honored her wishes and didn't say a word.

Slowing her steps before the other women saw her, she motioned her brother away, backing deeper into the labyrinth of the gallery. He made his excuses, his footsteps echoing on the hardwood floors, growing louder as he neared. He met her in an intimately secluded corner where she'd stopped to sit on a simple stone bench.

The cool, smooth seat faced a *karesansui* garden, the dry landscape of rocks and crushed granite seeming to flow like water beneath potted juniper. Annabel could believe she was far removed from the city as she sat and listened to a soft breeze blowing on hidden chimes.

Devon sat beside her, curled his fingers over the lip of the bench and hung his head. ‘‘Let me see them.’’

‘‘See what?’’ she answered, pretending cluelessness.

‘‘C’mon, Annie. Off with the shades.’’

‘‘Don’t call me Annie,’’ she barked softly as she pulled the glasses from her face and tucked them into her bag.

Devon gave her a sideways glance, then a shake of his head. ‘‘You better get some sleep between now and next week. If Luc Beacon gets a look at those purple half-moons, you’ll be kissing that shoot goodbye.’’

‘‘It’s called Photoshop, Devon. It cures a multitude of physical sins.’’ Though she knew her brother was right. The heavy makeup, hot lights and long hours of the shoot would exacerbate the problem. She definitely needed sleep.

‘‘I don’t think physical sins are responsible for that shade of purple, sweetie. That’s more than late hours and too much nightlife.’’

If only her brother had a clue as to what her nightlife entailed these days. ‘‘How’s Trina?’’

‘‘You’re not here to talk about Trina,’’ he said, moving his elbows to his knees and lacing his hands. ‘‘But you’re welcome to tell me about Chloe Zuniga.’’

Annabel huffed and turned a sharp look on her brother. ‘‘Forget it. She’s involved, and is simply going through a minor crisis.’’

‘‘Hey, I’m involved and am simply going through a minor crisis.’’

‘‘Are you sure?’’

Devon was silent for a moment before he picked up the Zen garden’s rake and began to drag it through the crushed gray-and-white granite. ‘‘It’s not minor, no. She met someone willing to give her what I won’t.’’

"A ring."

He nodded, continued to make random patterns with the rake as he combed it through the gritty sand.

"That was fast."

He shrugged one shoulder. "Seems it's been going on awhile."

Her brother grew silent, and Annabel wasn't even sure she knew what to say. Neither of them had ever dealt well with emotional complications. What they both understood was work, pouring their energies into attaining success.

Setting goals, even when in grade school, had given brother and sister a strong sense of self and made them survivors. Which was why relinquishing that control to another—or for another—came at such a high price.

Placing her hand on his shoulder, she cleared her throat. "I'm sorry, Devon. It's for the best, obviously, but that doesn't make it any easier to accept."

"Accept what, exactly? That we're both in our mid-thirties and no closer to being ready for a relationship than we were when we left home?"

Annabel gave a little laugh. "Which home would that have been? The one in Spokane? In San Francisco? In Portland? Vancouver? Fairbanks? Seatt—"

"Yeah, yeah. Point taken." He dropped the rake back to the edge of the garden and pushed himself up. "It wasn't the moving back to live with Grandmother I minded, you know?"

"I know."

"It was just that there was never any real reason for it. Not a one of those men our mother went after was worth a flying f— fig."

"Hmm. Is Trina responsible for your fruit curses?"

Devon blew out a huff. ‘‘She thought my language needed to be refined.’’

Much the same way Annabel had been trying to civilize Patrick. She crossed one leg and swung her foot, shaking off the pinpricks of guilt shaming her into admitting she had no right to change him.

And then her foot stopped as realization dawned. She was trying to change him, to make him a clone of the masses so that he would bore her and she could regain control of her world. The world he'd turned upside down when he'd backed her into that alley wall and kissed her defenseless.

‘‘Annie?’’

‘‘*Don't* call me Annie.’’

‘‘Then don't sit there and zone out on me.’’

‘‘I was just thinking that if your language was an issue with Trina, I can see why Chloe would snag your attention.’’

‘‘Liar. You weren't thinking that at all.’’

True, she wasn't. She was thinking that it was time to flay herself open and expose the mess she was in. She took a deep breath, uncrossed her leg and laced her hands primly in her lap. ‘‘I'm in trouble, Devon. Big trouble. Trouble like I've never known before.’’

His brow furrowed. ‘‘Man trouble.’’

She nodded.

‘‘You're in love.’’

She nodded, then just as quickly shook her head. ‘‘I don't know.’’

‘‘What do you know?’’ he asked softly after a moment filled with only the sound of chimes in the wind.

‘‘That I can't stop thinking about him. That he makes me feel safe when I didn't even know I felt otherwise. That he makes me smile.’’

"And?"

"I let down my guard when I'm with him. Way too easily." She sighed.

Devon chuckled. "Then good for him. It's about time someone cracked those walls of Jericho you've built so high."

"I built them for a reason."

"I know." He paused, went on. "But you're not our mother, Annie. You're not going to make the same stupid choices."

"I'm afraid that's what I'm doing now," she said, so softly Devon moved back to sit at her side.

"Tell me about him."

She wasn't even sure she knew where to begin. "He's younger."

"A boy toy, huh?"

"Exactly what I thought at first."

"And now?"

This time she was the one to reach for the rake and try to clear herself an obvious path through her personal quagmire. "Now I realize he's more of a man than any of the ones I've known."

"He must be quite impressive. After all, I've met a few of your beaux."

"Beaux?" Annabel laughed. "Is that more of Trina's influence?"

Devon shook his head. "No. That's how I've thought of the men you've let into your life. They've wooed you, but have never become anything more to you than trophies. What I've never figured out is if it's the chase that amuses you, or if it's that they turn out to be less than you expected once you give in."

"Are you accusing me of being a snob?"

"Aren't you?"

She looked away because he was hitting too close to a truth she seemed to be holding in a rusty bucket, a truth that was seeping away as she lost more and more of the control that had kept her safe from men like those who had used their mother.

"His name is Patrick, by the way."

"I know."

She turned her head sharply, her raised brows questioning.

"Chloe mentioned him and the impact he appears to be having on you." A slow, lazy grin spread over Devon's face. "A good impact, Annie. Chloe said she's never seen you so happy. Or so human."

Human? Ha! Annabel blew out a gusty huff. "He's dangerous, Devon. He's wild. I wonder at times how close he is to coming unhinged. Or how much of that attitude is a ruse."

"I'm sensing kindred spirits here."

"That doesn't mean we make a good fit."

"It also doesn't guarantee you won't. Why don't you give him a chance, Annie?"

She pulled in and blew out a long shuddering breath. "Because I'm scared?"

"Of getting hurt? Or of falling in love? Because I've gotta say, hurt shouldn't be an issue. That's one thing we both are experts on working our way through."

"And falling in love?"

"Once you have an answer to that one, you let me know."

8

CHLOE SAT AT THE FAR END of the horseshoe-shaped bar in Haydon's Half-Time, going over the spreadsheet she'd written to keep track of the catering details for Devon Lee's New Year's Eve showing. Details such as linens and crystal and flatware. Alcohol and ice. Tables and uniforms and cleanup.

Sydney and Macy and Lauren and Poe would share the grunt work. Chloe only hoped the five of them would be able to manage, especially since Poe's RSVP list had grown from sixty to eighty this past week alone. *P* might not literally stand for *promptly* in the acronym, but Sweet Pete in tennis shoes, what was up with all the last-minute decisions?

Sweet Pete in tennis shoes. See? She had it in her to curse creatively. She was doing her best to be the woman Eric wanted, to tone down her potty mouth—a toning-down she needed to do anyway, working with young girls as she did these days.

She knew Eric was proud of her for that, for following her heart and returning to school for her Master's, for making the change from fashion career to establishing gUIDANCE gIRL's mentoring model. And she hadn't done it to impress him. She'd done it for herself. gUIDANCE gIRL was a program she could've used as a teen.

Making counseling and peer services available to troubled girls rather than advising on lip gloss and nail color went a long way to satisfying a restlessness Chloe had thought she would live with all of her life. A restlessness she'd battled until she'd met Eric, and he'd shown her that stability existed outside of fairy tales.

Now she had to figure out where her tranquility had gone.

She drummed her fingers along the sides of her laptop, staring at the screen and the numbers and schedules that no longer made any sense. And wasn't that exactly the way her days were going lately—nothing making sense? Even the rusty-red henna designs on her palms were more ordered in their intricacy than her life seemed to be.

Glancing down the bar to where Eric stood, towel thrown over his shoulder, smile wide and eyes twinkling as he chatted up a group of regulars in for a beer and their nightly fix of ESPN, she thought back to the night almost two years ago she'd come to Haydon's Half-Time to ask him to do her a favor.

He'd been wary of her *and* her favor, and the memory made her smile. Hell, she'd never expected he'd take her up on her three-dates-for-three-wishes offer. But she'd been scared of screwing up what she had at gIRL-gEAR back then, and desperate enough to ask for his help in salvaging her reputation and her bad-girl name.

For so long since then she'd thought she'd found her happily-ever-after, but now, watching Eric at work, seeing him in his element, she wasn't sure of anything. He was the same man he'd always been, the one with whom she'd fallen in love. All she could wonder about was where she'd gone so wrong in making herself over that he didn't love her as much anymore.

Sensing that he'd looked her way and caught her sightlessly staring, she grabbed a cocktail napkin and feigned removing a speck of pretzel salt from her eye. Blinking away what she could of the moisture, she glanced up into Eric's frown.

"What's wrong, princess?"

She remembered how much she'd hated that endearment, yet now couldn't imagine hearing anything else. "Nothing. I bit too hard into a pretzel and my contact lens caught the shrapnel."

"Hmm," Eric said, obviously aware there wasn't a basket of pretzels within his arm's length, much less hers. "I thought you might've been crying."

"No. I'm not crying." She was lying, of course, and wanting to rub his face in the fact that she was crying over him. But that was childish, and she was trying not to be, so instead she gave him her sexiest smile. "Is there anything I can do in the kitchen, maybe? To help you get out of here early?"

He seemed to consider her questions, but she was convinced that what he was considering instead was what lay in store should he have to spend time with her at home. Lately he worked at least six nights a week; she was certain he'd thought about working seven.

"It would be nice to have more time together, Eric." He certainly didn't have to stay until closing every night. He employed a perfectly competent manager who was up for the task. "I can't make all those babies you used to talk about on my own, you know."

"I dunno, Chloe." Eric pulled the towel from his shoulder and wiped a circle on the bar surface next to where she'd set up her mini-office. "Tim mentioned cutting out early, and I pretty much told him to go for it."

Nothing about the babies. Why wasn't she surprised? "So you have to lock up. Again."

Lips pressed together, Eric nodded almost curtly before tilting his head in the direction of her laptop. ''Besides,'' he said, his tone sharpening with more censure than she'd ever heard from him, ''I figure you're pretty busy with your party planning.''

Chloe rolled her eyes. ''Don't tell me you're still in a snit over my helping out Poe?''

''I don't do snits, Chloe.''

''Then what do you call your attitude?'' she retorted. ''You've been pissy about it ever since I told you I'd agreed to give her a hand.''

Eric's towel went back over his shoulder none too gently. His face took on an equally testy expression, and he kept his voice low. ''It's like I told you then. I would've appreciated you checking with me before you committed to bailing out Poe.''

Chloe felt anger stir beneath her incredulity. ''Since when do I need your permission to help out one of my girlfriends?''

''Hell, Chloe. I never said you needed my permission.'' He leaned closer, lowered his voice, but kept the heavy-duty tone. ''But we're a couple. And basic courtesy says we okay things with one another just in case.''

''Come on now, sugar. We've been together long enough for you to know that Miss Manners is not my middle name.'' And that was it. She was out of here. She closed out her spreadsheet program and slammed shut her laptop.

He hadn't said anything that would've pissed her off ordinarily, but nothing she'd been feeling lately was ordinary in the least. And so it took less than nothing to light her fuse. She bit off the foulest words she knew.

Eric grabbed her by the wrist, tightly enough to force her to look up. ''I had plans, Chloe. For us.''

Easy for him to claim after the fact. "Would've been nice of you to share. Or have the basic courtesy to okay them with me. Just in case."

"Surprise plans." He released her, reached again for his towel as if needing to keep his hands busy. "But I guess they'll just have to wait, won't they?"

Yeah, they would. Same as the apology she wasn't quite ready to make. She would've made it, she really would have, if the idea hadn't left her feeling too exposed, too totally...vulnerable and raw.

She tucked her laptop into her computer case, situating dislodged CDs, a printer cable and the power supply. She took her time, knowing the case was in need of her attention even less than Eric needed to dry his hands.

How in the hell had they let themselves sink this low?

Finally, she looked up, calling on years of spine-stiffening techniques to keep her shoulders back and her chin high. "I suppose you're right. Surprise or not, they'll have to wait."

Eric gave a tired sigh and shake of his head. "I might as well let Tim have New Year's Eve off, since I won't be needing it, after all."

"What? You'd scheduled the thirty-first off? New Year's Eve?" Oh, God. That much he could've told her. She'd had no idea. "I thought with the crowd you're expecting you'd want to be here."

"There's a reason I pay Tim what I do," Eric said softly. "But, yeah. I should've known better than to try to surprise you. Especially since you've been so busy lately."

"Me, busy? What about you?"

"Overcompensating, I guess. I can pull a late shift here and save on staff overtime instead of watching TV at home alone."

Now, of course, she felt even worse, felt her bottom lip tremble and her eyes fill with tears she wouldn't be able to blame on any pretzel. If she'd been busy, it simply had been to keep her mind off losing him.

She reached out a hand, and he took it, pulling her closer and kissing the backs of her fingers. "I ruined everything, didn't I? I'm sorry," she murmured.

"No, princess. You didn't ruin anything." He smiled at her in that way that caused her heart to tumble, her knees to shake, her anger to seem wholly unjustified. "I tell you what. I'll take New Year's Eve off anyway. Maybe you could use another bartender?"

"Oh, Eric." The apology she'd tried to swallow earlier choked her again. She nodded rapidly, wondering if any other man could be so wonderful. "I really could. We're going to be cutting it close as is."

"Then that's the plan."

"Yo, barkeep!" called a voice from down the bar. "How about you make time with the lady later and get me a beer?"

When Eric rolled his eyes, Chloe opened her mouth to put the bastard in his place. Eric saw her intent and leaned across the bar, shutting her up with a quick, scorching kiss. "That's Big Bert. I spiked a volleyball onto his head during a game this summer, and he hasn't quit harassing me yet."

Oh, gawd, when was the last time he'd given her such a kiss? "Big Bert? As in—"

"Tall, beefy and bleached blond hair that sticks out like a headful of feathers."

"Now, that's funny," she said, and laughed, feeling the first tentative easing of the heaviness that for so long had weighed down her heart.

Eric backed a step away. "Lemme take care of Bert. But we're on for New Year's Eve, okay?"

She nodded. It had been hard to let herself fall in love with this man, yet he was so very easy to love. She sighed, praying that maybe they'd just taken the first step back to where they'd been, and hoping the rest of the trip would be free of detours.

ONE THING PATRICK WOULD never again take for granted was the value of being connected in a city the size of Houston.

Being Ray's brother, and Ray being engaged to Sydney, and Sydney being Nolan Ford's daughter, and Nolan being one of the city's major money men meant that arranging an interview with the executive chef at Tony's Restaurant without a single cooking class under his belt was a piece of cake.

No, a piece of a triple-chocolate tart with a cognac crème anglaise. Yeah. That had impressed the hell out of everyone from the manager to the maître d'. And he hadn't done so badly showing off his seared sea bass and bay scallops with garlic sake sauce, either.

He was definitely feeling more positive about his future than he had since graduation. A degree in business administration. What the hell had he been thinking studying a subject that bored him to tears?

He'd aced it, but had never felt the least bit of interest or excitement the way he did when deciding between mango-grilled chicken or broiled snapper and plantains when cooking with Soledad.

Heading to the far end of Tony's parking lot and his El Camino, which seemed to have muscled its way into this moneyed neighborhood, Patrick laughed. He actually laughed. Out loud. Laughed, and liked the feeling of his abs contracting as he did. Life was looking good.

Things with Ray were getting better. Their relationship wasn't what Patrick would consider one hundred percent, but they were rediscovering more of the easy camaraderie that had always been a part of their brotherly bond. And if this job panned out, Patrick would feel a lot more legitimate than he'd felt in a while.

It wasn't about the money; Patrick had his future sister-in-law to thank for his good fortune in the hard cash department. Though Sydney and Ray weren't yet married, her father had done what he could to put Ray's mind at ease by financing a search effort to locate Patrick. So between the reward put up by Nolan Ford's venture capitalist firm and the bounty the FBI had put on Russell Dega's gang—both of which should've gone to Soledad—Patrick was doing okay. He'd saved most of that bundle, except for what he'd plunked down on the El Camino. And what he'd used to buy Annabel at the bachelorette auction.

He opened the car door, slid into the seat and shoved the keys into the ignition. But he didn't start the car right away. He thought, instead, about how much of his current state of mind he owed to the last eight weeks of her company.

He wondered, not for the first time, how truly difficult it was going to be to let her go. Not because he'd grown to depend on her strength to keep him on the straight and narrow, but simply because he'd miss her.

The things he felt for her were so different than what he'd felt with Soledad. That relationship had been about dependence and survival, and separating the two was one thing he'd never been able to do.

But with Annabel—

Slam! Whoa! Patrick jumped, jerked his head to the right and wrenched his body away from the door. An eternity of seconds blinked by as he took in the walking cane wedged to his door, the hand at the other end, the car blocking his El Camino from behind and the face of Russell Dega.

A face Patrick had last seen twisted with fury and vowing revenge.

Instead of the long hair Dega had always tied with a bandanna, he now wore bronzed streaks in a spiky cut that was colored dark brown. A goatee and mustache hid the scar bisecting his chin, black slacks and a black turtleneck hid the others. But the Euro-trash look did nothing to civilize the murderous glint in his black eyes.

"Mr. Coffey." Dega smiled without emotion. "It's good to see you again."

Patrick felt his teeth on the verge of grinding to dust. His heart lodged like a fat wad of unchewed food in his throat. "Can't say I share the sentiment, Russ."

Dega laughed, still with no feeling. "No, I'm sure you don't. But then the last time we saw one another, you were making off with information I needed, while I was getting shot. I would've been in touch sooner—" he gave a carelessly deceptive shrug "—but bullet wounds take time to heal. And then there was the matter of letting the heat die down."

Patrick didn't say a word, but cast a quick glance to his right and the mirror there, back to his rearview, moving his hands from the steering wheel to his lap. The bulk of the knife in his pocket settled into his palm—

"Hands where I can see them." Dega punctuated his order with three sharp raps of his cane on the car door. "Who knows what tricks you have up your sleeves, and

I'd hate to have to kill you before getting what I've come for."

His heart beating all the way to his eyeballs, Patrick stared through the windshield at the flames licking over the hood of the El Camino, though what he really saw was Soledad facing the business end of Dega's semi-automatic.

"I don't have shit that belongs to you." He growled out the words.

"So you say now." The other man again tapped his cane. "Maybe I should ask that hot piece of ass you've been busy sticking it to."

Son of a bitch!

Patrick went for the door handle. Dega stumbled; Patrick took advantage. He dug into his pocket for the knife. He had one foot out the door and on the ground when Dega came back, kicking the door closed on his shin.

Patrick bit down on a howl. He sat still, refused to release Dega's gaze. The knife-blade pain in his leg had his eyes stinging, but his mouth worked just fine. "You touch her, I own your sorry ass."

Dega pushed harder on the car door. "You give me what I want, you'll never see me again."

"I couldn't get that lucky." Blood welled where his skin had broken, and began to trickle inside his boot to the cuff of his sock.

"You're out of luck, Mr. Coffey. I know what Soledad gave you." Dega bounced the car door with his cane. "She told me just before I shot—"

Motherfu— Patrick lunged, but Dega had the leverage and full use of his limbs. This time he threw the weight of his body and the force of his good hip at the door.

The bone snapped. *God-freaking-damn.* Patrick pushed out a panting grunt, ready to puke up his guts.

His eyes rolled back; sweat ran from temple to jawline, from his nape to the crack of his ass. His teeth crunched together. "You asshole."

"Payback, Mr. Coffey. We can get together at a future date and compare the condition of our limps." Dega pushed away from the car, the motion grinding bone edge on bone edge.

Patrick bit down on his tongue until the pressure finally lessened. He breathed, breathed, found what he could of his voice and said, "The only future date we have will be a threesome. You, me and the needle in your arm delivering a dose of potassium chloride."

Dega tossed back his head and laughed. "And here I assumed you'd want to shoot me yourself. Finish the job your *federales* botched so badly. Soledad never did show you the safe room under the house, did she?"

Patrick could only groan.

"It was tough to tunnel into, even before being shot all to hell. And it was obviously impossible to find, or I wouldn't be standing here now. A generator, medical supplies, enough food to last several weeks. Not exactly paradise, but close."

He'd never even left the island. The bastard had been there all that time. "You'd better watch your back, Russ."

"I certainly will, Mr. Coffey. I certainly will." Dega bounced the door on Patrick's leg, which had gone blessedly numb. "But most of the time I'll be watching that beautiful back belonging to Miss Annabel Lee."

Patrick forced his eyes open, his gaze back to Dega's. "I told you—"

"And I told you." Dega leaned in with a growl. "I want the information Soledad gave you...." He let the rest of whatever he was going to say trail off, glancing up as a police cruiser rolled through the parking lot one row over. "Hands on the steering wheel, Mr. Coffey."

"You can't run that fast, Russ," Patrick said, gauging time, distance and pain factors should Dega bolt. The cop couldn't be that far away—

"I don't need to run."

Patrick turned to find the foot of the cane inches from his face. The cane was hollow and nicely outfitted with a gun barrel now aimed straight at his Adam's apple.

Dega's thumb hovered over the single button in the dog's-head handle. "In fact, I'm quite sure you'll agree that I have nothing to run from."

"You must not want that info too badly if you're willing to wipe out your only chance for retrieval."

Dega's expression grew confidently smug. "I always thought you were a reasonable man, Mr. Coffey."

"Sure. I'm reasonable." He was also teetering madly at the edge of consciousness. "Just make sure you've got me chained to a tree trunk or caught in a car door and you'll get your way, no problem."

"Where is it?"

"In a safe place."

"Of course. Where?"

Patrick shook his head, sliding his far hand from the steering wheel to the bench, and praying like hell he could pull off this bluff. "Not here."

"Of course not," Dega said, his attention divided between Patrick and the police cruiser now slowing behind the El Camino blocked in by Dega's car.

Patrick kept his eyes on Dega's face. "He's running your plates, Russ. You'd better hope you have your paperwork in order."

"The beauty of rental cars and the best documentation

money can buy. He'll discover nothing more than what I want him to know."

"And what would that be?" Patrick's hand had reached his pocket.

"I said keep your hands where I can see them. On the steering wheel. Now," Dega said with a snarl. At the same time he raised his free hand to signal to the officer that he was on his way to move his illegally parked car. The cruiser drove on.

"Temper, temper, Russ." Patrick didn't keep his hand where it was at all, but moved it closer toward his pocket. "You can hardly fire that thing—"

Dega fired. The bullet ripped into the passenger seat with barely more than a *thwup*. Patrick swallowed hard. The throbbing in his leg was nothing compared to the explosive pounding of his heart. He swore his ribs had cracked. "Damn. And I just bought this car."

"Then I'm sure you'd like to remain alive to enjoy it." Dega returned the foot of the cane to the ground. "I'll be in touch to arrange the return of my information. Before I walk away, however, I'd like you to take note of the landscaping van parked at the rear of the lot."

Patrick glanced into his rearview mirror and saw the back end of a white panel van. "You mowing lawns these days?"

"If I have any trouble making it to my car or getting out of the parking lot, my associate will be on his way to visit your Miss Lee."

"You bastard." Patrick spat out the words and moved his hands to ten and two on the steering wheel. He imagined sinking the knife blade deep into the other man's belly, but nothing was worth chancing Annabel's life. "Get the hell out of my sight."

"As you wish." Dega bowed mockingly. "Until we next meet."

Patrick watched the other man's retreat in his side mirror, and only when the luxury rental eased away did he push his own door open. The fire in his leg roared to life. He used both hands to lift his knee and settle his foot on the floorboard at an angle that took the pressure off his shin.

Then he dug for the phone at his waistband, leaning back his head and closing his eyes as he waited for an answer.

"Ray Coffey."

"It's Patrick. I need help."

ANNABEL PACED THE LENGTH of her bedroom, back and forth, back and forth, as Joseph Baron, an EMT assigned to the same fire station as Ray, tended to Patrick.

Ray simply stood at the head of the bed. Blood pressure, temperature, pulse, pillows and pain meds. So thorough and competent. So cool and detached and brilliantly able to cope—while Annabel remained totally helpless.

She also remained frightened, and so she wrapped her arms even tighter over her middle as she paced. A ridiculous endeavor, as holding herself did nothing to contain the sharp spiraling pulse of fear in her chest.

Patrick had suffered a fractured tibia. A compound fracture, yes. But his injuries could've been so much worse. He could have lost his life.

And she could've lost him.

The three men had arrived from the hospital only thirty minutes ago, after five hours spent in emergency. Patrick had refused to stay overnight and had signed himself out, demanding his brother bring him back to the loft. Ray had, but not without objection. He'd wanted to take him to his house, at which point Patrick had threatened to walk.

Annabel hadn't known a thing about his encounter with Dega or the hospital visit until way too long after the fact.

She paced even faster.

"Annabel."

At Patrick's one-word plea, she stopped, glanced over to see Baron packing his medic kit and Ray staring down at his brother's elevated leg.

"What?" she snapped, because she had no idea how she was supposed to react. Guilt set in immediately, a reaction so unfamiliar that she tightened her grip on her arms. "I'm sorry," she said, her voice calmer, her stomach still churning. "Do you need another blanket? More water?"

He shook his head, his eyes glazed and foggy, but his smile genuine Patrick. What he had to smile about, she had no idea, but she approached the bed until she could take hold of the hand he offered. The hand that would've indicated the extent of his fever if she hadn't known how high his temperature ran.

"Just stay here," he mumbled, close to falling asleep.

She glanced toward Baron. He nodded. "He's fine. Watch for a fever, or numbness in his foot. The meds will knock him out for a while, but he's good. You've got his prescriptions here. Just make sure he takes them on schedule."

"Even if you have to shove them down his throat," Ray added, staring at his brother with an expression that belied his gruff voice. He looked at Annabel then. "I'll take him out to the house, no problem."

"No." Patrick's eyes shot open. "I want to be here. I've still got ten days left on my lease."

"His lease?" Ray asked.

Annabel's jaw tightened. "An inside joke."

"But not a very funny one," Patrick muttered, squeezing her hand as he drifted off.

Annabel forced her gaze back to Ray, swallowing as best she could to clear her throat. "I have your numbers. I'll call if he gets out of hand. Or out of bed."

"No need." A tic pulsed in Ray's jaw. "I'm crashing on your couch. I'm on duty at six, but I need to see him through the night."

Annabel tucked Patrick's limp hand beneath his blanket. "You're welcome to stay, of course, but I can handle him."

"I know. It's handling Dega I'm more concerned with."

She had to admit she shared Ray's concern. "There's an agent watching the fire escape, and the elevator requires a code."

"Which the bastard is just canny enough to break."

"He's obviously not your garden-variety bandit," Baron added, hoisting his pack on his shoulder.

"He's a stupid son of a bitch," Patrick mumbled through closed eyes and a mouth that barely functioned. "Thinks I have information. I don't have shit but a broken leg and a bad haircut."

Arms crossed, Annabel reached up to press her fingertips to her mouth. She rolled her eyes, but still couldn't keep a grin from spreading over her face. "And here we have your not so garden-variety patient."

Ray met her gaze. "Don't hesitate to wake me up if he gets contrary. If his fever spikes. If he needs—"

"I'll wake you, Ray." She placed a hand on his shoulder and turned him toward the door, when he so obviously didn't want to go. "I'll lock up after Joseph, then find bedding for you. I'm sorry I haven't yet furnished the guest room.''

''The couch is fine. I've slept in worse places.''

''Me, too,'' Patrick muttered. ''In the mud, in the rain, tied to a tree.''

Pain sliced through Ray's eyes before he managed to mask it. Baron moved a hand to the center of his colleague's back and guided him out of the room. Annabel followed, glancing briefly at the man lying naked where she'd slept alone for so many years.

The thought of what could have happened to him, the realization that he might not be lying here now had things gone down differently, was more than she could bear. Catching back a sob, she turned the lamp on the bedside table down low.

''Annabel?''

She glanced over at a nearly unconscious Patrick, looking into his bleary but beautiful eyes. ''Yes?''

''I love you.''

9

SHUTTING THE BEDROOM DOOR quietly behind herself thirty minutes later, Annabel tightened the sash on her robe before heading into the kitchen.

She thought a cup of herbal tea might help her relax enough to get to sleep, since the shower, though soothing, had done nothing to take the edge off her nerves.

Since walking Baron to the door and gathering bedding for Ray, she'd checked on Patrick twice before heading to the shower. He'd barely moved a muscle, and seeing him getting the rest he needed pleased her in so many ways—even if defining those ways was more than she was capable of doing tonight.

She was still off balance from his woozy declaration of love, though she was well aware of the drug-induced basis for his statement. He didn't love her any more than she loved him...*did he?* They were simply bedmates, and short-lived ones at that...*weren't they?*

Love had nothing to do with their association. Once Patrick was feeling more himself, she was certain he'd recant what he'd said. She was simply bracing for the inevitable and ignoring the nagging reminder that, if she was as uninvolved as she claimed, she wouldn't have to brace.

She yanked the towel from her hair and roughly squeezed most of the water from her short razor cut. Shaking the layers into place, she tossed the towel into the kitchen's laundry closet. She'd just reached for the teakettle when she heard someone close the balcony door.

Ray.

Kettle in hand, she made her way around the lava lamp bubble sculptures and into the main room.

Crossing from the balcony to the sofa, Ray glanced her way. She lifted the kettle. "I was about to make a cup of tea. Can I get you anything?"

Shaking his head, he dropped onto the far end of the sofa, his legs outstretched, head slumped back. The bedclothes she'd brought him earlier remained stacked on the coffee table. "I'm fine."

She didn't think he was fine at all. "You need sleep. The guest room facilities are yours to use if you think a shower might help."

He looked over as she sat on the opposite end of the sofa. "Did it help you?"

Chagrined, she set the teakettle on the floor at her feet and tucked her legs beneath her. "That's why I was going to try the tea."

"Yeah, well, I'm not even sure a bottle of Jack would help me at this point." He wearily scrubbed both hands over his haggard face.

She understood his sentiment well, just as she agreed with his unspoken caveat that alcohol was best left out of this situation.

"Poe, what are you doing with Patrick?"

She bristled at the bluntness of the sudden question, but then relaxed. Ray was Patrick's brother; his concern was legitimate and went far beyond a broken leg. And Patrick had said that he loved her....

Annabel tightened the belt on her robe. "I'm not quite sure how to answer that, Ray. I certainly never thought we'd still be keeping company when he bought me off the auction block eight weeks ago."

Ray huffed. "Yeah, that was something. I don't think anyone saw that coming."

"There's a lot to Patrick that no one sees," she said softly, realizing as she did how much she believed it.

"I still can't believe you got him to cut his hair." Ray paused, then added, "You've really been good for him. He's seemed more…alive since seeing you than anytime since he's been back."

She wasn't sure how she felt about that responsibility, that compliment, about the idea that she was capable of such a positive impact when most people agreed she was difficult, if not an outright pain in the ass.

"He's not a bad guy, Ray. But I'm not sure he knows that."

"When I think of everything he went through…" Ray let the sentence trail off, though Annabel could see by his pained expression that the thought wasn't as easy to let go.

"He doesn't blame you, you know."

"He's told me."

"But you still blame yourself."

His answer was a simple nod, and she waited, sensing he had more to say. The room was dark, lit only by the light over the stove, which reflected off the open area's white walls. From the end of the hallway, she heard Patrick's snore, and she couldn't help but smile.

"It was my idea to book the cruise. I'd just finished my Master's thesis. That, and the fact that Patrick managed to hang on through four years and actually graduate, was worth celebrating. There were a lot of times my folks didn't think he'd make it."

"His grades were bad?"

"Hell, no. He aced everything. He just didn't give a shit about his degree and partied his ass off for four freakin' years."

"Where did he go to school?"

"Texas A&M. Same as me. Because of me," he added hoarsely, shifting on the sofa, bringing his legs up and leaning forward, his elbows on his knees. "The cruise was going to be his last fling. He swore he was going to get serious, straighten up his act, lay off the booze. He was still such a kid." Ray buried his face in his hands. "What a goddamn way to have to grow up, tied to a goddamn tree."

He looked so miserable Annabel wished she was better equipped to offer comfort. "He told me about fishing. About cooking. He wasn't always tied to a tree." She paused, unsure if she would be revealing a confidence, then added, "He even had a lover."

At her strangely painful revelation, Ray glanced over. "What?"

Nodding, she looked away and reached for the memento box on the coffee table. She didn't speak again until she held her grandmother's jade pendant. Rubbing her thumb over the gold inscription, she took a deep breath. "Her name was Soledad. Apparently she'd been Dega's mistress years before the kidnapping. He'd never intended to let Patrick live, but did so to humor her."

"Wait. I knew about Soledad. He told me about her, but not about her being his lover. Or about her keeping him alive?"

Annabel nodded. "That's what he says. And that it wasn't always a sure thing that she would succeed. Apparently she contacted the authorities on a trip to Key West for supplies. She also made a deal with them that

Patrick would get the reward money should anything happen to her.''

Ray hung his head. ''I didn't know any of this. I mean, I knew she'd been the informant, and the part about her being Dega's mistress at one time. Patrick told me that much. But none of this. None of the details of their...relationship. Or Dega wanting to kill him.'' He wrung his hands together. ''It's like Patrick had this whole other life, and I never even knew.''

''I'm not sure he wanted you to know.''

''Why wouldn't he?''

''It's just a guess, Ray. I don't know this for certain. But I get the sense that he wanted to spare you the dirty truth along with the hurt.''

''But he told you.''

''A disinterested party.''

He shook his head. ''I don't think you're all that disinterested.''

She shrugged one shoulder, returned the pendant to the memento box, then reached for the teakettle and set it on her lap. ''I've enjoyed him a lot....''

She stopped, feeling her voice catch and threaten to break. She held tight to the teakettle's handle, fearing if she didn't, her shaking hands would give her away.

''But?''

She glanced over. ''But?''

Ray smiled gently. ''It sounded like you were about to qualify that with a 'but.' ''

''My life is about to undergo a major upheaval. I may be moving. I'll certainly be changing careers. We're both high maintenance, and I'll have a hard enough time keeping myself up and running. I won't have the energy or the skill to fix Patrick, too.''

''Only Patrick can fix Patrick...but I hear you. He's

never been easy to live with.'' Ray studied her thoughtfully. ''So his comment about his lease being up is about splitting from your place here.''

She nodded.

''And from you.''

She said nothing.

Ray huffed. ''Why do I think you're no happier about that than Patrick sounded?''

ANNABEL SLEPT FITFULLY, dreaming of wicked walking canes come to life, car doors refusing to close, bullet holes that led to deep dark rabbit holes where the Mad Hatter wore a colorfully coiled snake on his head.

She kept her back to Patrick and stayed as far to the other side of the bed as she could, touching him with the soles of her feet anytime she came awake. She wasn't even sure she awoke or if she simply never really slept. The latter seemed a more likely scenario.

He was no hotter than usual and he didn't toss or turn. She was thankful for all of that, knowing sleep was what he needed more than anything.

She needed sleep, too, but her exhaustion was more of the crash-and-burn sort, and her subconscious obviously recognized that it was easier to keep her wits in focus than to try to regain them from slumber's depths. Of course, that meant she lay there with way too much on her mind.

Beyond imagining the horror of what had happened earlier in the day, she thought of her talk with Patrick's brother. Both subjects were better than caffeine for keeping her mind buzzing, and between the two it was Patrick's whispered claim of loving her that had played repeatedly now for hours.

''I meant it, you know.''

She squeezed her eyes as tightly as her chest seemed to close around her fast-beating heart. "I hate it when you do that."

He chuckled softly. "You're just saying that."

"No, I mean it. You scare the spit out of me when you wake up without making a sound." Not to mention seeming to know exactly what she'd been thinking each and every time.

"Yeah, yeah. Go on pretending you're mad. That way you don't have to deal with the truth."

"You're delirious."

"I'm perfectly sober and alert."

"You're on medication."

"For my leg. Not my heart." He pulled in a deep breath, blew it out slowly. "I can tell the difference in the pain."

It took her a minute to open her eyes, what with the constriction in her chest. How in the world was she supposed to deal with knowing how much and in how many ways he was hurt? Carefully she rolled over to face him. "Do you need another painkiller?"

"No," he murmured softly. "I need you to scoot your butt over here and put your head on my shoulder."

Doing that appealed to her on such a deep level that she was almost too frightened to move. She wasn't sure how to disconnect her concern over his injury from that for his safety. Or how to separate either of those from her more basic sense of caring for him because of who he was.

Then, strangely, it occurred to her that perhaps she wasn't supposed to. That the weft and warp of her feelings were too tightly woven to separate the individual threads.

"I'm waiting over here."

Swallowing the lump in her throat, she inched toward him, feeling as if this moment might mean more than any other they'd shared. It was the sense of vulnerability, the way the darkness hid the same multitude of sins exposed in the bright light of day. There were no prying eyes, no need for defenses. This was simply her and Patrick and nothing more.

"Speed it up, woman, before I fall back asleep."

Sighing heavily, she moved against his side, her head on his shoulder where he wanted it to be. She curled her hands between their bodies, uncertain with his injury how far to take her caress. "Happy now?"

He wrapped his arm around her and urged her to come even closer. "Getting there, though feel free to touch. Just leave Mr. Happy and the boys alone."

She rolled her eyes; he was such a guy. But she did as he asked, enjoying the heat of his skin. "Mr. Happy?"

"Umm," he murmured, his fingers threading in and out of her hair. "Make that Mr. Not-So-Happy. He's on a sort of self-preservation quest. Giving the boys a vacation."

"After today? I should hope so. The three of them came awfully close to the wrong end of a gun."

"That's not it at all, though that car seat business pisses me off." He grumbled under his breath. "See, this is where women get it all wrong."

Frowning, she stopped rubbing her fingertips over his ribs. "Get what all wrong?"

"The relationship between a man and his dick."

She waited a minute, at a totally uncharacteristic loss for words, before saying simply, "I see."

"No you don't. But there's no reason with your history that you should."

"I haven't told you anything about my history with men's dicks."

"You don't have to. You're pretty easy to read, you know."

"No, I don't know." She'd always thought herself an impenetrable and blank canvas.

"Well, you are." He held her even closer. "You bristle so easily when you're challenged."

She started to do just that but kept her mouth closed in an effort to be valorously discreet. And because she didn't want to prove him right.

"You see, a dick can be a wonderful thing."

Lips pressed together tightly, she allowed herself a quick roll of her eyes, even though what she most wanted to do was smack him silly. Or laugh.

"But there are times it can earn a man a world of hurt." He moved the hand that had been toying with her hair lower, massaging the crest of her shoulder.

"I was going to say 'I see,' but not being master of my own..."

"Bat and balls?"

"Yes. Bat and balls. Since I have no personal experience owning a set, I obviously cannot see."

"Exactly." He turned his head slightly. "Did you know you also speak very formally when a conversation bothers you?"

"This conversation doesn't bother me. I'm hardly a virgin or ignorant about the workings of the male anatomy."

"That's not the conversation we're having."

"Oh?"

"Uh-uh. We're talking about why I had sex with Soledad in the heat of danger, but why I now won't make love with you."

Delirious *and* delusional. ‘‘You have no business making love now period.’’

‘‘I could easily make it my business. But I’m not going to.’’

‘‘I see,’’ she said, the answer becoming automatic, though she didn’t really and had no idea how the conversation had turned to Soledad and sex.

Patrick nodded his head, his chin brushing over her bangs. ‘‘I thought you might.’’

The one thing she did see, however, was that his level of cognizance remained too high for someone under the influence of the pain medication he’d been given. Then again, he was the one who could drink a platoon beneath the table and never feel a thing.

‘‘I needed Soledad as a sort of confirmation. She tried to keep Dega from killing me because he wanted to, and there was a time or two he tried.’’

Patrick had told her some of this in the abstract, enough that she’d been able to share the same with Ray. But still Annabel’s stomach turned over, hearing Patrick speak so casually about having attempts made on his life. ‘‘What happened?’’

He shrugged; she felt the movement beneath her head where it rested on his shoulder. ‘‘I motored out once in a flat-bottom boat, and he tried to mow me down. Never knew I could hold my breath that long.’’

Annabel snuggled closer and again gave in to her desire to touch him, moving her hand soothingly over his chest. He moaned as she adjusted the pressure of her massage.

‘‘Do you know how good that feels?’’

‘‘I know how good it feels to touch you, yes.’’

His heart thumped harder beneath her hand. ‘‘Well, it

feels damn good to be touched. I never realized how good until you showed me."

She bit back her question about Soledad, feeling petty for entertaining the thought that what she and Patrick shared now was better than what he'd had then. That hardly mattered. She'd never before considered that the quality of their time in bed meant anything more than physical compatibility. But it almost seemed as if that was what Patrick was trying to say. And the possibility that he was right floored her.

She continued to play her fingertips over his chest, across his collarbone, down his sternum, making her way to his abs, which were rippled and taut. His moan deepened, and she thoroughly enjoyed the sensation of the tickling rumble.

"I'd give anything to be buried inside you right now." He spread his legs wider in that way he had of showing her where he wanted to be touched.

Oh, how she wanted the very same thing. But no matter how much she longed to crawl over his body and take him as deeply inside as their intimate fit allowed, he wasn't physically well enough. The groan he released as he resettled his injured leg told that tale. And she wasn't so desperate or so selfish that she'd take advantage.

"You're hurt, Patrick," she reminded him softly. "There will be time for that later."

"Just keep doing what you're doing."

She did, asking, "You'll let me know if I come close to ruining the vacation down there, right?"

His only answer was to grunt. Still, she kept her hand above the waistband of his boxers. As much as she would have enjoyed reaching deep between his legs to pleasure him in the ways she knew he loved, she did nothing more than curl up even closer to his body.

She rubbed her palm over his far shoulder, down his biceps to his elbow and forearm before lacing their fingers together in a sensuous in-and-out motion. He tried to hold her hand still, but she slipped away to explore his chin and jawline, the width of his neck, circling her fingertips behind his ear.

She knew how good such pressure felt from all the times he'd done the same to her. Giving offered as much pleasure as receiving, a truth that had never been more of a reality than when practiced with this man.

He turned his head toward her and brushed his lips over her brow. She shivered at the contact, so sweetly simple, so incredibly tender even while it drew her nipples into tight buds.

Her arousal was unexpected, yet she welcomed the flush to her skin, the tingling at the apex of her thighs, the quickening deep in her belly. She loved the way her body responded so effortlessly and intuitively, as if knowing no man but Patrick could satfsfy her needs.

"I want you, Annabel," he whispered, his breath fluttering the hair on her forehead.

She couldn't count how many times she'd heard those words, but she'd never before listened to them, felt them, taken them to heart and believed them. Cuddled up to Patrick's side as she was, she experienced all the things she'd blocked out in the past. The sense of free-falling within his protection. The idea that he needed her, that she could give him what no other woman could. The possibility that what they shared in bed was only the iceberg tip of the depth of their relationship.

She shivered and confessed, "I want you, too."

They lay there for several long minutes, silent but for the twin beating of their hearts and fingertips stroking bare skin and silk pajamas. It was the first time in her life she'd felt this full, this satisfied, without having removed her clothing or done more than touch a man with purely innocent intent.

And then Patrick sighed, a sigh of resignation, not one sleep-induced. "Wanting you the way I do is hard when I know where we're headed."

The fact that she was unable to turn his "hard" comment into a double entendre proved that she was having an equally difficult time with their situation.

"I know," she said, not even pretending that she knew what to say.

"It's just that I can't make love to you and pretend it's only sex. It's not. Not anymore." His stroking fingers slowed on her shoulder, then moved up to caress and tease the shell of her ear. "Being with Soledad was about staying alive. But making love with you is about living."

Annabel squeezed her eyes closed, but instead of blocking the scope of his words, she saw his face and body, the look in his eyes as he held her gaze when he came. She was so out of her element she couldn't even conceive of a response. All she could think about was the very real possibility that sending this man away was going to be the biggest mistake of her life—no matter all the reasons she had for doing so.

"I want to be with you, sweetheart. All the time, not just in bed. I want—"

"Shh." She pressed her fingertips to his mouth. "Right now all that matters is that you sleep."

He nodded and, thankfully, didn't say another word. She wasn't sure, however, if she wouldn't be better served to take her comforter and pillow to the guest room and make a bed on the floor.

Her mind reeled from the tempest of her emotions, questions and possibilities and nary a solution in sight.

Staying with Patrick? As a couple? God, she didn't even know the first thing about making a relationship work.

She'd spent the last twelve years avoiding entanglements, keeping the promise she'd made to herself to never fall prey to an unsuitable man. And that was exactly what she'd done. The walls of Jericho her brother had so recently accused her of building too high had come tumbling down, and now she faced the very dilemma she'd never wanted to encounter.

Not only had she let a man into her life as well as into her bed, she'd picked the most unsuitable one she could find. He was too irresistible. He was young and vulnerable. He was too traumatized to differentiate the natural process of healing from the act of falling in love. He was way too smart not to wake up soon and regret such a huge mistake.

And he was far too deeply embedded in her heart not to break it when he left.

SELECTING EIGHT wineglasses from the set of stemware she kept in the hallway storage closet three nights later, Annabel thanked the Fates that she'd planned her Christmas Eve dinner as a group effort.

Certain that she and Patrick would no longer be an item on December 25, she had never enlisted his help in putting together the food for the evening. A very good thing, since her panic over New Year's Eve had escalated once she realized the far-reaching effects of his injury, which was barely seventy-two hours old.

He'd assured her he only needed crutches, maybe a wheeled desk chair to get around in Three Mings' kitchen. She'd rolled her eyes at the claim. Thinking of Patrick issuing orders to Devon's kitchen staff was as frightening as it was amusing, though at least they had those resources available. She swore that if they all made it through the New Year's Eve showing, she would never volunteer her partners for anything again.

Of course, they wouldn't be her partners much longer. The thought nagged at Annabel as she continued to arrange place settings on the table in the dining alcove. She knew she was doing what had to be done, giving up her position at gIRL-gEAR to follow her dream. That didn't mean the change would be an easy one to make.

Her consuming fascination with the human face had determined so much of her life's direction. The modeling, her position with gIRL-gEAR's cosmetics division, her studies, of course, but also her early comparisons of her own face with Devon's. He'd teased her about her obsession with their differences—his sharper features; his nose, which was definitely Roman, while hers was flatter with a strangely snobbish tilt that had served her well.

Her fascination had probably been responsible initially for her affair with Patrick, too. He'd been so compelling, what with the way he would hide behind his long gypsy hair, giving her mere glimpses of his bone structure and the wicked gleam in his eyes.

He'd tempted her beyond belief with his moodiness even though a childhood of experience with her mother's emotional swings told her to stay the hell away. Yes, her mother's problems had been a true mental illness. And while Patrick's ups and downs were more situational, they were very, very real.

There were times, like now, when she was glad she'd ignored her own advice. She couldn't imagine not knowing Patrick Coffey, never learning of his multifaceted personality, experiencing his attention. His devotion brought to mind master and slave as they battled for dominance. Even as she felt beset with a longing, an urge to ignore years of self-preservation instincts and simply give in.

She'd just placed the last bright plate of her casual plum-colored Fiestaware on the table when she heard the *tha-dump thump, tha-dump thump* of Patrick's crutches as he made his way from the bedroom down the loft's long hallway. She stood on the far side of the dining room table as he came into the room through the kitchen's back entrance.

He wore a pair of black dress pants he'd borrowed from his brother, having ripped open the side seam of the left leg and meticulously pinned it back together over his cast. His shirt was starched and white, and though tucked in, it hung loose on his frame. She wondered if he'd bought it without trying it on, forgetting his body wasn't of the same build now as the one he'd once garbed in clothes dressier than T-shirts and jeans.

His tie was a beautiful burgundy-and-hunter-green dressed-for-success paisley. She could so easily see him circulating through a corporate happy hour or office Christmas party. Then again, the silver hoop still twinkled in his ear.

She hid a grin behind the fingers she pressed to her lips. He was so adorable, having dressed up for her and her guests even if he hadn't been able to tame the whole of his savage beast. And, yes. She found herself quite taken with his cleaned-up and barely restrained bad boy self.

He'd stopped in the center of the kitchen to adjust the ends of his tie, and when he realized she was staring, he glanced up with a self-conscious grimace. "I look like a freak."

My freak, she wanted to say. "You look fine."

His glare conveyed his disagreement. "I've always wondered about your taste in men."

"Which men would those be? All the ones who came before you?" If asked, she doubted she would be able to name a single one. What a blur the last few years—and men—had been. "Or was that a backhanded reference to yourself?"

He gave up fidgeting with his tie and took hold of his crutches again, crossing the kitchen until he stood in the dining alcove on the opposite side of the table. And then he grinned—a cocky and wickedly devilish grin that had her curling her toes in her black velvet pumps.

"You know there hasn't been a man before me worth remembering." Balanced on one crutch and his one good leg, he used the other crutch as a pointer and gestured toward her. "I'll bet you can't put names to the faces you do recall."

"I really do hate how you do that," she said, though these days there was much less venom behind the statement that had become their shared private joke.

"I knew it." He smacked the foot of the crutch against a table leg. "Houdini had nothing on me."

"I don't think Houdini was a mind-reader."

Patrick thought for a minute before his mouth twisted wryly. "Yeah. But he made a hell of a lot better escape artist than I did."

No. Not tonight. After this last wild and crazy week, she refused to let this evening end with another of Patrick's disappearing acts. *End.* What was she saying? He rarely made it through a meal's first course when there were more than the two of them present.

Tonight was important, a gathering of friends, a last holiday hurrah before launching into the New Year and her new life. But this evening was also for Patrick, a simple first step back into the society he'd shunned now for too many long, lonely months.

She wasn't going to let him walk out on her, to let him sulk and avoid the simple human contact it seemed so hard for him to make. He needed to make it for himself, yes, but for his brother, too. And a small intimate party with no pressure or expectations seemed the best place to start.

Then inspiration struck. Reasoning and logic be damned. The potluck dinner might not interest his palate enough to keep him around, but an appeal to his more visceral hunger might help ensure he stayed for the meal—and for more.

10

"I WANT TO SHOW YOU something," she said, determined that he wasn't going to slide into one of his famous Patrick funks.

"What?" He was back to fiddling with his tie, avoiding her gaze, though he finally glanced up when she didn't respond.

Now that she had his attention, she wasn't going to let it go. Wearing a knee-length, long-sleeved, formfitting dress of red silk, she circled the table, breathing deeply of the spicy ratatouille, mandarin chutney and roasted chicken she had yet to remove from the oven.

Patrick's gaze traveled from her bare legs to the dress's neckline, which was as wide as it was deep. He didn't say a word, but he didn't have to. The tic at his temple was nearly audible. And when his chin came up and his nostrils flared, she knew he wasn't inhaling the aroma of the food.

She stood there between the table and the bar that divided the kitchen from the dining alcove, her gaze locked on his, which she held captive. Captive was good. Captive was what she needed to make her plan work. Reaching back with both hands, she took hold of her zipper and slowly eased it down—slowly, because she wanted him to imagine the separation of each of the teeth.

The dress parted and began to slide from her shoulders. When her zipper hit bottom, she shrugged off the garment. The neckline caught on the buds of her bare nipples; she dipped forward and the silk slid all the way to the floor. Ah, yes. She had his attention now.

Patrick reached for a chair and sat. Perspiration glistened at his temples and his Adam's apple bobbed. She loved his reaction, loved knowing how to read him, how to tempt him. Loved, as well, how her own heart beat faster watching his arousal grow.

She stood there completely naked but for her black velvet pumps now hidden in a puddle of red silk. Seconds quietly ticked by, and her skin grew warm, even damp and fevered, beneath Patrick's gaze.

"Annabel?" His voice a husky rasp, he shifted his hips and widened his legs where he sat. "What are you doing?"

She stepped out of the dress and turned in a complete circle. She wanted to be sure he got an eyeful, that he knew what was in store, that he had to do nothing to have her but stay. "I'm offering you dessert."

"Dessert?" He lowered one crutch to the floor.

"I'm yours, Patrick—"

He moved his free hand to her waist, ran his palm over the curve of her hip to her outer thigh. Gooseflesh pebbled her skin. Her nipples tightened, and a shudder ran from her shoulder blades to the base of her spine.

"—with one caveat."

"Caveat my ass." He wrapped his arm around her beneath the swell of her bottom and pulled her forward. "C'mere."

She placed her hands on his shoulders and, frowning, tried to back away. "Patrick, wait. Dinner first. You stay, you don't run out, and then you can have dessert."

He shook his head and opened his mouth over her

belly, swirling his tongue in and around her navel. ''Any-time, anywhere, any way. That was the deal.''

''Yes, but—''

''No buts. Now, here, standing exactly as you are. That's what I want.''

She shuddered as he slipped a hand between her legs, but couldn't close her eyes. This was not going at all as she'd planned. ''That's not what I meant. Our guests will be here any minute.''

He opened her folds with his thumbs, exposing her clit, which had grown hard and tight. Leaning forward, he blew warm breath over the knotted nerves. She gasped, shivered, looked down and watched as he pressed the flat of his tongue hard against her.

He opened his heavy-lidded eyes and glanced up, meeting her gaze as he lapped his way in and out of her sex. Her heart pounded. She'd wanted to give him reason to sit through dinner, not seduce him. Or be seduced.

She should've known better, because it wouldn't have mattered now if the guests were on the way. She'd never known this pleasure with another man. Pleasure that deepened each time she and Patrick came together. Pleasure that had once been no more than his hard body and her willing one, but now, she feared, was so much more.

Using the only corner of her mind capable of thought, she listened for the elevator bell, hearing nothing but the thud of her pulse in her ears. The rest of her senses had coiled into an explosive spring between her legs, where Patrick played using his fingers and tongue.

He opened her fully, separating her labia and exposing her damp inner flesh. His gaze still holding hers, he slid the point of his tongue up one side of her sex and down the other, making teasing dips into her sheath.

Her thighs quivered and her knees threatened to collapse and take her to the floor. She wanted to hang on, enjoy, relish every stroke, but the intensity was too great, her desire beyond reining in. He left her breathless with the ways he fed her hungers and knew, even now, how near she was to coming. She saw the truth as a wicked gleam in his eye.

She wanted to tell him to hurry, to finish her, to take down his pants and invite her onto his lap. But she said nothing. Her voice had long since vanished, her throat gone dry from her quick choppy breaths. She knew if she told him to hurry, he'd make her wait forever. And if she told him to wait, he'd do just that, knowing too well the ways her mind worked.

Saying anything quickly became moot. Patrick knew exactly what he was doing, exactly how to bring her off in fierce and fiery sparks. She was wet, so incredibly wet. Moisture trickled down her inner thighs. She smelled her scent and her arousal heightened. She brought up her palms to cup her breasts, her fingers to tug at her nipples.

He pushed one thumb into her, spreading his fingers over the curve of her bottom, sliding one intimately between her cheeks. His thumb pressed deeper, finding that pillow-soft spot of keen sensation inside, then withdrawing in a rhythmic motion timed to that of his tongue. He licked his way through her folds, one side then the other, swirling around her clit before sucking her into his mouth.

He stopped only once to whisper, ''I love you,'' before delving deep with his tongue.

That was all it took. She cried out, her legs spread wantonly, her hands moving to his shoulders for support. She shuddered, shivered, quaked where she stood, unable to do anything but give in.

Patrick continued to suck her, to finger her, to apply a teasing pressure where he knew she wanted him to play. Not even the chime of the elevator distracted him from seeing to the end of her undoing. His attentiveness remained, even as he began to ease away. He moved his mouth upward, kissed the round of her belly, the one spot she was never able to exercise away.

That disconnected thought finally returned her to the present, and the sound of the elevator motor whirring in the shaft. She took a step back from his hands, looked down at his reddened mouth, his chin glistening with her juices. Panic set in as she grabbed her dress from the floor, and she couldn't find any words to say.

"I know, I know." Patrick grabbed up his crutches and hoisted himself to his feet. He thumped his way to the kitchen sink, where he turned on the water. "You hate how I do that."

She watched him pump liquid soap into one palm and carefully wash the lower half of his face. She watched him rinse just as neatly, keeping his cuffs and his collar dry. She watched him reach for a paper towel and blot the water from his face before turning off the water and facing her again.

"See? Good as new." He frowned, taking in her state of dishabille with a smartly arched brow and a grin that was entirely too cocky. "Were you going to get the door or would you like me to do that?"

His question jarred her out of her trance. She rolled her eyes and shook out her dress. What the hell had just happened? All she'd been wanting to do was convince him that it wouldn't kill him to stay and face what normally sent him running. Now *she* was the one battling the urge to flee, to get the hell away, as far away as she could.

Patrick Coffey was a dangerous man, and she couldn't afford to love him.

TWO HOURS LATER, Patrick sat back in his chair, glaring at Annabel, who sat way the hell at the opposite end of the dining room table.

It wasn't a hateful glare but one of aggravation. She'd seated six people between them, as if she needed a defensive line as well as the distance. Protecting her goal, as it were, with Chloe, Macy and Syd sitting in a zigzag formation with Eric, Leo and Ray.

Swirling the last half inch of his fourth glass of wine, Patrick decided to open a brewery specializing in alcohol of a proof sufficient to intoxicate any poor soul unable to get drunk. Getting drunk right now sounded like the best time a guy could have.

Especially since he'd sat through one hundred twenty minutes of drinking and dining and chitchatting. It was enough to drive a man to take up the bottle. Oh, yeah. It had. And damn little good it had done.

He'd played host to Annabel's hostess, answering civilly when questions came his way. He didn't have a lot of anecdotal input when the conversation turned to careers and Annabel's forensic fetish. He doubted there would've been much interest in his chef's apprenticeship under Soledad, though news of his recent interview at Tony's Restaurant did earn him a round of applause.

He'd really started feeling like a circus freak then, sitting there with fourteen eyeballs aimed his way, the cuffs, collar and tie he wore being the least of his annoyance. Hell, if he'd known everyone shared Annabel's obsession with his private life, he would've propped his cast on the corner of the table and given a graphic rendition of his injury, followed by sweeping tales of life on the high seas.

Fortunately, Ray had seen Patrick's edgy discomfort with what felt like microscopic scrutiny, though it was really nothing more than attentive curiosity, and had swept the post-interview parking lot incident under the table. Patrick appreciated the save. It gave him time to catch his breath and rein in his temper. He would've walked off to deal with the stress except his crutches made for a lousy getaway vehicle.

And then there was the small detail of having promised Annabel he'd stay.

With Eric and Ray talking over Haydon's Half-Time's Superbowl plans, Patrick kept his gaze trained on the far end of the table. Macy, Sydney and Leo had moved to the living room to kick back and digest, leaving Annabel to lean forward and listen intently to Chloe's whispers. The room wasn't that large, nor the table overly long, but having the two men at his side talking sports, Patrick could hear nothing of the female conversation.

He supposed they could've been discussing the New Year's Eve showing, but Chloe's glum expression led him to believe otherwise. More than likely it was personal, and that meant Annabel would be pawing through the other woman's baggage the same way she pawed through his. Not that what they were talking about was any of his business.

It just said a lot about who Annabel was, the way others sought her help and advice, getting her to bail them out of trouble and then turning around and doing the same for her. He liked that about her. It was one of so many things. More than he could ever list, yet as a whole had stolen his heart.

But the thought of her pawing sent his mind right back

to dessert. Not the pecan-fudge pie sitting unfinished on his dessert plate, but her sweet juices he'd lapped up earlier.

He'd never intended to go at her when she'd dropped her dress to the floor, but she'd acted as if he was the one she was tempting, when he knew better. Sure, he was easy. He was the guy and he had the dick. That didn't mean he was the only one to get off on her naked body. Even now she had her hands on her skin, one elbow on the table's edge and her hand unconsciously stroking the hollow of her throat.

As he looked on, the fingers she'd had pressed to her collarbone drifted beneath the neckline of that wild red dress she wore. It wasn't an obvious sexual touch, but a case of absentminded stroking as she talked. An innocent touch, but one that still managed to fire him up in a very big way.

"Hey, Patrick."

He whipped his gaze to the side. "What?"

"Dude, don't bite off my head," Ray said. "I was telling Eric about your pitching arm."

"Heh. I haven't thrown a ball in years."

"Still, playing college ball says a lot about the arm you did have," Eric said, glancing from one brother to the other.

Ray reached for the bottle of wine Annabel had left on the table, and refilled his glass. "Yeah, doofus here screwed it up his junior year in a game of coed touch football."

Eric chuckled, leaned farther onto the forearms he'd braced along the table's edge. "Can't say I wouldn't have been tempted, too. I ended up losing my Major League dream to my rotator cuff."

Patrick shook his head. "Man, that had to be tough. I

wasn't even close to that caliber and kissing my arm goodbye pretty much blew any reason I had for staying in school.''

Frowning into his drink, Ray shook his head. ''Can you believe I never put that two and two together? I knew you had a jones for the game, but I thought that was just you playing so you didn't have to study.''

''Yeah, well...'' Patrick's mouth twisted. ''It was. I might've had the arm, but I never had the discipline. If I had—''

''You wouldn't have been playing coed touch football,'' Eric finished for him.

Patrick nodded toward the other man, though he looked straight at Ray. ''What *he* said.''

Ray leaned back and laughed. ''Guess I wasn't exactly the brother's keeper I claimed to be.''

''You kept me just fine. You and your size twelve boots. I figured I'd better toe the line or I'd be digging leather out of my ass for years.''

Eric laughed. Ray chuckled. Patrick grinned and lifted his wineglass. His gaze cut to Annabel as he drained it, and he was glad there was no more than a swallow left or he would've choked to death.

Her head was bent down slightly as she listened to Chloe, her lashes slightly lower, but her eyes were pinpoint sharp, her focus on his face. Her mouth was what got to him, the way she held her lips in a bow that seemed more an effort to hide a smile than anything. He didn't know what he'd done to draw her smile, but it wasn't her expression that mattered.

No. What mattered was the relentless tease of her fingers playing in the neckline of her dress. She leaned at an angle that exposed more than the swell of one breast.

He could see the dark circle of her areola, and the cherry tip of her nipple.

Neither of the men at Patrick's end of the table faced her direction, their chairs clustered off to the right of his. With Chloe's attention on her hands twisting in her lap, and Annabel's back to the living room, she was in no danger of being found out.

But she was in danger of being tossed onto the table and having her legs thrown over his shoulders. This woman was going to be the death of him. The absolute death. And he wouldn't have it any other way.

"Ray, sweetie, are you about done here?"

Hearing Sydney's voice, Patrick glanced from Annabel to his soon-to-be sister-in-law in time to catch Sydney's grin.

"Dude's reminiscing over my not-so-glorious glory days. He definitely needs to go home and sleep off that mountain of food he's been shovelling in." In fact, Patrick decided, reaching for the crutches propped on the wall at his back, it was time for everyone to go. He pushed himself to his one good foot and braced his weight on the crutches. Annabel took his unspoken cue and got to her feet, as well.

"I guess we should go," Ray said, groaning as he forced himself out of his chair. "Don't want to keep Santa waiting."

Sydney hooked her arm through Ray's. "Let me help Poe clean up this mess first—"

"No." All eyes turned on Patrick. "I've got her, er, it. I've got it. I'll help her." Could he have been more obviously horny? "I'll help her."

Sydney fought a grin with a frown. "Are you sure? It won't take ten minutes."

"He's sure," Annabel said, making her way around

the back of the table. "We're just glad all of you could come. The company has been wonderful." She was right. As much as he'd pissed and moaned, it had been. Though not half as mind-blowing as hearing her refer to the two of them as "we."

"The best part was her not making me cook." He gave her a wink as she sidled up beside him. She smiled in return—right before sliding a hand down his back to cup his ass.

With the kitchen bar on his right, Annabel and the table on his left, he knew no one could see where she'd planted her hand. But that didn't matter, since the view from the front was rapidly becoming as scenic as Everest.

"Good luck with Tony's," Macy said, as Leo helped her into her quilted denim jacket. "They'll be lucky to have you."

"Thanks," Patrick answered, feeling the first tingling beads of sweat on his brow.

He shook the hand Leo offered, then returned Sydney's one-armed hug before casting a sideways glance at the woman with her fingers probing between his legs. He cleared his throat. "Let me get the elevator, then I'll be back to help."

Her pulse beating visibly in the deep V of her dress, Annabel nodded, saying her goodbyes to Ray and Sydney as Patrick walked away. Eric and Chloe were already at the elevator. Patrick pulled back the grate, hit the code for the door and rolled it up on its tracks.

He shook Eric's pitching hand with his own, sharing a moment of male bonding that was rare. Chloe pushed past them and got into the elevator; Leo and Macy followed. Sydney kissed Patrick on the cheek before following Eric inside.

Ray was the last to go. He took hold of Patrick's offered hand, then pulled him into a brotherly bear hug. "We'll see you and Poe out at the house tomorrow, right?"

Patrick nodded as his brother backed away. "Not sure what time we'll be there."

"Whenever. It's an all-day-long, come-and-go sort of thing." He stepped into the elevator car and grinned. "Thanks for dinner. And thanks for staying."

Patrick tried to keep a straight face—and failed. It was good to see his brother smile. He waved as Ray pulled down the rolling door.

Once the car was on the way to the ground, Patrick made his way to the kitchen at his crutches' top speed. *Anytime, anywhere, any way.* That was the only thing he could think about—especially once he reached the kitchen.

It was empty save for a sinkful of dirty dishes and a red silk dress on the floor.

WITH HER EYES CLOSED and leather coat drawn tight against the evening's chill, Chloe slumped into the curve of the Mustang's bucket seat for the short ride home through Midtown.

For the most part the evening had gone well. Eric had been attentive if not as solicitous as Leo had been with Macy or as openly affectionate as Sydney with Ray. And then there was the way Patrick looked at Poe, which had caused even Chloe to shiver.

She wasn't sure Eric had ever looked at her like that, as if wanting to singe off her clothes with his eyeballs. Then again, she knew he had, and more than once, though a particular mechanical room on one of the lower floors of the Renaissance Hotel was the first incident that came to mind. The way he'd wanted her then... She shivered and sighed and curled in on herself even more.

"You cold, princess? Say the word and I'll up the heat."

The comeback to his double entendre didn't even make it all the way to the tip of her tongue. She missed that fiery passion they'd once shared. "No. I'm fine."

"You sure?" he asked, moving his hand from the stick shift to her knee.

She wanted to touch him, wanted to remind him of how hard it used to be to keep their clothes on around each other. She wanted to know if he remembered the Renaissance Hotel, or the strawberry shortcake she'd made of his body.

"I'm good. Don't worry about me."

He returned his hand to the steering wheel, and she felt him sit straighter in his seat. "I do worry about you, Chloe. That's part of loving you. It bugs me that you haven't been yourself lately."

Her eyes came open at that. She turned a bit in her seat, leaning back against her door as, arms still crossed, she faced him. "You think that *I* haven't been *myself?*"

He pressed his mouth into a line, and nodded. "I'm trying not to be a pig about it, but it's like you're on permanent menstrual cycle."

"Well, sugar, I guess that's better than being on permanent spin."

"Spin?"

"Yeah, you know. Turning a situation so that your viewpoint is the one people see."

His tight expression quickly became a frown. "I'm trying not to seem dense over here, but you've lost me. What is it that I'm supposed to be spinning?"

Men! Were they all this incredibly clueless? "Our relationship, Eric. You'd think there wasn't anything going on with us, judging by what all of our friends think. We're the only ones who don't seem to be moving forward, making plans. It's like we've stalled, and I'm not sure why.''

There. She'd said it. She'd given him an opening to spill the gripes, the complaints, the bitching and the moaning, all that he'd been holding back. But he didn't say a word. At least not right away.

He simply kept his eyes on the road ahead. She stared at him for a long time, for what seemed like ages though was no more than seconds. Seconds became suspended while nigh on two years of their time together unwound in her mind like a movie reel. He'd broken into her house once, like William Hurt had broken into Kathleen Turner's in *Body Heat,* wanting her that much, needing to set things right before they lost another day.

Now their days seemed nothing but a blur.

''What is going on with us?'' he finally asked, his voice low and tense, a restrained whisper. ''It's obvious that you're unhappy, but I can't fix anything until you tell me what's broke.''

Oh, why the hell not? She'd had just enough wine to loosen her inhibitions and with the Red Hot Chili Peppers as background music she was sufficiently pumped. ''Okay then. You used to talk about wanting kids. Now when I bring up the subject, you change it. Every single time.''

Eric ground his teeth. The light of the moon and that from the streetlights glinted off the hard lines of his jaw. ''We're not ready for kids, Chloe. Not to mention that I'd like to get married first.''

She pushed away his comment about marriage. It was the issue of babies confusing her most. ''What do you mean, we're not ready for kids? That's all you used to talk about.''

''I do want kids. Eventually. But you don't decide to have them just because your friends are starting their families. Baby-making isn't like scrapbooking. It's not a trendy little hobby.''

Is that what he really thought? That she wanted his babies in order to be fashionable? ''Macy doesn't have anything to do with this.''

He snorted. ''Hell she doesn't. You've been baby-obsessed ever since you heard she was pregnant.''

''Maybe that's because it got me to wondering why you'd changed your mind.'' She drew her coat even tighter.

''I haven't changed my mind, Chloe,'' he said, his voice softer now, more patient, more like that of the Eric she'd fallen in love with instead of the one she couldn't even coax into bed.

He cleared his throat and went on. ''My foster family was amazing. If I'd gone to live with them as an infant, I'd never have known my folks weren't my birth parents. I want that sort of security for my kids. Our kids. I'm not going to be bringing babies into the world when I'm not certain a family is what we both want.''

''And you don't think that's what I want,'' she said over her audibly pounding heart. She wasn't sure she'd be able to hear his reply, fear ringing as it was in her ears.

''I don't know what you want.'' He shifted down for a red light, gunned the Mustang and shoved it back into third at the green. ''You started gUIDANCE gIRL. You went back to school. Don't get me wrong. I admire you like crazy for going after what you want. But it's like nothing you do satisfies you, like you have to keep looking."

Chloe blinked, not knowing what to say, blindsided at hearing her own words coming out of Eric's mouth. She'd thought him unsatisfied with her; he thought her unsatisfied with herself. She was at a loss, a total loss, even as she knew he'd hit on a corner of the truth.

She wasn't happy. Or satisfied. But she had no idea where to find, even to look for, the root of either emotion. Swallowing hard, she closed her eyes again, wondering why she found flirting with Devon Lee so easy, yet talking to Eric brought her nothing but a big fat ache to the heart.

She heard him fiddle with the temperature controls and shift into a turn before he asked softly, "Why would you think I'd changed my mind?"

She huffed. "Because you never come to bed with me anymore. Because we're lucky to have sex every couple of weeks."

He didn't respond to that immediately and when he did it wasn't at all what she'd expected to hear. "The bar's not doing so well. I've cut back on the staff, which means I've been working a lot of extra hours. I know you know that—"

"But I didn't know the part about the bar," she interrupted, opening her eyes and straightening in her seat. "Why didn't you tell me?"

He shrugged. "I didn't want to worry you."

"So you decide not to sleep with me so I could worry about that instead?" Men! Arrgh! Couldn't live with 'em, couldn't feed 'em to the dogs. "All I've been doing is fretting and wondering why you've been ignoring me. And the fact that you have has really pissed me off."

He reached over and squeezed her knee. "I really am sorry, Chloe."

Well, she hadn't exactly been Miss Merry Sunshine. "Is there anything I can do? Rearrange my classes? Get Deanna or someone at the office, Rennie maybe, to take over more of my gUIDANCE gIRL duties?"

Eric chuckled.

"And now you're laughing."

"I know. It's not funny. It's just that if we'd talked about all of this sooner—"

"We, sugar?"

"Right. If *I'd* talked about all of this sooner, maybe we wouldn't have to figure out how to get back to where we were."

The fact that he wanted to, that he recognized they needed to, that he thought they'd be able to... She allowed herself a private smile. No, their issues weren't *all* about the trouble Eric was having with the bar. A lot of this was about her strange inability to find herself.

But for the first time in months, she felt a flicker of hope.

"Uh, Eric?" she asked after a minute or two of staring out the window. "Where are we?"

"Hmm. About two hours out of San Antonio."

"San Antonio? What the—" She turned her head sharply. "Aiden's. We're going to see my brother?"

Eric nodded. "Jacob and Melanie are already there. I talked to Rennie this morning. She begged me to bring you out. Said Aiden was moping because he wouldn't get to see his baby sister for Christmas."

"What about his baby brothers?" She'd been too depressed to plan anything for the holidays. The thought of seeing Aiden lifted her spirits, which Eric had already sent flying.

"Actually, Colin and Jay are there already. Richard's supposed to arrive first thing in the morning."

Chloe didn't even try to disguise the sob that escaped from her throat. "I can't believe this. We haven't all been together in... God, it's been years."

"So Aiden said."

Chloe launched herself toward the driver's seat as far as her seat belt allowed and threw her arms around Eric's neck. "Step on it, sugar. Give these horses their head. We don't want to keep Santa waiting."

11

THE BATHROOM OFF the master bedroom had definitely been designed for baths rather than showers.

The stall in here, unlike the one in the guest room, was relatively narrow and utilitarian, while the tub was a massive piece of marble, square and deep and orgy-size.

Patrick was ready for an orgy. A wet and wild orgy for two, though managing such with his leg in a cast was going to be a superhuman feat. He was up for it.

Not to mention being *up* for it.

Having grabbed a white plastic garbage bag and a roll of duct tape from beneath the kitchen sink in a half-hearted effort to keep his cast dry, he stood in the bathroom doorway and shucked off his clothes. Tie, then shirt, then boot and belt, pants and boxers, until he stood jaybird bare with a stiff second and third leg.

He leaned on one crutch, holding the garbage bag in the same hand, while in his other hand he held Annabel's dress. He made his way into the bathroom, figuring he'd find her up to her breasts in bubbles. No dice. She was in water, all right, but it was clear, tinted a pale green, obviously salts or oils or whatever women bathed in that turned their skin to silk.

Speaking of silk… He wrapped the hand holding her dress around his cock and began to stroke. Annabel turned her head to the side on her bath pillow and watched, her gaze never meeting his but focused on the bulbous head of his penis as he shoved it through the silk.

"That dress cost four hundred dollars."

"I'll replace it."

He continued to stroke. She continued to watch. He moved his gaze from her face to her body, to her breasts and her nipples, which tightened as he stared. The tempo of his stroking increased, increased further when she drew up her knees and spread open her legs.

He swallowed hard, watching as she smoothed the fingers of one hand down her belly, over her dark patch of hair to her clit. He stroked as she circled the knot with her fingertips, stroked as she pinched it and tugged. He then took the silk and began to rub circles over his cock's head, sweat beading, heart beating, watching Annabel slide one finger, then another down through her folds.

He watched her finger herself; she watched him stroke. He wanted to come, to make her come, but not this way. He wanted to shove himself inside her—fingers, cock, tongue, he didn't care. He wanted to be there and feel her spasms. He wanted her to come for him, with him, because of him.

And he sure as hell wasn't about to say no when she pulled her fingers from her sex and crooked one his way.

He hobbled another few feet into the room, watching as she stood, water running down her sleek body. That's what she was. Sleek. She had the curves he wanted in a woman, no poking ribs or jabbing hipbones. She was her own class of muscle car, hot and sexy and wild under the hood.

He imagined her painted with flames, and the image fit, as did the fantasy of making love to her on the open road in the seat of his car, her legs spread wide as she straddled his lap, her back arched, her breasts thrust forward....

She raised her brow and her hands went to her hips. "If you're determined to use my dress to get off, I'll get back to my bath. But if you'd rather use my mouth..."

Four hundred dollars was nothing. He tossed the dress to the floor, his gaze on Annabel as she stepped out of the tub, easing down to sit on the square edge. He moved forward—step, clump, step, clump—and still she crooked her finger. Wanting him closer. Wanting him where she could slide one hand between his legs and wrap the other around the base of his cock.

He sucked in a breath as she did.

She pressed her lips to the ridge beneath his head and held him there, using her tongue to swirl and tease the tight skin and the slit. He groaned, one hand flat on the wall, the other gripping the handhold of his crutch. He slid his good foot out to the side until it hit the baseboard against the wall. That was good, yeah. Now maybe he wouldn't fall flat on his ass.

Besides, Annabel had this thing about him spreading his legs. She got off on playing with all the goods, and he couldn't find any objections to raise. Not anymore, when she had his implicit trust. He especially wasn't going to object now that one of her hands fondled his balls and the thumb of the other teased the seam beneath the head of his cock.

His knees shook. His pulse raced. A quickening of nerves sizzled at the base of his spine. Annabel continued to perform magic with her mouth, in a rhythm that increased the closer to coming he came. She measured his readiness with her fingers pressed to the bulge on the near side of his ass.

And then it was too late to think about pulling away.

The warmth of her mouth, that incredible heat and moisture, her tongue that swirled, her fingers that probed... Hell if he wasn't going to come all over the place.

He moved his hand from the wall to the back of her head and unloaded into her mouth. He thrust once, twice, standing still then as his body convulsed and a visceral burst of sensation fired at the base of his cock.

Annabel stayed with him all the way, matching her tempo to his need, easing back when she knew he'd grown too sensitive to touch. He shuddered, shuddered again, a third time before he was spent.

And then there was nothing left to do but pull out of her mouth. He glanced down through bleary eyes in time to see her lick her lips and smile. Merry Christmas, but he loved this woman. His heart ached with how very much.

Shivering, she slipped back into the water, swirling her hands in and around and beneath her bent knees. "Too bad about that cast."

"Why's that?" He croaked out the words, giving up and dropping down to sit on the edge of the tub.

"I've got warm water and soap and a lot of body parts I'd love to have you wash."

The look in her eyes... His next breath caught on a strangled groan. Recovery time, hell. He reached for the trash bag and taped it securely beneath his knee—right before sliding bottom first into her lap.

"DINNER WAS FUN." Swearing that Patrick's body temperature was perfect for reheating the cooling water, Annabel cuddled back against his chest.

He slumped farther down on his spine, his arms around her middle, his bagged and casted leg hanging over the edge of the tub. "Dessert was even better."

"Which dessert?" Oh, but she loved the feel of him, his strength, his warmth, the nice soft package of his penis tickling her bottom. "The one before dinner, the one after or the one I ate just now?"

"The last one, definitely." He growled out the words, his sex beginning to stir. "Feel free to indulge anytime."

"I'll think about it," she said, and spoke the truth. She loved taking him into her mouth. The change of textures from shaft to head, ridge to seam amazed her; the idea that she was able to please him so thoroughly thrilled her no end.

Even now, feeling him thicken and pulse against her hip brought a corresponding arousal to bear deep within her body. Warm water lapped at her nipples, swirled and eddied between her legs when she shifted position.

Contentment enveloped her as she rocked back into the cradle of his arms. Temptation followed, teasing her with the possibility that she didn't have to give this up, didn't have to let him go. Confusion was the last to set in. *He loves me, he loves me not. I love him, I love him not.*

Why were complications so very...complicated?

She toyed with his fingers as if plucking at flower petals, keeping his hand from drifting lower on her belly even though she clenched her inner muscles, preparing for his penetrating touch. "I'm glad you stayed tonight."

"Where was I going to go?" he asked, working his hand free from hers and sliding both up her rib cage to cup her breasts.

She was getting way too used to this, she admitted, settling as close as possible to his body. If not for his heat, she wasn't sure she'd be able to tell her skin from his. "Where do you usually go when you walk out on a meal?"

He shrugged the shoulder on which she'd laid her head. "Since most of the time I'm cooking at Ray's house, I head out to the pool."

"Water baby," she teased.

"I got spoiled after three years of having the Caribbean in my front yard. I swam off a hell of a lot of frustration and stress."

"Physical exhaustion makes for great therapy." She slid a palm down the outside of his thigh, from his hip to his knee, circling her index finger over the intricacies of his tattooed snake.

"It also makes for shaping a lazy frat boy into a lean, mean sex machine." He pumped his hips against her.

She didn't even try to fight her smile. "You couldn't have been too lazy, playing college baseball and all."

He playfully tweaked at her nipples. "What's up with this eavesdropping crap? That was a private men's-only conversation."

"You don't think I would've been interested to know about your pitching arm?"

"Nah." One hand started drifting down her belly again. "You don't seem the pitching-arm-groupie type."

She rolled her eyes. "I'm female, therefore I'm not sports-minded. Is that it?"

He snarled. "Are you getting all snotty on me?"

"Answer the question."

"It's not about you being female. It's about you being Annabel." He nuzzled his cheek to hers. "The only time I've seen you break a sweat is in bed."

"That's because I work out at the Memorial Athletic Club for *Women.* Ouch." She slapped at his hand, which was busy pinching her belly, then wiped the splashed water from her face.

"Just measuring your body fat."

"If I'm not entitled to know about your pitching arm, you sure as hell have no business knowing about my body fat."

He stopped pinching and slid both hands over her inner thighs, spreading her legs as he did. "I haven't thrown a ball in years. I've thrown coconuts and dates, pitched fish heads and tossed ammo belts. But no baseballs to talk about."

She felt her legs quiver, her pulse race. Yet at her back his heartbeat remained steady and sure, as if mentioning ammo belts in the same breath as baseballs was no big deal. Amazing man that he was, he'd learned to cope. She wasn't sure her character had that same sort of resilient strength, otherwise Devon wouldn't be harping on her refusal to leave Jericho. And she wouldn't have freaked earlier and thought about running away. God, she was becoming her own worst contradicting nightmare, she mused, moving her hands to the backs of Patrick's, where they rested on her thighs.

She twined their fingers together. "It's hard to think about the danger when we're here, like this."

"Then don't." His thumbs began drawing circles in the creases of her thighs. "Think about how we're going to get out of going to Ray's tomorrow."

She laughed softly. "It's Christmas, Patrick. Of course we'll go out to Ray's," she said, realizing how her statement branded them a couple.

"Hmm."

"Hmm what?"

He drew his thumbs along the lips of her sex until she forgot how to breathe. "I grew up in that house, ya know? But it stopped feeling like home awhile ago. It feels like Ray's place now. And Sydney's."

"As well it should after they've lived there as long as

they have,'' she said, contracting her abs and moaning as the stroking of his thumbs grew more intimate.

He continued to toy with her, to tease her, pressing over her entrance but never dipping inside. ''I guess I'm going to have to get a place of my own here soon.''

''I guess so,'' she said, only halfway listening, much more involved with the arousing work of his hands.

''Especially since you'll be kicking me out of here in another week.''

''That's true.''

''Humph.''

''Humph what?'' She turned her head toward his.

''You were supposed to say you've changed your mind and don't want me to go.''

''I see,'' she said, frowning to herself when he moved his hands back to her thighs, then to her knees, where he left them.

Feet flat on the floor of the tub, she grabbed the edge for leverage and stood, turned, then sat back down to face him. She leaned against one enameled side. He leaned against the one opposite and sat with his casted leg draped over the tub's edge near her shoulder. She slipped her right leg beneath his raised thigh.

Her left leg, well, she ended up with her knee bent and her foot on the far side of his hip. The contortions put their bottoms in full contact, with Patrick's balls pressed against her and his partial erection nudging the lips of her sex. He didn't say anything for several long seconds, and with his arms stretched out along the tub's edge, he appeared to be comfortably biding his time.

But then he pushed his hips forward. His cock was now fully hard.

She felt the probing tip, saw the pulse beating at the base of his throat, and wanted more than anything to reach down and guide him into her aching sheath. But she waited, certain what he was feeling was more than desire. She saw it in his eyes, which sparkled with a glimmer of pain.

He cleared his throat before speaking. "I'd feel a lot better hanging out here until Dega's behind bars."

She leaned to the side just enough to rub her cheek against his knee, which was near her shoulder, and then with complete honesty replied, "I have to say that would make me feel better."

His tension lifted as visibly as if she'd pulled on the curtain's ropes at stage left. She kissed his knee, nuzzled her nose against it. "What if it takes longer than you think?"

"Then I'll be around for a while."

"Well," she began, feeling strangely impish, as if the decided course of action allowed her to push away her misgivings as well as her fears. "I have been meaning to finish furnishing the guest room."

"Guest room?" His arms came down with a splash. "What kind of crap is that?"

Teasingly, she went on. "You can choose your own color scheme, of course. And accessorize the space yourself."

"I'm not staying in the friggin' guest room, Annabel. I'm staying with you."

She pressed her lips tight to hold off a laugh at his endearing adamancy. "Do you realize that when you're thirty-six I'll be forty-three?"

"Yeah, and when I'm ninety-six you'll be a hundred and three." The hoop in his nipple twinkled, as did the one in his ear. "What about it?"

"Nothing really." Looking down, she swirled her fingers through the water between them, brushing ever so lightly over his groin.

He gasped, sucking in a sharp breath. "You think I'm too young for you?"

"I think you're young, yes." She leaned forward, took his nipple ring between her teeth and tugged, letting go and teasing his tight nub with her tongue.

"And you're just entering your prime," he managed to mutter from between gritted teeth.

She sat back, cocked her head, moved her fingers down beneath his balls. "Is that so?"

"Oh, yeah." He closed his eyes, let his head fall back, and groaned. "By the way, have I ever told you how glad I am that you keep your nails short?"

"I see," she said, demonstrating thoroughly how very short they were.

"You're not a guy, so I doubt that you do." He blew out a series of short panting breaths, then released a seriously satisfied sigh. "But you can definitely feel."

"Like that?"

"God, yes. You're the only woman I've let touch me like that. Hell, you're the only one who's ever wanted to."

"I like touching you, Patrick. It…stimulates me." She circled her clit before testing her own readiness.

"And here I thought I was the one getting a rise out of it."

"And what a nice rise it is," she said, wrapping her hand around him.

His eyes burned brightly. "Then a proper show of appreciation is in order."

"There's nothing proper about what we do together, Patrick." At that, she took him deeply inside.

Neither one of them moved. They simply sat there,

joined in the most intimate mating of bodies, staring into each other's eyes. She felt as if for the very first time she knew the purity, the immeasurable depth, the passion of Patrick's soul, and she could no longer deny her love.

"I want to kiss you," he finally said, his voice a raw whisper, his eyes growing red-rimmed.

She shook her head, although she couldn't deny how much she wanted the very same thing. "No, you don't. You'll taste too much of yourself."

"No," he said, shifting his hips forward so that he buried himself even deeper within her body. "I'll taste us."

And then he cupped his hand to the back of her head, pulled her to him and drove his tongue into her mouth.

ANNABEL DIDN'T CARE that Patrick wanted to stay at the loft to do what advance prep he could for Friday night's showing. She wanted him with her at Devon's gallery for Luc Beacon's Tuesday morning travel-ad shoot.

Since the incident with Dega a week ago, she hadn't let Patrick out of her sight. She had no idea why she thought she could keep him safer than he could keep himself. But there it was. Her need to know he was out of harm's way was as real as the cast immobilizing the leg Russell Dega had fractured.

The depth of trouble Patrick was in went beyond what she'd convinced herself she was willing to overlook. She was still too scared to tell him that she loved him. Admitting it to herself had been hard enough. But speaking the words, lowering her walls, opening her heart to a man whose stability she still wasn't sure she could trust... She shook her head.

Soon, but not yet.

Once this shoot was out of the way. Or maybe once

they'd made it through New Year's Eve in one piece. Only three days remained until Devon's showing. Her stress level, which had skyrocketed this time last week, still hadn't safely splashed down. It would, though, of that she was fairly certain. What she didn't know, couldn't anticipate, was the frame of mind she'd be in once it did.

Standing in front of the single floor-length mirror in the gallery studio's small dressing room, Annabel adjusted the belt on the cargo-style jumpsuit she wore and pondered again her current pickle. Not the pickle of wearing what looked and fitted like a leopard-print parachute and did nothing for her very fine ass, but the pickle of loving an unsuitable, dangerous and inappropriate man.

She would have to tell him how she felt. But dealing with the emotion had her reeling and unbalanced, even while feeling strangely…giddy. She smiled for no reason way too often. Patrick had caught her in the act and once actually backed away. That, of course, had started her giggling.

She'd chased him threateningly through the loft, giving his gimpiness a head start, laughing maniacally as they'd tumbled onto the sofa. For a long time after, they'd simply lain there in one another's arms, breathing together, silent in their communication, speaking with their heartbeats and their fingertips and quiet brushes of lips.

She'd never in her life experienced anything like those amazing moments, lying on him as much as at his side, their legs tangled, her head in the curve of his shoulder, his arm around her back, keeping her from tumbling to the floor. This love business was frightening, exhilarating and too uncertain—all emotions she'd long thought unhealthy in their inability to be controlled.

Of course, here she was out of control and wearing a parachute; each time she moved she expected the material to deploy, what with its *swish, swish, swish* as she walked and its refusal to cling to any of her curves. She'd worked with Luc Beacon often in the past and had always trusted his judgment. But, good grief, what in the world had he been thinking? She looked so much better in Lycra.

The travel agency that had hired the photographer to shoot the ads for their summer campaign was looking to promote a new "Sex and the Safari" tour package. Said package was aimed toward single female professionals who wanted to let down their hair, kick out of their Manolo Blahniks, and run wild with nubile young jungle boys.

The running would all be done in a climate-controlled and catered environment complete with Grecian pool and spa, Finnish sauna and twenty-four-hour Swedish massage. The pool, spa, sauna and massage sounded like heaven, but Annabel doubted that before knowing Patrick Coffey she would have been able to see the jungle boy appeal. Now, however, she was a full proponent of getting naked and savage. At least with her savage.

What she was not the least enamored with was this outfit.

Muttering to herself, she gave up on doing any sort of accessorizing with the belt she'd been given to wear. Her hair had been slicked back, her makeup appropriately applied in sweeping strokes of olive and dust. She'd laced the drawstring hems of both pant legs tight above the Manolo Blahniks out of which she would be kicking.

She'd even ditched her bra and left the jumpsuit open from stem to stern.

She turned this way and that in the dressing room mirror. It wasn't a bad look; it just wasn't her. She cast a frowning glance at Luc's assistant for a second opinion. "Well?"

Gennie smiled, taking the belt Annabel offered and grasping it close to her chest. "You look awesome, Ms. Lee. Luc is so going to die."

"I'd rather he wait until after the shoot," Annabel said, heading for the door. "I don't plan to star in his skydiving fantasy again."

The dressing room opened onto the hardwood floor at the rear of the dark high-ceilinged studio. Camera strapped around his neck, Luc stood off to the side talking to Patrick, who sat in a plain folding chair.

He still didn't look thrilled that she'd appointed herself his baby-sitter, but at least he hadn't called a cab and vanished while her back was turned. And, really. She did like having him around. In fact, just as it had on Christmas Eve, his decision to stay put a new bounce in her already swishy walk.

Umbrella reflectors and lighting equipment clamped to C-stands sat clustered around the room. Luc's safari set consisted of a bamboo hut mock-up with a hammock suspended from the thatched roof. Nearby, handler at the ready, two parrots perched on a bamboo bird stand. As critical of the backdrop as of her own appearance, Annabel decided Luc was just not in his element today. The set needed serious sexing up.

She considered how to do just that while she followed Luc's posing instructions. Bracing a hip on the hut's porch railing, she stood with a parrot on one shoulder, another on her arm. Lounging in the doorway, she turned her head in profile. Standing with her feet spread wide in the stilettos, she held on to the porch support beams as a wind machine tried to blow her away.

Finally Luc stopped. He scrubbed a hand over his near-white buzz cut, rubbed behind his black-rimmed glasses at his eyes, which were bleary. "I'm not in love with this, Annabel. It just doesn't say sexy to me."

Taking a deep breath and stepping out of the glare of the lights, Annabel glanced over at Patrick, who was standing now and leaning on one crutch. He shrugged, his earring twinkling, and reached one arm overhead and stretched, left, right, back, twisting one way, then the other. The motion of his body was so naturally sexy... Inspiration struck. "Gennie, would you bring me that belt?"

With Luc looking on, Annabel took the belt from his assistant and motioned Patrick forward. Eyes rolling, and obviously reading her mind, he stripped off his shirt. Gennie twittered. Luc cleared his throat. He started to speak but stopped—Annabel had predicted he would—as he watched Patrick peel off the snap-away warm-up pants he wore over his cast and the single sandal he had on.

"Amazing," the photographer muttered, his gaze taking in Patrick's coiled tattoo. His eyes widened further as Patrick clumped past him toward the set across the room, grumbling under his breath the entire way.

"What do you think, Luc?" Annabel asked, knowing the effect the head of the snake in the small of Patrick's back had at first viewing.

"Brilliant," the photographer said, looking down to adjust his camera's settings. "Utterly, frighteningly brilliant."

Annabel turned to Patrick as he ducked beneath the

thatched porch, his expression petulantly glum, the thud of his crutch on the hardwood floor emphasizing his mood. "I know, I know," she said, reaching a soothing hand to his cheek. "You feel like a freak."

"Freak, hell," he grumbled. "I feel like a piece of meat."

"You are a piece of meat," she whispered into his ear, biting the lobe and slipping the belt she'd previously had no use for around his neck like a leash.

Patrick glanced at the strip of faux black crocodile she held in her hand. His eyes sparked, his mouth twisted, his nostrils flared. "You're going to pay for this, sweetheart."

She gave a gentle tug to the belt, tweaked the ring in his nipple, managed to keep from pulling his mouth down to hers. "Exact your price, jungle boy."

"You'd better believe that I will."

In front of them, Luc's camera began to whir. "Ah, yes, Annabel, you angel. This is the sexy I was looking for. Keep it up. Don't stop."

"I'm wearing my friggin' underwear here," Patrick growled to no one in particular.

What he was wearing was a pair of very formfitting, long-legged briefs in basic black. Annabel shivered. "Women won't be able to resist."

"The ad will sell millions," Gennie added breathlessly.

Patrick snorted. "Millions of pairs of my underwear?"

"No." Luc shook his head, continuing to shoot. "We'll Photoshop them right off of you."

"Oh, that's even better," Patrick said, and Annabel laughed, turned, tugged on the belt as if leading her pet. He grabbed hold of the faux leather and forced her back. "Aren't we supposed to be posing here or something?"

"No, no. This is perfect," she insisted. "This is the attitude the ad needs. 'Sex and the Safari.' Hot studly jungle boys and the women who keep them leashed."

He groaned and leaned closer to whisper, "This won't go up on a billboard, will it?"

"The agency probably won't use our faces at all. Just our bodies. It's all about sex and anonymity," Annabel answered, then realized Luc had stopped shooting. She shaded her eyes and glanced beyond the blinding lights to where he stood with his eye to the camera, his hands still. "Luc?"

"Huh. Strange." He shook off the comment and began shooting again.

"Strange doesn't even cover it," Patrick said.

"Down, boy." Annabel tugged on his leash and returned her attention to Luc. "What's strange?"

Letting his camera hang on its strap, Luc walked toward them, stopping at the edge of the set. He stared at Patrick's leg, blew out a curious huff. "Did you know your tattoo looks like it's written in code?"

Annabel's heart thumped. Her gaze shot to Patrick's, then to his leg where he was staring, his mouth a grim line, his temple throbbing. Her voice croaked out in a whisper. "What do you mean, a code?"

Luc shook his head, shoved his hand over his hair again. "Code's probably not the right word. It's just the way the design is laid out."

"Show me," Patrick demanded.

"Okay, look at the pattern of the scales." He pointed as he spoke. "It's balanced and symmetrical. At least the sections that are red, blue and green."

"And the yellow?" Annabel asked, nearly breathless.

"That's the thing. The bars of yellow seem random, but they're not. Turn around," Luc ordered Patrick with a spin of one finger. "It starts here." Annabel studied the snake's head, where Luc pointed out the first series of yellow markings. "This is the key. There are ten individual shapes right here, and they're scattered the length of the snake."

"Ten shapes," Patrick repeated, staring down at the part of his thigh he could see. "Zero through nine."

"I'm probably imagining things, but I design a lot of mandalas." Luc looked from Annabel to Patrick as each stared. "It's Sanskrit." He gestured as if at a loss to explain. "A ritualistic geometric design. Colorful. Symbolic of the universe. They're used in Hinduism and Buddhism to aid in mediation. Which is why the pattern stood out."

"The code," Patrick said, looking down at Annabel.

She got to her feet, loosened the leash from his neck. "Sorry, Luc. Shoot's over. We've got to go."

12

"I CAN'T BELIEVE it's in his tattoo," Sydney said. "I never would've guessed."

"I know," Annabel replied. "The photographer I occasionally work for discovered it today."

"Discovered what?" Ray asked, walking into the kitchen and sliding the patio door closed on its tracks.

"The code," Sydney said. "The information Dega wants from Patrick. Soledad hid it in his tattoo."

"What?" Ray's voice raised the rafters. "How do you know? And why the hell didn't someone tell me?"

"She is telling you, Ray," Sydney replied. "They only found it today."

"We're still in the dark as to exactly what the information is going to reveal," Annabel added. "We left it in the hands of the FBI."

Snapping up his sweatpants in the small private study off the kitchen, Patrick shook his head, listening to his brother and the two women go at it in the other room. He'd closed himself in here earlier, while Sydney and Annabel worked on throwing together a quick dinner of burgers and fries.

So much for the downtime he'd desperately needed.

He'd spent the four hours before arriving at the house bare-ass naked, or near enough, having literally every inch of his tattoo scrutinized, measured, photographed and scanned in the FBI lab.

He'd spent the last thirty minutes doing his own study while sitting in the same chair his and Ray's father had sat in every night after dinner for years. Patrick supposed he'd been looking for the same peace and quiet, the same sense of privacy their dad had come here to find.

The room had been off-limits then; as boys, they were only allowed in by invitation. As a kid Patrick had been awed by the room, had spoken in a whisper anytime he'd been inside. Later he'd come to realize that this study, and not the family room, was the true hub of the household. Out of it bills were paid, home remodeling contracts analyzed, decisions made on family vacation destinations.

Sitting here now, swiveling from side to side in the cracked leather desk chair, which had to be thirty years old, Patrick realized that their father had probably loved this room for another reason, as well.

It kept him near their mother, who had puttered endlessly in the kitchen and family-size breakfast room. Patrick realized that fact because he liked sitting here and hearing Annabel's voice nearby.

After he and Annabel had made the drive from the FBI office to the Woodlands and filled in Sydney as she arrived home from the office, Patrick had come in here to unwind, to get a grip, to wait for Ray to arrive home. And to decide if the pain and the cash would be worth removing the tattoo.

He wasn't sure he wanted to live beneath the specter of Russell Dega for the rest of his days. What he wanted was the normalcy of family life this room caused him to feel.

And he wanted it with Annabel.

Unfortunately, plans for his future—their future—were going to have to wait, as would any thoughts of returning the skin on his leg to rights. He was branded with more than a memory of Dega and the time Patrick spent with Soledad.

Patrick was carrying what might turn out to be a record of not only Dega's piratical activity but years' worth of Caribbean crime.

The FBI steganographer had nearly burst out of his pants with excitement at seeing Soledad's intricately primitive encryption. He'd been the last, thank God, in a long line of feds today to pick and paw at Patrick's leg. If Patrick had been subjected to one more analysis or examination or hand on his ass, he swore he would've come unglued.

Annabel had kept him from bolting. She'd done nothing more than be there for him, even if he'd only seen her in passing as he'd been escorted and wheeled from room to room, from ass-grabber to ass-grabber. He'd known then that his brother would go ballistic at being left out of the fun. Calling Ray any earlier wouldn't have done any good.

But now, yeah, Ray deserved his answers.

Patrick pushed up to his one good foot and shook his pant legs back into place. It was time. Time to come clean, to tell his brother and their respective women his torrid tropical tales. He grabbed his crutches and, with one last look around his father's study, hobbled out to the kitchen.

Sydney and Ray started talking to him at once. Annabel just looked up and smiled, a smile that Patrick swore made his heart stop beating. Her eyes warmed. Her expression softened.

If he hadn't been such a cynical bastard, he would've sworn what he was seeing was a reflection of the consuming emotion that left him unable to breathe.

Leaning heavily on both crutches, he held up a hand to stop the flood of questions. "I'll answer everything, anything, I promise. But can we please eat first? Annabel's been keeping me on a short leash and hasn't fed me a thing all day."

DURING A DINNER THAT nobody but Patrick really seemed interested in eating, Annabel listened to him describe to his brother Luc Beacon's suspicions about the strangely symbolic patterns in the tattoo, and the hours spent with the FBI that followed.

Not surprisingly, Ray hadn't eaten but half of his man-size burger with bacon and cheese. His attention was fixed on his brother. "It was not a pleasant return to Barbados without you, I can tell you that. I kicked my own ass repeatedly for ever letting Dega take you off the schooner, and then I went after everyone else at least twice."

Patrick dragged a home-style fry through the pool of ketchup on his plate. "I'm surprised you made it home in one piece without sinking the schooner in the process." He glanced briefly at Annabel, winked and smiled. "Ray hasn't always been the rational man you see before you today."

Sydney sputtered. "Who says he's rational now?"

"And that's why I have you, cupcake," Ray mocked. "To keep my Dr. Jekyll from turning into Mr. Hyde."

"What I'm trying to do is keep you from going after Dega. I don't care what you say. You cannot bring him down on your own, Ray." Though her eyes were damp with tenderness, Sydney's voice was businesslike and stern.

And Ray looked none too pleased that she was obviously airing his privately dirtied laundry. "Anything I do, it won't be because I've gone off half-cocked. I'm not stupid."

As Annabel looked on, Patrick's head whipped from his brother to Sydney and back. "Going after Dega? What the hell is that crap if it's not stupid?"

Leaning forward at the table, Sydney spoke to Patrick even though her gaze remained fixed on his brother's guilty face. "Exactly what I've asked him more than once since that bastard broke your leg."

"Sydney?"

At Ray's soft query, she turned. "Yes, Ray?"

"You said bastard," he said with all seriousness, and Annabel had to hide her grin.

"I did, yes. And I meant it." Sydney stabbed a fry with her fork and gestured with it. "You are not going to change the subject on me, Ray Coffey."

"And you sure as hell aren't going after Dega," Patrick added in a voice Annabel wasn't sure she'd ever heard. A voice that was low and lethal, threatening in its certainty, uncompromisingly brutal and sharp. "You don't know him, Ray. Yeah, sure, you've seen what he can do. You've heard secondhand stories...."

Patrick let the sentence trail off, not for effect, she knew, but to gather his bearings, to center himself and find his reality. He looked back at his brother then, his expression just this side of savage and set off by the gleam of the hoop in his ear. "Secondhand stories aren't worth a shit. Not when you haven't heard mine."

Ray nodded slowly, sat back in his chair. "So? Tell me."

Patrick stared down into his plate. "What do you want to know?"

"Everything," Ray said fiercely. "But mostly about Soledad and the tattoo."

"No," Sydney said. "I want to know how you learned how to cook."

"That, too," Ray added. "But not so much how as where. This island have four-star kitchen facilities or something?"

"Or something, yeah." Patrick chuckled under his breath, and the sound had Annabel sighing with relief. It was so good to know he had it in him to relax and enjoy his brother, even in the face of his previous and rather ferocious insistence that Ray mind his own business. "I might've been tied to a tree half the time, but trust me, Russell Dega lived in style."

"I don't get it," Sydney said. "I thought the island was primitive. Uninhabitable. Not..."

"Paradise?" Patrick asked.

She nodded. "Exactly."

"He'd been pirating long enough to have a palace to rival Saddam's." Patrick returned to his ketchup and fries, nodding as he swallowed. "No shortage of money, which meant no shortage of generators or fuel. The biggest building was fairly basic, a sort of barracks where most of his crew stayed. Where I stayed when I wasn't shackled. But the house he lived in, that Soledad lived in, was twice this one's size."

Annabel's eyes widened. "You're kidding."

"Nope. And it wasn't just the size of the place. It was the extravagance, the cypress and cedar and walls of glass." Patrick reached for his beer and drained the bottle. "Then there was the underground hangar for his helicopter."

Ray's "What the hell?" came on top of Sydney's "Oh, my God." Annabel had the same reaction. She hadn't heard any of this. All this time she'd imagined him living like Tom Hanks's character in *Castaway*—not in a resort to rival Nolan Ford's vacation home off the coast of Belize.

"This is getting way too James Bond," Ray finally said, dragging both hands down his face.

"It took him years to design and to build it," Patrick continued. "He'd send different men to the States for supplies, bribe others whose skills he needed. He'd pay their way from Miami to Kingston or wherever, then bring them out to the island in the chopper, blindfolded and bound so they had no way of knowing where they were or how to get back."

"And they went for this?"

"It was untraceable cash, Ray," Patrick said soundly. "And you can't discount the loyalty given a man as charismatic as Russell Dega."

"Soledad told you all of this?"

Patrick nodded at Annabel's question. "She'd been with him since the beginning. She'd seen it all. The loyalty part she didn't have to tell me. I witnessed that myself."

"How exactly did Soledad fit in?" Sydney asked.

"She was one of his earliest acquisitions."

"He bought her?"

"Not really." Patrick swirled another fry through ketchup as he responded again to Sydney. "Dega actually grew up in Miami. Same as Soledad. Late seventies, early eighties. He got his Master's in engineering by the time he was twenty-two."

Ray snorted. "A freakin' whiz kid."

"A genius. Literally."

"That's not hard to believe," Annabel offered. "To pull off what he did? That's not a simple feat."

Patrick shifted in his chair. "Soledad was his only

weakness. And I'm pretty damn positive I wouldn't be alive if she hadn't been."

Ray bit off a curse. "If she knew what he was doing, what the hell was she doing with him?"

"In the beginning? Getting out of a bad situation. Poverty, abuse, typical crap used to justify a life of crime. Except she was a straight arrow. Her mother was dead. Her father ran a tattoo parlor way the hell deep in Little Haiti." Patrick's mouth twisted. "Guys came after her all the time. She was raped at least twice."

Shuddering, Annabel took a deep breath. "And Dega was her savior."

Patrick gave a single nod. "Took her out of hell and dropped her into heaven. She tried to repay him by watching his back until she realized the extent of what he was into. It was mostly drugs back then," he said, answering the unasked question Annabel was certain the others had, as well. "Dega was pretty much his own cartel before he decided to take over the Caribbean. By then she was embroiled and knew too much. He wasn't ever going to let her go."

Frowning, Ray crossed his arms over his chest. "And she sure as hell guaranteed he wouldn't let you go, either, spilling her guts like that."

"He wasn't going to let me go, anyway. She knew that. Knew that neither one of us would leave the island alive. That's why she talked in the end. She didn't tell me much of anything at first, but eventually..." He took a breath, shifted in his chair, stretched out his injured leg. "Eventually she talked about everything. It was a kindred-spirit thing, I guess. We were in the same boat. I was a willing ear." He shrugged. "That's the most sense I can make out of it."

Annabel reached across the table and took hold of his

hand. It was time to change the subject. She sensed Patrick reaching a critical edge, a precipice, and she laced her fingers with his. "She learned to tattoo from her father, didn't she?"

"And cook from her father's mother. Dega made sure she had anything she wanted or needed. It was a game with him." Patrick's voice caught, cracked; his eyes grew watery, but he held tight to her hand. "Knowing he could take it all away at any time."

"You don't have to do this now." God, but Patrick had gone through so much, Annabel thought. Both he and Soledad. The urge to push up from the table and take him in her arms was overwhelming. "Not if it's too—"

"Too hard? It's never going to be easy, sweetheart. I told you that." He squeezed her fingers. "But this has been a long time coming. And I need to get it done."

"Poe's right, Patrick. We've never wanted to push you," Sydney said, her head canted slightly with a gentle smile. She reached for Ray's hand. "We've always wanted to know. I hope you don't think we didn't want to know."

"Hell, if I were you *I* wouldn't want to know," he answered with a sharp laugh.

Ray placed his arm along the back of Sydney's chair, looking at her as he spoke. "Not knowing has been killing the both of us."

"Yeah, I can see that you're wasting away to nothing over there," Patrick said, ribbing his brother.

"I'm being serious." Ray glared back. "You're always sulking or goofing or walking off. Talking to you about anything hasn't exactly been a piece of cake."

Patrick took a deep breath. "Talking hasn't done me a lot of good for quite a while. I got used to walking off, figuring it was better than having Dega cut out my tongue. But talking's coming easier these days.''

''I should hope so,'' Annabel said, trying to keep a straight face. ''What with all the work I've done on you.''

Patrick gave her a look that lost its harshness when his eyes twinkled. ''My lot in life. Always have women working on me.''

''Did it hurt?''

He glanced over to Sydney. ''Annabel making me talk?''

Sydney shook her head, giving Annabel an eye-rolling glance. ''I can't get used to hearing Poe called Annabel. She's always been Poe. And, no. I meant the tattoo.''

He gave a shake of his head, grimaced, then nodded quickly. ''Like hell. Or parts of it did.''

''It must've taken forever.''

''A good while, yeah.''

''And you had no idea what she was doing.''

''Not a clue.'' He continued his conversation with Sydney. ''I knew she was proud of her work, and her timing makes me think the FBI will find a lot of information on Dega's activities once they decipher it all.''

''What do you mean, her timing?'' Ray asked.

''Just that Dega had this thing about showing off the goods. He'd have Soledad come out to the dock and watch the boat being unloaded. Proving himself, I guess. Strutting his feathers. And that gave her the firsthand particulars on which boats he'd boarded and the cargo he'd taken.''

''Too bad he wasn't familiar with pride going before a fall, and all that,'' Ray said, reaching for his beer bottle. ''Guess he was disappointed we didn't have crap worth ripping off. Then again, the way you kicked his ass, he was probably more about getting his pound of flesh than anything.''

Annabel lifted a brow, pulling her hand from Patrick's. ''You kicked his ass?''

He rolled his eyes before grabbing another handful of fries from the serving platter and turning to Sydney as she asked, ''Why did he board your schooner in the first place, do you know?''

Ray shook his head. ''Wrong place, wrong time. That's about all I can figure.''

''He was looking for a yacht that was supposed to be in the area,'' Patrick said, squirting a new pool of ketchup onto his plate.

Ray snorted at that. ''And he couldn't tell the difference between our schooner and a yacht?''

Patrick's first response to his brother's question was a quick shrug. ''It wasn't there and that pissed him off.''

Annabel glanced from one man to the other. ''He couldn't get what he wanted so he took what he could, right?''

''He'd take anything he could get a good buck for. But he'd also take a souvenir. Notching his bedpost or whatever. I have a feeling that's what Soledad recorded somehow. Either the dates of the heists or the names of the boats, and then the accounts and storage locations where the money went.''

''If they weren't together, what was the point of his showing off?'' Sydney asked, frowning. ''Or was he trying to win her back?''

''Nope. It was more like he wanted her to see what she'd given up when she'd given up on him.''

''That would make her revenge make sense.'' Ray pushed away from the table, grabbed another beer from the fridge, offering one to Patrick, who nodded.

"I don't think anything about this makes sense," Sydney said with a sigh.

Patrick took the beer from his brother. "It would if you'd known Soledad. Dega guaranteed she wouldn't leave him, at least not alive. So she did what she could to take him down." He stared at his bottle. "For so long I thought she'd failed, that we'd both failed, but knowing she may win in the end makes her death a lot easier to deal with."

Sydney started gathering up the dirty dishes, as if putting an end to the subject of death and the long silence that followed. "It's hard to believe that amazing snake holds so many secrets."

Patrick chuckled softly. "It looks like an average snake to me."

"There is nothing average about that snake, Patrick," Annabel said.

He wiggled both brows. "Glad you think so."

Annabel rolled her eyes. "We're trying to be serious here."

"And you're doing an excellent job."

"I hate it when you do that."

"No, you don't. You love it when I don't take things too seriously. In fact," he added, his expression wickedly bright as he sat back in his chair as if surveying his harem, "I'll bet *you* love *me*."

Sydney, having moved from the table to the sink, gasped, then turned her attention to Annabel. "Well?"

"Well what?" Annabel answered. She was going to kill him right where he sat. Right in front of witnesses.

"Do you love him?"

No way was she going to get into this here and now and with an audience. She narrowed her eyes in Patrick's direction, hoping her voice wouldn't break, and said, "Only in his dreams."

THE DRIVE HOME from Ray and Sydney's passed in silence for the most part. Patrick slumped back in the passenger seat of Annabel's Jag and dozed. Or pretended to doze.

He was wiped out, exhausted beyond belief. But he also felt better about his life, his future, his relationships, than he had for approximately fifty-four months.

There were times, thinking about his life of five years ago, that he might as well have been watching a bad B-movie or reading dishwater-dull fiction. He'd been so lacking in ambition that the kid he'd been then now bored him silly.

Given a choice, he wouldn't have picked growing up tied to a tree as the way to go, but he'd made it through. The only thing left to do was rid society of Russell Dega.

And convince Annabel how miserable she'd be if they didn't spend the next fifty years together.

He rolled his head to the side and took in her profile, which was sharp and stunning and punched him in the gut every time. "Forty or fifty? You pick."

Her brows came down in a small frown, and she kept her eyes on the road. "Forty or fifty what?"

"Years. With me. I figure if we decide on a time frame now," he hurried to add, sensing her stiffening in her seat, "we won't run into any of those awkward arguments later about you being too old or me being unstable."

"I see." That was all she said.

"Do you?" As tired as he was, he was more aware of the ticking clock than he was of his need to sleep. "What do you see? Tell me."

"I see that you're not going to be easy to get rid of."

He watched her try to hide a grin, yet he wasn't quite confident that they were on the same wavelength. Her grin was a bit too tight, her fingers too rigid on the wheel. "The age thing and the Dega thing aside—"

"As if we can push either one of them aside..."

"The age and the Dega thing aside—" he growled the words again, shifting in the seat to better face her "—I've never figured what the big deal is. I'm not going to get in the way of your career, and I'm not going to sit back and let you support me."

"That's good to know," she said with a huff he didn't take seriously.

"We're outstanding together in bed, and we even get along when we're not." He gestured with one finger. "Yes. I distinctly remember you telling me that you liked me."

"I do like you. In fact," she confessed, pulling in a deep breath, "I...like you a lot."

"Well, hell," he said after a jaw-grinding moment of recovery. "I was hoping to hear that other *L* word just then."

She shook her head as if love was beyond her capacity to consider. "You frighten me, Patrick."

"We're going to get Dega, sweetheart. I'm not going to let him touch you, I promise you that."

"No. *You* frighten me."

Hearing those words spoken so softly... Damn. He looked at her, seeing the little girl she'd once been, the one who'd grown up too soon because she'd had to. "I'm not going to walk out on you, Annabel. I've walked out on a lot of situations, a lot of people the last few years. But I love you. And I'm going to be here for you."

She turned into the loft's parking garage and shut off

the Jag's engine before she said another word. Even then he wasn't sure she was going to speak, or that he was going to like what she had to say.

"I want to believe you. I want to trust you. And, yes. I want to love you." She looked at him briefly, glanced away just as quickly. "But right now I can't think straight, and I don't want to make any decisions without a clear head."

"What's to be clear about?" he asked gruffly. "Either you do or you don't."

"You're right. It should be that simple."

"But it's not." When she shook her head, he reached for the door handle and pushed his way out of the car. He didn't think he'd ever known a more infuriating woman in his life. But she was who she was, and he loved her because of—not in spite of—her nature.

They made their way down to the first floor of the garage in silence. The silence continued as they entered the loft's main hallway. If not for the rhythm of his crutches and his awkward step, he would've had nothing to listen to but the battling voices in his head.

Stay with her. Run the hell away. She's not worth the grief or aggravation. She sure the hell is.

They stood on opposite sides of the elevator on the ride up, still didn't speak as they reached the fourth floor. He reached for the handle and rolled the big door up on its tracks. Annabel pulled open the grate...and gasped.

"Patrick?"

He glanced toward her. She'd stopped in front of the elevator and was looking down at the floor. He followed the direction of her gaze. Fury rose in an enveloping cloud as he took in the splintered memento box and the jade pendant of her grandmother's, now crushed to dust.

In the middle of it all lay a box of Dega's sweet Jamaican cigarettes. Patrick reached for the box and read aloud the note carefully printed on the cardboard. "'New Year's Day, Mr. Coffey. I'll be in touch.'"

Annabel sobbed at his side. He took her in his arms and held her while she cried. The stakes had just doubled. This was beyond personal now. This was about a threat made on the woman he loved.

Russell Dega had just provided the final nail for his own coffin, and Patrick couldn't wait to swing the hammer.

13

CHLOE RAN DOWN THE BACK stairs of the house she shared with Eric, heading from the bedroom to the kitchen. Poe was going to kill her for being late, especially after swearing she'd arrive at the gallery in time to help with the setup and prep. But all the world's good intentions wouldn't have done her a bit of good when she couldn't find her tie or the cuff links that went with her tuxedo shirt.

She remembered having them in the kitchen earlier, but could've sworn she'd taken them up to the bedroom with the cummerbund and shoes. Hopping off the bottom step in her trouser socks, her tuxedo shirt hanging to midthigh, she rounded the corner, sliding across the floor à la Tom Cruise in *Risky Business* and stopped.

Eric stood in the middle of the room, the stainless steel refrigerator to his right, the matching stove to his left. He was dressed similarly to her, but he was dressed completely, from bow tie to cummerbund to black patent dress shoes. He was so beautiful, his blue eyes twinkling, that it took her forever to find the breath to speak.

And then what she said wasn't at all what she wanted to say. "Have you seen my tie and my cuff links?"

Eric shook his head, a grin playing at the corners of his mouth. "Poe's going to have your hide for being late."

Chloe huffed. "And whose fault is that?"

"I'm pretty sure you were the one who insisted on an afternoon nap to rest up for tonight," he answered, his cocky expression tempting her to blow off the showing and take him back to bed.

"Well, I meant to go to sleep a lot earlier than I did. Plus I was pretty exhausted by the time I did fall asleep."

"And you were just plain pretty while you slept."

Her heart began racing in response to the tenderness in his tone. She rubbed the bottom of one foot over the top of the other as prickly cactus nerves began tickling in her stomach. "You watched me while I was sleeping?"

He nodded. "Not for the first time, either. I like seeing you relaxed."

"Why?" she asked as calmly as possible, taking everything too personally these days. "You think my stress level is contagious or something, sugar?"

He shoved his hands into the pockets of his pants, hunched his shoulders and smiled. "It's not good for you, but I don't think it's contagious. Watching you sleep, though, is more about how beautiful you are. And about how much I love you."

God, but she was a hormonal basket case, getting weepy at everything these days. Her eyes welled and burned and she had to sniff back the burst of emotion. "Oh, Eric. I love you, too."

"I know you do, princess." His face grew solemn. "But I've been afraid lately that you don't love yourself."

Love herself? What was he saying? She shook her head, took a step farther into the kitchen and gripped the edge of the black marble countertop. "I don't understand."

Eric blew out a heavy breath. "I fell in love with you,

with the good, the bad, the ugly, all of it. You going back to school, doing that for yourself and for work... I'm in awe of all you manage to juggle."

"But I'm not devoting enough time to us, right?" Her pulse had reached maximum velocity. "That's what you're going to say."

He shook his head vehemently, his eyes losing their sparkle. "Oh, Chloe, no. If you haven't devoted enough time to us, I'm doubly guilty."

"But the bar—"

"That's no excuse. I should've been home more. I should've been here for you, in bed with you."

"This isn't about sex, Eric. Yes, I've bitched about you not coming to bed, but that's because I've missed having you to hold close." Her voice broke. "Just having you close, holding you—hell, we don't even have to talk. But when you're with me, life seems to fall into place so much easier."

"I know." His voice was raw. "That's why it's so hard for me to see you miserable and not be able to do a damn thing to make it better. I don't think I can make it better, princess. I think whatever it is you're looking for you're going to have to find on your own."

"And you're cutting me loose to do that, right?" she asked, moving her fingertips to her temples. She was so dizzy...*so dizzy*....

"God, no." Eric moved two steps toward her and reached out with one hand. "How the hell could you even think that?"

He looked so miserable, his face pinched, his eyes weary, that for a moment she wondered the very same thing—until his words "on your own" came back to pound in her head.

"Then what are you saying, Eric?" she asked, and braced herself for the blow.

He rubbed a hand over his eyes, then caught and held her gaze. "I'm saying that I want to take the journey with you, that I want to be by your side whether you need me there or not."

His gentle explanation was so far from what she'd expected that she lowered her hands to her sides and remained silent. She didn't know what to do, what to say. Eric appeared to swallow hard as if pulling himself together.

And then he reached back into his pocket and dropped down to one knee, a black velvet jewelry box in one hand.

Chloe gasped, feeling as if her heart would burst through the walls of her chest. Her knees threatened to give out, but she stood where she was, afraid to do anything to ruin the moment. The thought of his proposal… How many times had she woken from this dream?

This had to be real. She would die if this wasn't real.

"Falling in love with you has been the best part of my life. Living with you, learning about you and from you, sharing the ups and downs of our lives…all of it has made me a better man."

She hugged herself tightly, holding on to the fluttery sensation evoked by his words. "Oh, Eric."

"Let me finish," he said, shaking his head to cut her off. He opened the jewelry box to reveal a stunning rose topaz with a diamond on either side set in an antique gold band.

Taking the ring from the box, he looked up into her eyes. "I want to spend the rest of my life with you, Chloe. I want to be your husband. I want you to be my wife. One day I want that Little League team of babies we've talked about."

She couldn't help but giggle—with joy, yes, but also with nervousness. There was more that he hadn't yet said.

He cleared his throat. "Thing is, I don't want you to marry me because Lauren and Anton got hitched, or because Sydney and Ray are going to, or because Macy and Leo are populating the world with little wild child attorneys."

He took a breath and rushed on. "I want you to marry me because I'm the one you want. Because you think of me the way I think of you, at the strangest times of the day and for no other reason than that I love you. I want you to marry me because I'm the first one you want to share your good news with, or tell the bad. I want you to marry me because you can't imagine coming home to anyone else, the way I can't imagine this house without you in it. I want—"

"Shh, shh." Chloe dropped to her knees in front of him, wrapped her arms around his neck and nuzzled her nose to his. "You talk too much, sugar. You don't let a girl get a word in edgewise."

He grinned with his lips only inches from hers. She wanted to kiss him, but instead she took his face in her hands and caressed his cheeks, loving the rough feel of his late-in-the-day beard. "I've been a pain, I know. And lately I've been more of a trial than any man should have to deal with. I'm working hard to get my act together, but I've been so afraid that I'm going to lose you in the process."

"Chloe—"

"Shh." She moved her fingertips to his lips. "Let me say this while I've got the balls. You signed on for a lot when you fell in love with me, and a day hasn't passed that I haven't wondered if I was being fair to you. I love you, Eric. I love you with all that I am, more than I thought it possible to love a man.'' She pulled in a painful breath. ''But I've always thought you deserved someone better.''

''Better?'' He looked at her as if she couldn't have said anything to confuse him more. ''There is no one better than you, Chloe.''

And then he kissed her, tenderly yet with a restrained hunger and need that told her the truth. He loved her. *He loved her.* She pulled back and looked into his eyes, wishing this moment would never end.

''I want to marry you, Eric. I want to be with you forever because you're the only man I trust with my heart.''

He took her left hand from his face then and slid the ring onto her finger before bringing her wrist to his mouth for a kiss. ''I want to laugh, I'm so happy.''

She stared at the ring, amazed by the sense of all being right with the world for the first time in her life. That feeling bloomed fully when she looked back into his eyes. ''I want to cry, my knees hurt so bad.''

He did laugh then as he helped her to her feet, helped her find her tie and cuff links, and helped her realize that she'd found the one man in the world with whom she was meant to spend the rest of her life.

ANNABEL PACED the gallery's main showroom, her steps slow, her smile ready, her hands laced together at her waist, threatening to cut off her circulation. She did her best to appear serene, to let the soft classical music soothe her, to enjoy the guests' laughter, the clink of ice and crystal, the aroma of rich perfumes and even richer food.

None of it was happening.

Chloe was late. Sydney, Macy, Kinsey and Lauren were already circulating among the guests with trays of drinks and food items from the buffet. Patrick was downstairs in the Three Mings' kitchen, no doubt instilling righteous fear into Devon's staff. Devon was mingling like the master of ceremonies he was, commanding both respect and attention and remaining quietly humble through it all.

She supposed she was the only one who knew she was pacing rather than simply walking through the crowd, seeing to the food and the drink, exchanging pleasantries and pointing out various artists' works and discussing the creative politics of the day. But her stomach burned, her chest ached and she swore she was on her way to a full-blown panic attack. All she could think about was Patrick downstairs on crutches with no more than a knife—granted, a hell of a knife—and Dega's promise to seek him out tomorrow.

"You've outdone yourself, Annie."

Annabel started, then smiled sweetly at her brother. "Don't call me Annie, and I can only take partial credit."

"That's right." His face deserving of the big screen, his body an Armani vision, Devon glanced from one end of the room to the other. "Where is Miss Zuniga?"

"I don't know. I'm assuming wherever it is she's there with Mr. Haydon. Eric. Her significant other."

Devon laughed, causing heads to turn toward the deep lyrical sound. "You're a good friend. Almost as good as you are as a sister."

The look she gave him called him on his bullshit.

"The credit I was referring to belongs to Patrick. I just hope he's not..." She let the sentence go unfinished, not even certain what it was she hoped. What she did know was that she wished she was downstairs instead of feeling like a useless piece of the decor up here.

Devon glanced from her face to her hands, the knuckles of which were as pale as the winter-white sheath she wore. "You hope what? That he hasn't used his crutches on the skulls of my kitchen help?"

Annabel couldn't deny herself a grin at how easily she drew that mental picture. It was Patrick Coffey in the kitchen with the crutches. "Funny, what a first impression he can make."

"He made a good one," Devon said, leaning closer to add, "You have my blessing."

"You're assuming I require it," she said huffily, though she had to admit the pleasure at having her brother approve of her choice in a man.

"I don't assume anything when it comes to you." Devon's expression grew intently serious. "Especially that you have enough sense to ask for help when *you* need it."

"What are you talking about?" Her frown relaxed as she raised a hand in greeting to one of Devon's patrons. "I asked both Chloe and Patrick for help, not to mention the rest of the girls."

"Annie, my dear sister," he said, reaching for her hand. "You have taken on the world for so long on your own that it will be nice for you to have someone to lean on."

Annabel looked into her brother's eyes, searching for a hint that he was teasing her about Patrick's suitability, or trying to get a rise out of her for involving herself with a much younger man.

She found nothing in his expression but care and concern. "I've always had you."

"And you always will."

"I'm frightened, Devon."

"Of Patrick?"

She shook her head. "Of making a mistake."

He laughed softly. "All this time and you haven't learned that life is all about mistakes."

"That wouldn't be such a bad thing if there wasn't the issue of what happens after."

"So, you mess up. You live with it. You move on. You survive. It's called life, Annabel." He stroked his thumb over the center of her palm, then looked up into her eyes. "Does he make you happy?"

She nodded. "Yes. He does."

"And there you have your answer." Releasing her hand after kissing the backs of her fingers, he moved away. "Now, let me go be happy as the man responsible for all you see before you."

"And what an arrogant man he is." She loved him to death, but meant every word.

"Yeah, he is," Devon agreed with a grin, glancing over her head. His eyes sharpened. "Ah, and there is your Miss Zuniga, looking extremely content with her man at her side. Excuse me while I give them both my regards," he said, his grin widening as he walked away.

Annabel watched him go, wanting more than anything for Devon to find love, to know what she'd discovered with Patrick—minus the fear, of course, that he might lose his life. Swallowing hard, she turned back to the room and caught Sydney Ford's eye as the other woman wove her way through the crowd. Sydney looked Annabel up and down. "You look amazing."

"Thankfully, outward appearances can be deceiving. I'm a wreck like even I can't believe."

"Why?" Tucking her empty serving tray beneath one arm, Sydney glanced around the room. "You've pulled off an awesome feat without a single hitch."

Annabel pictured the splintered memento box and crushed jade pendant left on the floor of her loft. Her throat constricted as if wrapped in the coils of a colorful snake. "None visible, at least."

Sydney's expression softened, her eyes conveying concern. "Are you worried about what's going on with Patrick in the kitchen?"

"As far as the food goes? No." Annabel took a deep breath. "But, yes. I'm worried."

"I'm sure he's fine. But I'll send Ray down if it would make you feel better." Sydney lifted both brows in question.

Annabel nodded. She didn't want Patrick to think she didn't trust him to take care of himself or to make it through the hectic evening without cracking the skulls Devon had teased her about. It wasn't that at all.

It was that she loved him and until Dega was caught nothing would make her feel better.

"COMING THROUGH!" Patrick called, using his good foot to propel the rolling desk chair the length of the kitchen. Getting from here to there on wheels only made sense in that it left his hands free to double-check the trays of food going upstairs.

So far, so good. Having a commercial kitchen to use, and one so convenient, had made this whole cooking on crutches business a lot easier to manage. Annabel had fretted all day that he'd need more help than he'd arranged with the Three Mings manager to have on hand.

But everything was coming together better than he'd ever thought possible.

The restaurant was hosting a private party, which had the kitchen hopping. Patrick needed only one prep table, and sharing the ovens and stovetops hadn't been the sort of hassle it could've been had the kitchen been open for regular business.

Still, he had to admit being surprised that Annabel hadn't been downstairs fifteen times by now to check on him. He liked what that said about the extent of her trust. Now to parlay that trust into an admission of love, and he'd be set for life. Yeah. He liked the concept.

He rolled on into the small office at the back of the kitchen. Time to switch the wheels for the crutches he'd left leaning against the room's file cabinet. He needed to whip up more rum cream and could hardly operate the mixer when sitting on his ass put the prep table at chin level—

Slam!

Patrick whipped his head back toward the door in time to watch Russell Dega, decked out in kitchen scrubs, turn the dead bolt. Patrick's stomach dropped to his feet; his heart shot into his throat. The Glock 10 mm automatic in the other man's hand guaranteed that no one would be getting out without a hell of a messy fight.

He hated the disadvantage of sitting, but stayed where he was. *Think, think, Patrick. Think.* Calm under fire. That was his priority. "Russell, my man. You're a day early. A dollar short, too, no?"

Dega's expression remained darkly blank. "The element of surprise, Mr. Coffey, though I doubt you're at all shocked to see me."

No, no. He couldn't say that he was. Time for a quick reconnaissance. His knife in his pocket. His brother upstairs. His crutches behind him on the file cabinet. A kitchen of deadly possibilities right outside the door...the closed and locked door barred by a Glock and a man without compunction.

It was either talk his way out of here or shut the hell up. He chose the latter.

"Come now, Mr. Coffey," Dega said, gesturing randomly with the gun, the silent stare-down having apparently gone on too long for his liking. "Give me what I've come for, and I'll be on my way."

At this point, turning over Soledad's information and allowing Dega to fly the coop sounded like a plan to Patrick. All but the part where he'd have to lose a leg. "Sorry, Russ. No can do. You said tomorrow. I didn't come prepared."

"You're trying my patience, Patrick." Dega spat out the words, considered him down the sight of the Glock.

Patrick rolled his chair six inches closer to the desk and didn't say a word. The phone was less than a foot away. Knock the receiver from the cradle. Punch a quick 9-1-1. That's all he had to do. All he had to do. He clenched his fist around his tingling palm.

Dega's expression remained devoid of emotion. "Not to mention that I see straight through your bluff."

"Yeah?" Patrick asked, stalling and distracting. "What bluff would that be?"

"That you would deliver to me Soledad's information at our next meeting."

"Our next *scheduled* meeting. Tomorrow." Patrick shrugged, sweat rolling between his shoulder blades. He braced an elbow on the desk. One more minute. *One more minute.* "Can't help you out tonight, Russ."

Dega's nostrils flared. His black eyes darkened. "You

have what is mine, and I'm prepared to get it back. At any cost,'' he added, sharply punctuating the last words.

A punctuation Patrick didn't need to understand the extent of the shit he was in. ''Including killing me?''

''If necessary.'' Dega barked out a menacing laugh, the sound deep and low and nearly soundless, which made it that much more eerie.

Patrick's mouth went dry. His mind raced. Adrenaline pumped through his veins. His minute was up. He swung his hand, knocked the receiver from the cradle, punched 9-1-1 before Dega's cane cracked against the side of his head.

The desk chair sailed back with the force, and Patrick went flying. Pain burst through his shoulder, exploded through his skull. The phone clattered to the floor nearby. Breathe, breathe, *breathe.* It took forever, but finally he gasped, pulled in a short ragged breath, peeled open his eyes. Then wished he hadn't.

The barrel of the cane gun was three inches away and aimed right between his eyes.

''Dead or alive, Mr. Coffey. It doesn't matter to me. I want the head of the snake in the middle of your back, and I'll skin it off of you if I have to.''

The head of the snake? Grimacing, Patrick pushed up to his elbows, then into a sitting position. He kicked the chair toward Dega, who swung it around the front of the desk and toward the far wall of office machines.

Patrick nodded toward the copier in the corner. ''How about we take a picture? It'll last longer.''

''That would still leave you walking around with my map. And I can't have that.''

''Your map?'' *What the hell?* What about coded account numbers and the like? The FBI was certain that's what they'd find. A complete record to replace the one destroyed in the raid on the island. But Dega wanted a map? "What're you talking about, your map?" Patrick demanded, scooting back against the file cabinet.

His crutches lay on the floor on his right. His knife, tucked deep in the left pocket of his snap-away pants, bounced against his leg. The odds weren't great, his head hurt like hell, but no way was he going to give up or give in.

With the Glock aimed at Patrick, Dega leaned a shoulder against the door, his cane in his hand, supporting the rest of his weight. "An armored-car heist and a bag of gold bars, Mr. Coffey. Many years before we settled into our profitable lifestyle, Soledad and I found a suitable rock of an island and hid the gold in a small cave. It didn't occur to me after we'd spoken last that your tattoo is the obvious key."

"And my tattoo tells you, what? How to get back there?"

"Along with the information of our activities she coded, I'm quite certain Soledad recorded the island's coordinates. She knew the information would eventually be deciphered. I doubt, however, she intended for me to be the one to use it. But with my records being destroyed and my memory not quite as good as it once was..." He gestured with the gun. "On your feet. We're leaving."

"I'm not going anywhere with you."

Dega didn't miss a beat. "Then you die here, and I take the map."

Stalling more than weighing options, Patrick asked, "And if I go?"

"Once I have my treasure, I'll leave you with a gun and a single bullet. Then you can decide how long you live."

"Sounds like paradise." He bit off the words, inching his hand toward his pocket. The knife was his best hope.

"Patrick?" Ray pounded on the office door.

Dega shifted to train the cane gun on Patrick and raised the Glock chest high toward the door. Toward Ray. "You tell him you're fine, or he's dead."

"Be right out, dude," Patrick called, hearing the flatness in his own voice and hoping like hell his brother believed him and didn't start anything stupid.

"Yeah, well..." Ray hesitated, his voice muffled. "Poe wanted me to check on you."

Patrick closed his eyes and pictured Annabel upstairs in her gorgeous white dress. His heart pounding, gut churning, he looked up slowly, and furiously met Dega's gaze. "Tell her I'll come upstairs in a few."

The idea of this bastard getting to Annabel... Patrick grabbed hold of the edge of the desk and one crutch and levered himself to his feet. "Good enough?" he mouthed, his hand, now free, reaching for his knife.

Dega nodded and whispered, "We'll give your brother time to get out of our way and—"

The door burst inward and caught the bastard's shoulder. Dega went flying, landed on his back, sliding headfirst into the copier stand. Patrick scuttled in reverse, watching the battering ram knock the door off its frame.

Uniformed officers pushed through, yelling at Dega. "Drop your weapon. Drop your weapon."

Then Ray was in the doorway. "Ray, no!" Patrick cried.

Dega raised the Glock.

"Drop your weapon!"

Dega fired once, twice.

Ray dived. Patrick threw the knife, followed his brother to the floor. Then he whipped his head up, searching out and finding—*goddamn, there they were*—the bullet holes in the ceiling.

Ray's throat convulsed as he swallowed. He glanced over Patrick's head toward the officers, then nodded. Patrick turned to see two of them backing away, guns lowered, faces solemn. He rolled to his one good knee. His brother helped him to his feet, handed him a crutch.

And then he couldn't move. He couldn't think. Couldn't respond. Dega lay on the floor, the knife quivering beneath his Adam's apple. Patrick stood there, leaning on his crutch and the arm his brother wrapped around him, and watched Dega's life flow away in a dark ribbon of blood.

"Your call got through," Ray said gruffly, his mouth at Patrick's ear. "I was coming down to check on you just as the cops showed up. When the dispatch came through, they were only a block away. I can't believe it. It's done. After all this time, it's done."

It was over, over. Patrick wasn't sure that he wasn't going to pass out. And then he heard Annabel's voice raised in argument with the police officers keeping her from the scene. He gave Ray a final hug. "I've gotta see her, man."

He was barely out of the office and into the kitchen before Annabel was in his arms. She held him so tightly he had to back into the door frame for balance. He didn't move. She didn't exactly cry, though heaving sobs rattled her chest.

His own breathing grew ragged and taut. His eyes burned. His throat tightened. He held her while officers shouted orders and radios crackled and sirens wailed through the open kitchen door. Even with the mayhem and an audience, Patrick did the one life-affirming thing he had to do.

He kissed her.

He cupped his hand to the back of her head and ground their mouths together. Passion wasn't a part of it, and his only desire at the moment was to sweep her into his arms and get the hell out of here. But he couldn't walk, and ahead lay a long messy night of questions and answers and paperwork....

He sighed, and she pulled away to take his face in both of her hands. Her makeup ran in jagged streaks down her pale face, tears spilling unheeded. "I heard the gunshots. I thought you were dead. I just knew you were dead."

He shook his head, pressed his lips to her inner wrist. "I'm too hardheaded and mean to let you off the hook that easily."

"Oh, Patrick. If anything had happened to you..." She pressed her quivering lips to his cheek, moved her mouth to the barest edge of his. So soft. So gentle. "I love you. I love you, and losing you would be more than I could bear."

He felt his grin start deep in his gut and stop to massage his heart before it hit his mouth. "Does this mean I don't have to move out tomorrow?"

"If you do, I'll never speak to you again," she said, and sobbed.

He considered for a moment the pandemonium, feeling nothing but relief, nothing resembling the guilt he'd expected over killing a man. But he had to know. He needed to know. "I just killed a man, Annabel. Are you sure you can live with that? With me?"

"Oh, Patrick, yes." She nodded quickly, her hair settling to frame her chin. "You acted in self-defense. How could I think badly of you for that?"

"Just making sure, sweetheart. Just making sure." He

reached behind him, where earlier he'd tucked a kitchen towel into the waistband of his pants. "Here. Fix yourself, woman. You're a mess."

With a sharp teasing glare, she took the towel and dabbed at her face before blowing her nose loudly.

"Ooh. My kinda sexy woman," he said, and ruffled her hair.

She growled. "I hate it when you do that."

"No, you don't. You love it," he said, and sighed. How could one woman make one man so insanely happy?

"You're right. I do." She smiled. "Almost as much as I love you."

Epilogue

ANNABEL STOOD AT THE BOW of the rented schooner, the brisk Caribbean breeze ruffling her hair. The skies were the blue of postcards, the water an unbelievably clear turquoise. The sun warmed her from the inside out with its brilliant heat.

With her arms wrapped around her bare middle, she watched the cove come into view—the very cove depicted in the head of the snake tattooed as a map on Patrick's back. Millions in gold bars. She had to laugh at the possibility.

The past six months had brought an amazing whirlwind of change to her life. At long last she had her degree, though she'd yet to leave gIRL-gEAR. She had time. She also had offers. It felt good to be wanted by three out of the four crime labs she'd queried. It felt equally good to know that, no matter her partners' regrets at seeing her go, they supported her decision.

But nothing would ever feel as good as loving Patrick Coffey.

She shuddered even now to think of New Year's Eve and all that had happened since. Patrick loathed the notoriety that had come from being a local celebrity, but Tony's Restaurant had never been busier. Patrick's reputation, in fact, had caught Nolan Ford's attention.

Sydney's millionaire father, having taken a big step backward out of the business of venture capital, was talking with Patrick about a future executive chef position at the restaurant he planned to open.

Life for all of the gIRL-gEAR partners was surging strongly upward. Macy's baby was due in another month. As tiny as Macy was, she never ceased to amaze the rest of the girls that she was able to walk with a belly that size. Chloe and Eric, as well as Sydney and Ray, had set wedding dates for the next year.

Melanie had moved in with Jacob and the two were discussing opening their own media firm. Lauren and Anton were as happy as a married couple could possibly be, though Kinsey and Doug were definite rivals for most newly wedded bliss.

And, finally, finally, *finally,* Annabel and Patrick were taking a real vacation. Unlike the time she'd had off at the end of last year, which hadn't been the least bit relaxing, this was a real trip away from their very busy lives.

He'd bought a house in River Oaks and was fighting off the attention of bored soccer moms and the upwardly mobile *Sex and the City* types on a regular basis. Annabel had seen it happen more than once.

Several times she'd stood at his home's front windows as he'd driven up and rolled out of his El Camino, his hair still cropped close, the sun glinting off his sleek designer shades and the hoop in his ear, his long, rangy body drawing hot female stares from the parade of SUVs and chic status cars that seemed to follow him everywhere.

She certainly didn't blame the onlookers for wanting what she had. Oh, no. She couldn't blame them at all. There was definitely something to be said for younger men. And even more to be said for savage beasts and jungle boys.

As if reading her mind, Patrick walked up behind her and slipped his arms around her waist. She leaned her head back against his shoulder, soaking up the heat of his bare chest on her back, settling into the circle of his arms and knowing she'd never felt more safe, more secure or more loved.

"You ready for this?" he asked, his voice husky near her ear.

She wiggled against him, feeling his nipple ring sear her back. "Do you really think we're going to find anything?"

He stepped back, turned her around. She laced her hands behind his neck; he moved his to her hipbones. His skin was bronzed and beautiful, his body ripped with muscle.

And she remembered the bad boy in the bomber jacket who'd kissed her senseless less than a year ago and was now the man whom she loved.

"Who the hell cares?" he said, his hands sliding up her rib cage and around to the small of her back. "I've got my treasure right here."

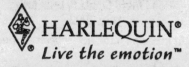

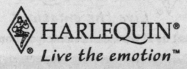

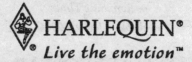

Dear Reader,

What a long, fun trip gIRL-gEAR has been! From six single professional females to nine committed couples...plus weddings, engagements and babies on the way!

Thank you so much for loving the stories and the characters of gIRL-gEAR. Leaving the series now, I feel as if I'm saying goodbye to friends. I want to come back in five years and hear the pitter-patter of little gIRL-gEAR feet.

Yes, I know. There's still Jess Morgan and Nolan Ford and now Devon Lee left hanging. Not to mention Chloe's brothers, Colin, Richard and Jay. Oh, and didn't Anton have a younger brother? And Macy was the youngest of how many siblings?

See? These characters have become like family to me. And walking out of their lives is going to be tough. But I'm strong. I will survive! Plus, I can always visit them again on the Web at www.gIRL-gEAR.com!

And you can visit me, too, at www.AlisonKent.com. The girls and I would all love to hear from you!

Best!

Alison Kent

Books by Alison Kent

HARLEQUIN BLAZE

24—ALL TIED UP*
32—NO STRINGS ATTACHED*
40—BOUND TO HAPPEN*
68—THE SWEETEST TABOO**
99—STRIPTEASE*
107—WICKED GAMES*

*www.girl-gear...
**Men To Do!

"I want to show you something."

Annabel refused to let this evening end with another of Patrick's disappearing acts. He rarely made it through a meal's first course when there were more than the two of them present.

"What?"

Now that she had his attention, she reached back with both hands, took hold of her zipper and slowly eased it down. Her dress parted and began to slide from her shoulders. Ah, yes. She had his attention now.

"Annabel?" His voice a husky rasp, Patrick shifted his hips and widened his legs where he sat. "What are you doing?"

"I'm offering you dessert. With one caveat. You stay, you don't run out and then you can have dessert."

He shook his head and wrapped his arm around her and pulled her forward. "Anytime, anywhere, any way. That was the deal."

"Yes, but—"

"No buts. Now, here, standing exactly as you are. That's what I want."

This was not going at all as she'd planned. All she'd wanted to do was convince him that it wouldn't kill him to stay. Now *she* was the one battling the urge to feel. Patrick Coffey was one dangerous man.